Dear Readers,

This is my first book set in the medieval period, a time in which women had special charge of family health. In these times of sudden violence, when disease ran rampant through whole populations, herbs were the first and best line of defense. The fabled demoiselles of tournaments, ivory towers, and flowing robes often found themselves using herbs to treat every ill from sword wounds to agues, as does my heroine, Juliana. The herbs mentioned in <u>Lord of the Dragon</u> are but a few the use of which was widely known. Troubadours may have written their finest poetry about delicate noble ladies, but as you will see in this story, these women shared a life of risk and danger with their men, and used their skills with herbs and healing to protect the ones they loved.

Please share with me now the world of Arthur and Guinevere, of Eleanor of Aquitaine and Richard Lion Heart.

Suzanne Robinson

Lord of the Dragon

Suzanne Robinson

Bantam Books
New York Toronto London Sydney Auckland

LORD OF THE DRAGON
A Bantam Book / September 1995
Grateful acknowledgment to The Metropolitan Museum of Art for
permission to reprint an excerpt from *HERBS FOR THE
MEDIAEVAL HOUSEHOLD* copyright 1943 by Margaret B.
Freeman.

ISBN 0-553-56345-9

Published simultaneously in the United States and Canada

Bantam Books are published by Bantam Books, a division of Bantam
Doubleday Dell Publishing Group, Inc. Its trademark, consisting of the
words "Bantam Books" and the portrayal of a rooster, is Registered in
U.S. Patent and Trademark Office and in other countries. Marca Regis-
trada. Bantam Books, 1540 Broadway, New York, New York 10036.

Katherine Ann Harrod, you were my first and best friend. It didn't matter how long we were separated or how far away you lived. We shared a world of imagination, adventure, and dreams, and I believe we'll always have that world in our hearts. My dear cousin, I dedicate this book to you with love and thanks.

Lily of the Valley

For apoplexy one soaked the flowers in wine for four weeks and distilled to make a liquor. This liquor mixed with peppercorns and lavender water and smeared on the forehead and back of the neck made one have good common sense.

• *Chapter 1* •

STEALING OUT OF A CASTLE WASN'T EASY. JULI-ana Welles shoved open her chamber door in the Maiden's Tower of the old square keep and found the landing deserted. Then she motioned for her maid, Alice, to follow. She clutched a sack in one hand and lifted the skirt of her overrobe in the other as she glided down the circular stair. Alice came after her holding a basket that clattered with each step. The basket slipped, and pottery jars shifted, causing a loud clink.

Juliana halted on the stairs. "Shhhh! Thunder of heaven, you'll wake my sisters and then we're undone."

Alice nodded vigorously, then gave Juliana a horrified stare. Her nose twitched; her head tilted back. She sneezed. Jars clacked as the noise resounded off the stone walls.

Juliana started, then glared at Alice. The woman was widowed, had borne seven children, and sometimes lacked the sense of a day-old lamb. Setting down her sack, Juliana held out her arms. Alice gave her the basket and picked up the sack while casting apologetic glances at her mistress. With their burdens redistributed, Juliana resumed her progress down the tower stair and soon led the way to an arcade that stretched the length of the great hall.

Light was streaming through the high, arched windows, giving the cavernous room an early morning glow of silver. As she entered the arcade, Juliana stopped abruptly and took shelter behind one of a line of thick columns decorated with spiral designs and carved garlands. Alice stumbled into her, then skittered into a shadow.

In the middle of the hall, near the great central fireplace, stood her parents, cousin Richard, her father's chaplain, steward, and several squires and clerks. The group was silent, which was unusual for any group that included her father. Juliana followed the direction of their stares and saw a herald's retreating figure. He passed near her on his way out, and she glimpsed armorial bearings—a rearing animal, the dragon rampant fashioned in gold on a field of green.

Juliana muttered the heraldic description to herself. "*Vert*, a dragon rampant *or*. Now who owns those bearings?" She couldn't remember. Dismissing the mystery from her thoughts, she was tiptoeing down the arcade when her father's bellow made her gasp and shrink against the wall.

Hugo Welles broke from the group at the fireplace and swept up and down in front of them, his thumbs stuck in his belt. "*Him!*"

Her heart had stopped bouncing against the walls of her chest, so Juliana gave her father an irritated look and resumed her tiptoeing. Alice hugged the wall and came after her.

"Did you hear what that smirking catamite said?" Hugo roared. "Gray de Valence in my tournament, for God's pity. He's come for vengeance, that's what. To make mischief and evil, that's what."

Cousin Richard's voice broke the tirade. "Forbid him."

Hugo's wide girth swung in his nephew's direction.

"Forbid him? How? Who would have thought that he'd come back after all these years, and as the de Valence heir? He had four older brothers, four. And they're all dead of disease, battle, or accidents."

Juliana paused upon hearing the name of this new visitor. Gray de Valence. An infamous name. She remembered her mother's whispered stories. Nine years ago, when she'd been but eleven, de Valence had been a new-made knight of eighteen years in the same household as Richard. Both had been sent to be fostered with a relative of Hugo Welles. A penniless youngest son, de Valence had achieved knighthood early by his skill and the favor of his liege, only to betray him. He'd seduced his lord's wife.

The liege lord raged and nearly killed his wife, but for de Valence he reserved a special penalty. Biding his time, he denounced the youth before a tournament crowd and took him prisoner. This measure ruined de Valence before the entire kingdom. Then, realizing that condemning the youth to live in shame was his greatest revenge, the lord ordered de Valence taken from England by his fellow knights. Richard had been their leader.

They returned a few months later with harrowing news of an attack at sea by pirates. De Valence had been taken prisoner, and vanished. Years passed during which rumors drifted from the Holy Land and beyond of a tall green-eyed slave of a heathen general in Egypt, a slave with the same hair of silken silver as the vanished Gray de Valence. Then, without warning, de Valence reappeared out of nowhere with a French title, a riding household of over two hundred, and a desire to destroy the knights who had turned against him.

That was only a few years ago. In that short time de Valence had befriended the powerful William Marshal, Earl of Pembroke. After the battle of Lincoln in which the invading French dauphin was driven from England, rumors again flew like black bats across England. The

Sieur de Valence had fought with a skill that rivaled both Richard Coeur de Lion and Saladin. The great barons of the kingdom stirred uneasily and muttered among themselves, sensing a rival who threatened to surpass them in skill and ruthlessness. No wonder Father was disturbed.

Juliana had reached the end of the arcade. "Gray de Valence," she whispered to Alice as she waited for her father to look in another direction so that she could leave unseen. "A phoenix risen from ashes. This miserable tournament may afford some amusement after all."

"Aye, mistress. He be heir to Stratfield now. Imagine that evil one inheriting the Stratfield castles and riches."

"Quiet," Juliana whispered, staring at her father. "Now, he's looked away. Hurry."

Clutching her basket, Juliana hurried for the doors that could be seen through an archway.

"Juliana!"

She jumped at the bellow that echoed from the roof beams. Jars clinked inside the basket, and Alice squeaked and scurried behind her, as she turned to face the striding figure of Hugo Welles. Lord Welles was a man whose body could have been made of stacked tree trunks— thick, gnarled, and dense of muscle. His ruddy face had grown even more red at the sight of his daughter. Havisia, his wife, trailed after him like a midge fluttering after a dragonfly.

Hugo halted his charge in front of Juliana, who set her jaw and squared her shoulders. Hugo's thick black brows lowered until they nearly hid his gray eyes. He almost shouted.

"Where are you going, daughter?"

"To Vyne Hill, Father."

Hugo threw up his arms and turned to Havisia. "We're to give a tournament tomorrow, and she's off to that ruined manor of hers."

"You said I could go, Father."

"When?"

"Last night." She'd asked him then because he'd had two flagons of ale.

"Last night? Last night? I don't remember."

"You did, my lord," said Havisia.

Hugo waved his hand impatiently. "No matter. I mistook myself. There's too much to do. What of the food, the linens, the— Now don't you try to dazzle me with your glares and glowers, Juliana Welles."

"Mother has Laudine and Bertrade to help her." She began to stomp back and forth. With each step her heels snapped against the floorboards, calling attention to the men's boots she wore beneath her rough woolen robe.

Her voice rose as she spoke. "Thunder of God! I've Vyne Hill to look after and no time for another tournament. The castle fills up with strutting rooster knights and simpering women. I've much work to do if I'm ever to get the manor in condition for me to occupy it."

By now her voice rivaled Hugo's roar. Her father winced and glanced back at the group around the fireplace while her mother rolled her eyes and sighed. Waving his hands at Juliana, Hugo lowered his own voice.

"Peace, peace, daughter."

Juliana's boots pounded a drumlike rhythm. Her basket clattered in time with her steps and she waved her free arm as she uttered a stream of oaths.

"Holy saints, scourge and pestilence!"

Juliana whirled on her father, her face a darkening pink. Her gray eyes might as well have flashed small bolts of lightning. If her hair hadn't been caught in a net at the base of her neck, it would have flowed about her like a black storm cloud.

She thought of another oath. "By our blessed Lady of Mercies—"

Hugo threw up his hands again in the face of his daughter's colorful and intemperate display. The whole of Wellesbrooke castle knew he could face battle with the French king's army with better fortitude than he could withstand Juliana's temper. Now he blustered and grumbled as he turned away from his oldest daughter.

"The lot of the damned, that's what I have, the lot of the damned to be cursed with so evil-tempered a daughter. I don't wonder she's without suitors. Her humor is as black as her color. And no doubt that devil's whelp of a stripping bandit will return to plague my tournament and make my suffering unendurable." Hugo turned to his wife. "He'll swoop down on one of my most important guests and take his clothes, I know it. He's done it before. An impudent thief and a black-natured, willful daughter. I must have the fortitude of a saint."

Havisia placed her hand on Hugo's arm and murmured words of comfort. A beauty in the accepted mode of white skin and golden hair, Mother had always pitied her eldest daughter for her coloring. Juliana watched her parents turn away, Hugo complaining, Havisia consoling. Her booted foot tapped against the floor. Slanting black brows drew together and her fingers drummed against the basket. She turned abruptly on her heel without another word and stomped out of the hall with Alice in her wake.

Holding her skirt high, Juliana charged down the keep stairs and out into the icy morning air. Winter had stayed late this year and hurled cold winds across Wellesbrooke in an attempt to forestall spring. The sun was floating up over the battlements now, and the castle was awake.

Cooks scurried back and forth between the kitchen building and the keep. Children chased dogs, a stray piglet, and each other around the yard in front of the boar pit. Juliana ignored the din issuing from the smithy, the armory, and the carpenter's workshop. Sparing no glance for the dozens of castle folk in the bailey, she turned her back on the newly constructed hall with its glass windows. Wellesbrooke wasn't the largest castle in the kingdom, but Hugo was determined to make it one of the most modern.

She marched past the brewhouse and laundry, and by the time she came to the stables her steps had lightened. She and her father often engaged in such clashes, but she'd grown accustomed to them. Their temperaments were alike, too alike to avoid noisy battles. In any case, her mood was foul because of the coming tournament. Hugo was holding it ostensibly to celebrate Yolande's sixteenth birthday. An heiress of great wealth, Yolande de Say had been entrusted to Lady Welles's training. Hugo, ever the wily maneuverer, was hoping to match the girl with his nephew Richard.

"Thunder of God, I hate tournaments," Juliana said under her breath as she waited for the grooms to bring her mare.

"But this be the last one before we move to Vyne Hill. You said so, mistress."

"Thanks be to God."

Juliana scowled across the bailey without seeing the shepherds, brewers, cooks, and armorers in her view. For her, tournaments had always been an occasion of humiliation. So had May celebrations, festivals, and feasts. So many occasions at which she sat while her sisters flirted, teased, and danced with suitors.

At Wellesbrooke on May Day last month there had been a feast and dancing. It was a custom for the youths and young men to gather flowers and make garlands for their favorite lady's hair, and this year as in most, Juliana went bareheaded. Oh, she had received a garland from her father, and one from his oldest retainer, Sir Barnaby. Tokens of pity. She'd thanked Hugo and Barnaby, separated the garlands and worn the flowers on her gown.

Barnaby appeared leading her mare. "Good morrow, Mistress Juliana."

Barnaby's years could be counted by the number of gray hairs that were rapidly obscuring his brown ones. Even his thick mustache was mostly gray. His skin was weathered like old wood and cracked like drought-dried earth. He had a small fief from Hugo and had known Juliana her whole life.

"Barnaby," Juliana snapped as she saw the mare's saddle. "You know well I ride astride on long journeys."

Blinking at her, Barnaby pretended surprise. "I forgot."

"When donkeys sing carols you'll forget," Juliana said. "Oh, never mind. I've lost too much time already. Are you coming?"

Juliana mounted her mare before either Barnaby or a groom could assist her. Barnaby shoved Alice on another mare.

"Aye, mistress. I'll follow directly."

Alice sneezed again. "Oh, mistress, you know how I am with horses."

"Alice, I'm not going to listen. The rushes on the floor make you sneeze, geese and chickens make you sneeze, new-dyed cloth makes you sneeze, horses make you sneeze. Pull your head-rail up over your nose."

Juliana arranged the voluminous folds of her overrobe and cloak and checked the set of her leg over the sidesaddle. Her eye caught the built-up heel of her right boot. All her footwear had to be made this way, for her right leg was a thumb's width shorter than her left. The sign of the devil, her chaplain said, a sign that Juliana was cursed and must guard against evil more than most. Her lips thinned and pressed against each other, forming a tight seam like that between the stones in the castle walls.

Hugo complained of her stormy temper, but who wouldn't feel disgruntled. Everyone either pitied her for her deformity or feared her as the minion of the devil. Alice said she brought much of it on herself by glowering all day long and by her contrariness. Juliana had no time for pleasantries. They did her no good.

"Well, come on, then," she said to Alice and Barnaby. She patted the sack fastened to her saddle. "We've over three hours' ride ahead and I want to get these herb seeds to Vyne Hill so they can be planted."

"We should take more men," Barnaby said.

He urged his horse alongside Juliana's as she rode across the bailey and through the gatehouse.

"No time, and I don't need them. Damnation, we're only going to Vyne Hill."

Vyne Hill was a manor left to her by the Countess of Chessmore after she'd saved the old lady's life with her herbal skills. Juliana had caused a scandal by insisting upon occupying the rundown estate. Hugo had ranted and bellowed, with his usual success. Mother had demurred, but Mother had given up finding a husband for her after that disastrous aborted marriage ceremony with Edmund Strange. Had it been a whole year? The shame still seared her as if he had rejected her last night.

Her parents had negotiated a marriage with Edmund, who was Baron Stratfield's nephew and cousin to Gray de Valence. Juliana had been uncertain, but obedient. The ceremony was performed. There was feasting and merriment, and then the bedding ceremony. Juliana's thoughts veered away from that memory. It was the reason she'd balked at having anything to do with another suitor. She secretly suspected that her parents dreaded trying to find her a husband of the proper rank almost as much as she.

Now, after a year's persistent refusal on her part, no one objected to her spinsterhood. She had convinced Hugo that she was like a Beguine, one of those religious women who took minor orders and devoted themselves to service in the world. Juliana suspected that, like herself, her family was looking forward to August, when she would move permanently to Vyne Hill. Then she would have peace, and so would they. In the meantime, it was a fine day for a ride.

She led the way beneath the giant iron teeth of the portcullis and out of the castle. Wellesbrooke castle had been erected on a spit of land that jutted out into the river Clare and divided the stream into two branches. The castle loomed over the divergence, connected to shore by two bridges, one over the east and one over the west branch.

Juliana threaded her way through the foot traffic on the west bridge—farmers bringing produce, huntsmen, reeves, bailiffs, women bringing dough to be baked in castle ovens. As so often happened, Juliana's temper improved with the distance between her and Wellesbrooke. Once off the bridge, she turned north along the track beside the Clare.

She rode in this direction through fields and then woods for over an hour. By the time she reached the stream that marked her turn eastward, she'd had her fill of Alice's sneezes and complaints about her delicate health. The maid was a big woman, plump, with burnished, flyaway hair and a nose that was always pink. Juliana was guiding her mare along a portion of collapsed stream bank when Alice moaned.

"Me back. Me back's near broke with riding this bony nag. Ah-ah-ah-ahchoooo!"

Juliana glanced back to see Alice's hands fly up to her face. The end of a rein flicked her horse's ear, and the animal bolted. Jumping the stream, it careened into the forest along a muddy track that pierced deep into the North Wood. Alice shrieked and bounced in the saddle.

"Watch your seat," Juliana shouted as she kicked her horse and rode after her maid.

Barnaby came after her, but he was old and rode much slower. Juliana plunged down the narrow track dodging branches wet from a night's heavy rain. Alice vanished around a twisting curve in the track. Soon all Juliana could do was follow the so   ' her wails. She swerved along the jagged path. Mud flew in her face as her mare galloped, but she urged the horse on, fearful that Alice would lose her balance and fall or be dragged.

She heard another scream, and then nothing. Rounding another sharp bend, she slowed and came to a halt. Alice sat in the middle of the path. While Juliana dismounted, the maid got on all fours, put her hand on her back and moaned.

"Me back, me poor back. It's broke, it is."

Barnaby joined them and sat on his horse gawking at the muddy and moaning figure of the maid. Juliana stalked over to her.

"Hush. Have you no pluck at all, woman? Here, take my hand." Juliana pulled the maid to her feet and began poking and prodding her to the accompaniment of Alice's groans. "Just as I thought. Nothing broken." She looked around and spotted a spray of ceramic shards. "Nothing except my herb jars, by God's grace. Thunder of heaven! If you've broken all my pots, I'll skin you, I will."

"I couldn't help it," Alice wailed.

Juliana winced at the sound, then sighed. "I know, Alice. Pay me no heed. This tournament has me right evilly disposed. You rest here. Barnaby, you find her horse, and I'll go back for the basket. I've no doubt she dropped it back there somewhere."

She walked her horse slowly back down the track. To the side, beneath a dead shrub, she spotted a squat blue jar. Dismounting, she hiked up her skirt and picked her way toward it through dead leaves and mud. She'd been wise to wear an old gown of coarse wool and one of her mother's oldest cast-off cloaks. The end of the garment trailed in the mud. Juliana stopped to pick it up and sling it over her arm. Then she began to pick up herb jars.

She worked her way down the path, leaving it occasionally to retrieve a pot. Her boots soon wore thick coats of mud. It was growing harder and harder to walk in them. She'd made a sack of the end of her cloak, and it was filled with small stoppered pots, each carefully labeled.

Juliana stopped for a moment beside a water-filled hole in the middle of the track. It was as long as a small cart. She remembered splashing through it when she chased after Alice. A little way off she could hear the stream churning on its way to join the Clare. She would have to turn back soon, but she was reluctant. She still hadn't found the jar containing leaves of agrimony, a plant with spiky yellow flowers. She needed the agrimony, for one of the daughters of a villein at Vyne Hill had a persistent cough.

The child, Jacoba, needed to drink a decoction of the herb flavored with honey. Juliana didn't want to admit that much of her ill humor arose from her concern about Jacoba and her desire to get to Vyne Hill as soon as possible and dose the little girl. Yesterday Jacoba had been worn out from the violent spasms. If she lost more strength, she could be in danger.

Clutching her cloakful of pots, Juliana searched the

woods to either side of the track for the small white jar.
All at once she saw it lying on the opposite side of the
path at the base of a stone the size of an anvil. So great
was her relief that she lunged across the track. She sailed
over the puddle of water, but landed in mud. Her boots
sank to her ankles.

"Hell's demons."

Stepping out of the ooze, she picked up the jar, bal-
anced on the edge of the mud, and bent her knees in
preparation for a jump. At the last moment she heard
what she would have noticed had she been less intent on
retrieving the jar. Hoofbeats thundered toward her. Tee-
tering on the edge of the mud, she glanced in the direction of the stream. Around a bend in the track hurtled a
monstrous giant destrier, pure black and snorting, with a
man astride it so tall that he nearly matched the size of
his mount. Juliana stumbled back. She glimpsed shining
chain mail, emerald silk, and a curtain of silver hair before a wall of black horseflesh barreled past her. An armored leg caught her shoulder. She spun around, thrown
off balance by the force of the horse's motion. Her arms
flew out. Pots sailed in all directions. Legs working, she
stumbled into mud and fell backward into the puddle. As
she landed she could hear a lurid curse.

She gasped as she felt the cold water. Her hands hit
the ground and sent a shower of mud onto her head and
shoulders. Juliana sputtered and wheezed, then blinked
her muddy lashes as she beheld the strange knight. He'd
pulled up his destrier, and the beast had objected. The
stallion rose on his hind legs and clawed the air, snorting
and jerking at the bridle. Those great front hooves came
down and landed not five paces from Juliana. More mud
and dirty water spewed from beneath them and into her
face.

This time she didn't just gasp; she screamed with fury.

To her mortification, she heard a low, rough laugh. She had closed her eyes, but now she opened them and beheld her tormentor. The knight sat astride his furious war horse as easily as if it were a palfrey. He tossed back long locks the color of silver and pearls as he smiled down at her, and Juliana felt as if she wanted to arch her back and spit.

Juliana scowled into a gaze of green that rivaled the emerald of the length of samite that draped across his shoulders and disappeared into the folds of his black cloak. It was a gaze that exuded sensuality and explicit knowledge. And even through her anger she was startled at the face. It was the face of the legendary Arthur, or some young Viking warrior brought back to life—wide at the jawline, hollow cheeks, and a bold, straight nose. The face of a barbarian warrior king, and it was laughing at her.

"By my soul," he said in a voice that was half seductive growl, half chuckle. "Why didn't you stand aside? Have you no sense? No, I suppose not, or you wouldn't be sitting in a mud puddle like a little black duck."

Shivering with humiliation as well as the cold, Juliana felt herself nearly burst with rage. The knave was laughing again! Her hands curled into fists, and she felt them squeeze mud. Her eyes narrowed as she beheld the embodiment of armored male insolence. Suddenly she lunged to her feet, brought her hands together, gathering the mud, and hurled it at that pretty, smirking face. The gob of mud hit him in the chest and splattered over his face and hair. It was his turn to gasp and grimace. Teeth chattering, Juliana gave him a sylph's smile.

"And so should all ungentle knights be served, Sir Mud Face."

She laughed, but her merriment vanished when she saw the change in him. He didn't swear or fume or rant in impotence like her father. His smile of sensual corruption vanished, and his features chilled with the ice of ruthlessness and an utter lack of mercy. In silence he swung down off his horse and stalked toward her. Juliana gaped at him for a moment, then grabbed her skirts— and ran.

AGRIMONY

This herb was recommended for healing wounds hurt with iron, for inflammation of the eyes, bites of poisonous beasts, convulsions, warts, and absentmindedness. For coughs and sore throats, it was said that one should gargle a decoction of the leaves mixed with honey and mulberry syrup.

• *Chapter 2* •

GRAY DE VALENCE SNAPPED A COMMAND TO his destrier and threw the reins over his saddle. Ire threatened to melt the palisade of ice that surrounded his emotions as he strode toward the black-haired witch who had dared to throw mud in his face. He mastered the urge to release the anger in an ungoverned torrent.

For years he'd longed for the day when he could confront those who had ruined him. He'd spent months planning his arrival at Wellesbrooke, where one of his betrayers lurked. He'd arranged every detail of his appearance, from his embossed-silver chain mail to the fittings on his saddle. And this insolent peasant girl had destroyed it all with her mud!

He felt the acidlike scald of anger in his lungs and chest and tamped it down. The girl had launched into a run, casting fearful glances at him as she struggled with muddy skirts and boots. Her rout and confusion made him smile. She stumbled out of the largest puddle only to encounter another filled with more mud. His long strides covered the distance between them before she could pull one foot out of the mess.

While she lifted a leg, she turned to glance over her shoulder at him. He was almost upon her and joyous at the prospect. She cried out and threw herself forward, but he grabbed her around the waist. He heard a clatter. Pots and jars spilled from the recesses of her garments as she twisted in his arms.

"Just God," he said coolly. "I'll lesson you in manners proper to a little peasant duck."

He stared down into gray eyes as welcoming as the steel of a sword blade. When he felt the meager blows from her fists on his chest, the corner of his mouth curled. She must have seen his smirk, for she ceased her attack abruptly. Dark brows came down over those damascened eyes, and he found himself unable to look away from their silver depths. Then he noticed that his hands seemed full of yielding flesh, pillowed in a softness he hadn't expected. His ire began to fade. Surrounding her with one arm, he drew her close and allowed one hand to slip beneath her cloak to run from her waist to her hip. He heard her suck in a breath.

"It's too fine a day to quarrel with a maid of such beauty," he murmured.

"I'm a little black duck, remember?" Then she kicked him, hard, in the knee.

Agony burst in his joint, and his leg nearly buckled. Cursing, he staggered and then got an arm under her legs. He lifted her, kicking and swearing, turned, and stepped into the puddle. His boot slipped; his injured knee gave way, and he pitched forward. The girl went flying, and he after her.

Dirty water flew in his face as he landed on his knees and collapsed onto something soft. Spewing water, he shook his head, slinging mud in every direction, while beneath him the girl gasped and squirmed.

"My chain mail," he growled, all nonchalance and detachment abandoned.

"Get off me, you knave!"

With her pounding him in the chest and ribs, he managed to plant both hands in mud and lift himself. As he rose, her legs came free, and she brought a knee up between his thighs, nearly ramming him in the groin. He cried out as her knee drove into his inner thigh. To protect himself, he dropped his whole weight down on her, into the quagmire of water and mud. He fastened a hand around her neck and pushed her head underwater, then let her up. She spewed water at him.

"Oh, plague-ridden sodding caitiff!"

He shoved her underwater again with a chuckle. "Curb your impertinent tongue. I've never encountered so errant a maid." She bobbed out of the water and writhed beneath him, nudging his sex. "Nor one who invited me to correct her so lewdly."

She went still at this last comment and gave him a look of such bewilderment that all his assumptions were overthrown. No woman of experience gaped at a man with such confusion. Suddenly, he was forced to look at the girl anew. Lustrous skin (beneath the mud), lips the color of wild roses, strong, strong arms and legs that could wrap around a man's back—and that stare of complete incomprehension. He'd mistaken insolence for experience.

"My error," he murmured. "You're untouched, or were until I touched you."

"What?"

More confusion. He smiled as he hadn't since Saladin had thrown him into a cell with three lusty female slaves.

"Damascened eyes," he whispered. "I've never seen the like."

She was still struggling with his meaning as he lowered his mouth to hers. Her lips were cold, but lush and pliant, and her mouth was hot. He felt rather than heard her cry. A shiver passed through her body and spoke to him of a virgin's terror. He had known terror and helplessness; he couldn't endure it in her. He lifted his mouth, and then his body.

Shifting to the side, he allowed her to get to her knees.

Whimpering, she struggled to rise, but he was sitting on her cloak and skirt. She tugged at them with both hands.

"Thunder of God! Get off, you lewd devil, or I'll put my boot in that licentious archangel's face of yours."

"Ah, the quivering virgin has recovered herself," he said as he lifted his hip to free her.

She yanked her garments free, but with such force that she toppled into the mud again. He threw back his head and laughed a deep, full laugh such as he hadn't uttered in years. Now she was so furious her curses had disintegrated into wordless sputters. She picked herself up, scrambled out of the puddle, and turned on him. Too late he saw the glob of mud in her hand. She threw it, and it hit him square on the nose.

It was his turn to indulge in wordless imprecations, and by the time he'd wiped his face, she had put two fingers in her mouth and was whistling. He heard three sharp bursts as he stood. A mare appeared at her side, and she swung herself up into the saddle. Kicking the horse, the girl deliberately sent the animal into the puddle. Great splatters of water and mud hit him.

He lunged at her. "Aaaahhrgh!"

His hand grabbed a small, muscled leg, but slipped as the mare lunged past him. He tried to hang on too long, overbalanced, and plunged to the ground on his hands and knees. He glared after the girl, thwarted and furious about it. She looked back at him as she cantered down the track, laughing.

Laughing! A woman with wild-rose lips and damascened eyes was laughing at him. He sprang to his feet and ran after her, but she vanished around a bend in the path before he could reach her. He stopped, chest heaving, fists clenched, and snarled. Then he looked down at himself.

His surcoat, chain mail, boots, every bit of him was

covered with mud. He glanced at his destrier, Saracen. The animal was ignoring him, calmly munching on new grass at the side of the track. Saracen was half covered in mud and would have to be groomed.

Just God. He'd ridden a little ahead of his men to put his thoughts in order before they got to Wellesbrooke, and now he'd be delayed even more. He was to meet his cousin Arthur and the rest of his company by the Clare. When they saw him, they wouldn't rest until they got the story of the mishap from him. What was he going to say—that a peasant maid had tossed him in a mud puddle?

"Unruly witch," he muttered.

He wiped his face and started trudging toward Saracen. Then he heard his name called. It was Arthur, and he heard Lucien as well. He was late and they'd come looking for him. Mounting Saracen, he turned the destrier toward the stream, but before he could go far, his young cousin, Arthur Strange, trotted out of the woods to meet him. He was wide of shoulder like Gray, quiet, and often wore a lost expression gained from having Edmund Strange for an older brother. Unlike Gray, he possessed hair that was more blond than silver. Arthur pulled up, stared, then covered his mouth.

Another young man joined him—Lucien, who was French. Gray scowled and stabbed glances at the newcomer. He was older than Arthur and thus had more mastery. His features settled into frozen gravity. He walked his destrier over to Gray. Lean, with hair of deep rich brown and eyes the blue-gray color of a rain-filled cloud. His irreverence and impiety often shocked more staid English knights.

"*Messire.*" Lucien's solemn expression didn't waver, nor did the dancing merriment in his eyes. "*Pauvre messire.* What has happened? Did you purpose to take a mud bath to make yourself more beauteous than you already are for this momentous tournament? I assure you. *Ce n'est pas nécessaire. Tu es de Valence le Beau.*"

"Lucien, go to the devil."

"Perhaps first, *messire*, we should go to the stream and watch you bathe."

Having lost almost her entire supply of herbs, Juliana had returned home early. She'd created a stir along the way, with villagers and travelers alike staring at her mud-caked self. Her remedy had been to fix her gaze straight ahead and glower into the distance. Back at Wellesbrooke her parents had been in the midst of greeting the Earl of Uvedale, legal guardian of Yolande. Father had shot her a look of such outrage that she'd ducked into the crowds traversing the bailey until the guest had been conducted into the New Hall.

She had stolen back into the keep and up to her room. There she gave instructions that more agrimony be delivered to Jacoba's mother at Vyne Hill. Then she bathed, using twice the usual amount of water to get rid of all the mud. Now she was ignoring Alice's questions as she had been since setting out on the return journey.

"Beg pardon, mistress," the maid said as she helped Juliana into another old kirtle, undertunic, and overgown. "You know how awful I am at riding. But I'll make it right, I will. You'll see. I'll have them herbs potted again by tomorrow. But how in God's name did you come to fall in the mud like that?"

Juliana was combing her wet hair. She was still so furious she expected steam to come out her ears. "I met a beast. A great, arrogant Viking beast riding on a black monster."

Alice, whose imagination was peopled with ghosts, unicorns, griffins, and other fantastic creatures, widened her eyes.

"A beast? What manner of beast?"

Dropping her comb, Juliana began to tie the side lacings of her overgown. "Another of those foul, prideful rooster knights come to tournament, no doubt. The knave is probably one of those younger sons who go from one to the other unseating their betters, taking their horses and armor and holding them for ransom. Bloated with conceit, he was." Her eyes narrowed as she remembered him straddling her and laughing down at her. "But I have no doubt he'll meet his match at Wellesbrooke."

Alice stared at her mistress for a moment, then began to shake her head vigorously. "Oh, no. Oh, no, mistress. Please, not this time. There are too many knights and barons about. Think of the risk."

Juliana spared not a glance at the maid as she walked to an alcove in which was set a window with a pointed arch. The shutters were open to let in sunlight. She knelt on a bench and leaned out the window to gaze over the sparkling blue of the river Clare, past a patchwork of fields to the forest beyond them. Dozens of knight's tents had been erected between the castle and palisade at the edge of the promontory. To her right the sun was sinking toward the hills. She drummed her fingers on the windowsill, deep in thought.

"Please, mistress, not again."

"You may stay home this time."

"Someday you're going to meet a man who'll turn your own tricks against you."

Juliana smiled. "There's not a man alive clever enough, or if there is, he'll be too full of his own male importance to reason out the solution."

Alice crossed herself and muttered a quick prayer. "God preserve you, my lady."

"I like to help God along in his care of me—what's that noise?"

Juliana leaned farther out the window and listened. On top of the keep the sentry was blowing his horn. She heard a shout. Her gaze swept the river valley and found a mass of riders poised on the west bank. Ranged along the river, they formed a long line of glinting metal and rich colors, the most dominant of which were green and gold.

"De Valence! I've no doubt he's as hateful as his cousin since they share the same evil blood." Juliana left the window and raced out of the room. "Come, Alice. Let's see this scandalous phoenix Father so dreads to meet."

She ran downstairs and shouldered her way through the throng of servants in the hall who were preparing it for an evening feast. Outside she saw her parents, their younger daughters, and their highest retainers hastily putting themselves in order as they rushed across the bailey to the drawbridge to greet the new arrival. Juliana ducked behind the dovecote before they could see her, then went to the stairs that led to the wall walk. With Alice protesting behind her, she gained the wall walk and dodged men-at-arms on her way to a turret beside the gatehouse.

Once at the turret, she hurried up a winding stair to the top. There she perched in an embrasure and watched as a standard-bearer rode across the west bridge. He bore a great emerald banner that snapped in the wind. The breeze tossed her hair in her eyes, and she brushed it away. When she could see, she beheld a winged golden dragon rearing on the standard. The wind made the standard furl and billow so that the dragon appeared to twist, snarl, and claw in attack.

Behind the standard-bearer rode a long line of men,

three abreast. Juliana surveyed their number. Thunder of heaven, there must be almost two hundred men! Only the most powerful barons had riding households of that size. This was indeed a powerful phoenix.

She searched the first line of men riding behind the standard-bearer and in the middle found de Valence by the colors he was wearing—an emerald-green surcoat of the finest silk over gleaming silver chain mail. A glittering dragon of gold breathed fire on his chest. She wished he would remove that great helm, for all she could see were black slits where his eyes should be.

Suddenly that great helm turned and tilted in her direction. Juliana ducked behind a merlon, then peered out at him. The black slits in the great helm pointed at her, and for some unknown reason, she shivered and couldn't make herself leave her hiding place. Thunder of God, she was frightened, and for no reason. Swallowing, she chanced a peek. To her relief, de Valence had ridden up to the gatehouse where her parents, sisters, and cousin Richard waited.

He pulled up his mount, a black destrier Juliana now noticed for the first time. A quiver of uneasiness passed through her. Ah, what a foolish thought. There was more than one black stallion in the world.

De Valence was still sitting on his horse. He gazed down at Hugo, who was giving a host's greeting. Hugo finished, and still de Valence sat on the black horse that was growing restive. He controlled the animal easily with one hand, then dropped the reins.

The stallion planted his hooves and went still. Silence settled over the welcoming party. Juliana noted that Richard, a knight of renowned prowess, was caressing the hilt of his sword. His hair as black as Juliana's, he had Hugo's girth and courage as well. There was much between him and this silver-haired lord. De Valence unfastened his great helm. Juliana leaned down from the embrasure to get a better view. A gloved hand pushed back the padded mail hood that protected his head, and she cursed. Silken hair the color of moonlight and pearls spilled forth in thick cascades that almost reached to his shoulders.

"The Viking!"

Alice, who had been craning her neck in the next embrasure, let out a low whistle. "Oooo, mistress, that be a fine, beautiful man, that be."

"Hush, Alice, you're babbling."

"But look at them wide shoulders," Alice said. De Valence swung a long leg over the saddle as he dismounted. "And such grace for so long-limbed a man. Look at your sisters."

Laudine and Bertrade stood behind Richard, their veils fluttering, their whispers almost audible behind their hands. Juliana glared at them as they fidgeted, giggled, and stared at de Valence like two twelve-year-olds. The whole company in front of the gatehouse seemed to churn and stir, so great was the agitation among the inhabitants of Wellesbrooke.

Even Richard, who was as refined and chivalrous a knight as any in Christendom, revealed his agitation. He bowed to de Valence, but watched him uneasily until the other must have uttered some pleasantry. Then he gave de Valence a slight smile and gestured toward the gatehouse. Hugo fell in step with his guest, and a wave of relief seemed to pass over the crowd.

Juliana crossed to the opposite side of the turret to follow the progress of host and guest until they disappeared into the new hall. Then she whirled on her heel and began striding back and forth while Alice babbled on about the magnificence of Gray de Valence, his great personal dignity, his unparalleled beauty, his obvious strength, his magnificent apparel.

"And did you see how he bowed to your mother? What grace, such a true, perfect gentle knight."

Juliana swept back across the turret again. "Be silent, Alice! What nonsense. Did I not tell you he's the Viking?"

"You mean the arrogant beast?"

"Aye, the arrogant beast of a Viking who attacked me in the mud. By God, no wonder he was so unendurable. It was Gray de Valence. The pompous cur. Evil-minded brute. Slavering, scourge-ridden blight— Oh, no."

An unexpected thought made her stumble. She righted herself and twisted her hands together, intertwining the fingers in a nervous habit she couldn't seem to break. There would be a welcoming feast tonight for all those attending the tournament. A feast and dancing afterward. *He* would be there. And he would recognize her.

"Thunder of heaven," she muttered.

She remembered his strength, how he'd lifted her as easily as she lifted her veil. She remembered his violence, the fury directed at her when she threw mud in his face. He could have broken her in half with one hand.

Juliana leaned against the turret wall as the enormity of the peril she'd been in dawned on her. She'd thrown mud in the face of Gray de Valence, a man her father feared, and who made Richard more than a little apprehensive, who like some demon had vanished from England into a land of evil heathens and survived. Gray de Valence, by God.

What was she going to do? She couldn't hide from him. Father would be furious if she stayed away from the feast tonight after she'd promised to be good. But the thought of confronting de Valence made her legs weak and her stomach queasy. What was she going to do?

"Alice, I've fought with Gray de Valence."

"Oh, mistress, I hadn't thought . . ." Alice joined her in pondering the difficulty. "Ah!"

"What?" Juliana asked.

Alice clapped her hands and chuckled. "This morning you were in your old clothes, mistress."

"Yes?"

"Well, mistress, you were bundled in one of them old wool gowns and a cloak with patches on it, and covered with mud besides. Just you meet him all cleaned up in your fine clothes. He won't recognize you."

Juliana frowned. "He called me a little black duck."

"We'll hide your hair. Wear one of your flaring hats with your wimple and barbette and put a veil over that. You'll look the gracious eldest daughter."

Juliana glanced across the bailey to the new hall. Through Hugo's expensive glass she could see wavy figures moving around. One of them wore green and gold; this one she knew possessed emerald eyes and a heathen ruthlessness she didn't care to arouse.

"Viking beast."

Wait. She couldn't let this man frighten her. After all, he was only a more fabulous version of those feeble-witted rooster knights she detested.

"Alice, I refuse to let him scare me. He was the one in the wrong."

Alice gave her a wary look. "Now, mistress."

"It's true." Juliana began to pace again, swiftly, with jerky movements that matched her temper. "He shoved me into the mud with his leg, the monster. I won't have it. If I have to hide and disguise myself, he's going to pay for it."

Juliana stopped to gaze at the new hall again. "Indeed, I'll make it my special task to make certain he pays. In a way that will mortify Gray de Valence as he did me."

She smiled then, a sweet nun's smile that caused Alice to groan and shake her head. Juliana left the turret then, with Alice dancing at her heels.

"Now, mistress, now mistress. You don't want to do this, you don't. He's not the kind of man to take such a thing without avenging himself. Think of your father, think of your mother . . ."

Juliana said nothing, but her smile grew wider and wider as she walked toward the keep. By the time she reached her chamber, she was grinning.

Sweet Violet

One of the fragrant herbs, violets were used in potage and for sauce, and in fritters and custard. They were good for sore eyes, falling fits, and drunkenness.

• *Chapter 3* •

THE NEW HALL AT WELLESBROOKE ECHOED
with song. A minstrel held the company spellbound with
his ballad of love and chivalry at King Arthur's court.
Between the tall glass windows that ran along one side of
the great room, gilded sconces were affixed to the wall
and bore the luxury of beeswax candles. Their sweet
scent filled the air and chased away the rougher smells
that lingered after dinner. Soft golden light flickered in
pools on the newly swept floor. Tables had been cleared
away, and Hugo and his most prominent guests sat on
chairs and stools on the dais before the fireplace. Ladies,
barons, and knights disposed themselves about the hall
in groups grown quiet with awe at the brave deeds ex-
pounded by the singer.

Surfeited on Hugo's venison, pleased with himself and
the preliminary success of his plan for revenge, Gray
reclined next to the Earl of Uvedale on a curved chair.
He'd taken care to practice the guile learned from Saladin, a man who could smile, compliment, and charm his
enemies while poisoning their wine. Hugo's wariness of
him had faded in the face of Gray's courteous demeanor.
Richard still eyed him uneasily, but he had returned
Gray's civility.

While pretending to listen to the song with as much
fascination as his fellow guests, Gray leaned back into a
shadow and looked around the hall. Hugo was a prosperous baron. Tapestries woven in Burgundy, Brussels, and

Flanders reflected their brilliant colors in the firelight. White walls bore paintings of the creation, the Holy Family, and the apostles. Sideboards still bore serving vessels of gold and silver, while myriad servants in dark blue and silver, the Wellesbrooke colors, gave further proof of wealth.

Hugo could keep his tapestries, his growing list of fiefs, and his precious plate. Gray wasn't interested in his host except as a means by which to reach the man whose lies had cost him his reputation, his honor, his freedom, and nearly his life. Richard. He dared not look at Richard Welles, who was ensconced in the midst of a group of admiring ladies. Gray closed his eyes and fought off evil memories. He couldn't afford a lapse now.

Later he would pay for his control with nightmares in which he relived the branding. Slowly, making certain he wasn't observed, he slid his hand up to press against the scar on his upper arm. How many times in the years since Saladin had given it to him had he imagined that the wound still burned?

Gray forced himself to lift his hand and put it on the arm of his chair. Glancing at Uvedale, he was relieved to see that the older man was engrossed in the ballad and hadn't seen the gesture. Uvedale had been most cooperative. He'd gone to the earl before supper and presented the letter from the king's justiciar and unofficial regent, Hubert de Burgh. On behalf of the young King Henry, de Burgh had given permission for Gray to betroth himself to the heiress Yolande de Say. He also instructed Uvedale to allow Gray to woo the girl in his own way. The earl wasn't to reveal this agreement until Gray consented.

A wily and jaded courtier, Uvedale had recognized the favor and power Gray must wield to obtain such a letter. The earl hadn't objected despite the fact that Hugo was rumored to be about to ask Uvedale to consider a match between Yolande and Richard. Now Gray was free to carry on with his scheme.

His hands almost shook with excitement and anticipation. A black veil of rage threatened to obscure his vision as he contemplated how near he was to avenging Welles's betrayal. He dared not look at the man who evoked such hatred within his heart. Just God, he longed to be free of it, for this hatred gouged deep scars in his heart, as if acid were slowly dripping on it and eating it to the core. Had it only been a few hours ago that he first faced Welles after all the years of degradation and torture of the soul?

Gray nearly strangled the chair arms as he pretended to stare at the minstrel. Of the three men who betrayed him to his overlord, Richard Welles had been his friend—and the one who captured him and took him to sea. During his enslavement, he'd staved off despair by conjuring up Welles's image, especially his traitorous face, when his captors beat him, played games with him, laughed at him.

It was a pretty face but a few years older than Gray; in youth it must have been more suited to one of those expensive boy slaves Saladin kept. Now an old scar earned in a tournament bisected one of his black brows, and beneath those brows gleamed chestnut-colored eyes as large as plums. Richard had one of those long, straight noses bequeathed by the Normans. He also had the Welles ebony hair and his uncle's bearlike girth that contrasted with the almost feminine beauty of his face. To his muscled bulk he added a great height that rivaled Gray's.

The image of this black-haired devil's spawn had helped Gray endure, and he still couldn't quite believe he'd survived long enough to confront the original. When he'd first known the humiliation of slavery, he had decided to kill Welles, but years of warfare had cured him of blood lust. Now he was going to use all the circuitous craftiness Saladin had taught him to prick and goad Richard until the bastard finally lost his temper and issued a challenge.

Then, before hundreds of onlookers, he was going to calmly and happily beat the man whose betrayal had made him a slave. Once he had Richard's heart beneath the tip of his sword, he would demand a ransom of his captive that would beggar him forever. Welles would lose his honor and his nobility in one stroke, a fitting recompense. Ah, life was good at last.

It would be even better if he could have found that disrespectful black-haired maid. He'd sent men in search of her to no avail. Of all his experiences since returning to England, one of the more disconcerting had been to find himself unable to forget mud-soaked softness and damascened eyes. Only confronting Richard for the first time had swept the memory from his mind—briefly. Gray shifted uncomfortably in his chair. He had to put aside the recollection or he would lose governance of his body as he had while bathing away mud in the stream this morning and several times since.

The minstrel had finished, and jugglers had taken his place. The performers were dressed in tunics of bright yellow and red trimmed with bells. One of them deliberately dropped the leather balls he was tossing on top of his partner's head, one by one. To his right, his cousin Arthur Strange laughed at the antics. It was good to see Arthur laugh, for of late his quarrels with his malevolent brother had wiped merriment from his face. Used to the far more sophisticated and lurid entertainments of Saladin's court, Gray only smiled out of a desire to appear polite. His gaze wandered away from the jugglers' simple tricks.

He was looking for the girl Yolande, to whom he'd been introduced briefly before they ate. She was delectably small, barely sixteen, pale and blond like a princess in a troubadour's song. The encounter had taken him aback.

"Oh, my lord," she had said, clasping her hands in front of her chin. "How exciting it must be to sail the seas and visit the Holy Land."

Stunned that she would consider being abducted and enslaved exciting, he'd stared at her for a moment, but she gawped at him like an enraptured heifer.

"I, er, I wasn't in the Holy Land, Mistress de Say. I was in Egypt."

All he got was a blank look.

"Oh," she said.

He had considered telling her where Egypt was, but her attention wandered, and he had been spared.

The jugglers were still performing. He glanced at Hugo's daughters, the voluptuous Laudine and the madonnalike Bertrade. There was another, older sister who had yet to appear. From what he'd heard, she liked learning a man's skills with weapons more than dancing. Arthur had heard rumors that she'd learned swordplay along with her father's squires. The Welles heir, Tybalt, and his younger brother, Fulk, were in France attending to fiefs held by the king of France.

Gray stiffened. Someone moved out of the shadow of an arch behind the dais. He saw the figure, but no one else did, so intent was the crowd on the performance of the jugglers. The dark shadow crossed behind the group on the dais. It moved into a pool of light cast by the fire, and Gray caught a glimpse of curves draped in the finest samite. The color of the sky just before total darkness— royal-blue sapphire—shimmered as the figure glided out of the light. Just before the woman joined the group comprising Yolande and the Welles sisters, he saw a fluted, stiffened cap, barbette, and silver caul.

Cloth of silver and sapphire, clinging samite surrounding a face not quite visible in the darkness. Intriguing. Could this be the missing sister? He hadn't given her much thought, but that one glimpse had startled him. What was her name? He'd forgotten, but any unmarried girl who held herself back from tournament festivities, appeared only late after a feast, and kept to the shadows, this was an exceptional maid, indeed.

"Arthur," he whispered. His cousin was laughing at the tumbling jugglers again. "Arthur!"

"Yes, cousin."

"That girl in dark blue beside Yolande de Say, who is she?"

Arthur glanced at the girl in the shadows. "I think that's Hugo's eldest, Juliana. Oh, yes, hmmm."

"What does that 'hmmm' mean? Come now. I know your appetite for gossip. What do you know?"

"Little," Arthur said, but he leaned nearer Gray and gave him a salacious look. "It's said she never recovered from being spurned by my brother. Indeed, Edmund said she vowed to kill him, and I've heard other tales of her foul temper and unruly manner. Welles can't rid himself of her, so he's resorted to allowing her to take minor vows and retire to some ruined fief she got off the Countess of Chessmore. She's reputed to be good with herbs and healing—"

Gray rose suddenly as the juggling ended. "Enough, cousin. She sounds far more unpalatable than her garb would betoken. Come. The dancing is about to begin."

With Eastern guile, he allowed his hostess to direct him to a group of dancers that included Laudine and Bertrade, but not Yolande. The heiress had already been whisked away to be linked with Richard. The musicians struck up on lute, harp, horn, and drum. Gray bowed to Laudine on his right and Bertrade on his left, then linked arms with both as they all formed a chain. Arthur was the leader, and he began to sway from side to side as the pattern dance commenced.

Gray followed Arthur's intricate steps easily, but soon found himself the object of Laudine's frankly interested gaze. Seldom had he encountered so open a look of sexual appraisal in a maid. Generous of figure, with dark gold hair like her mother, she gave him such a knowing look that he almost blushed. He looked away, only to encounter Bertrade's stare. The girl quickly lowered her lashes, and he was struck again by her resemblance to paintings of the Madonna. She looked up at him again. He blinked into the cool blue gaze of a beautiful saint and somehow realized that the look was meant to challenge a man to break through the façade of saintliness to the passion beneath.

"Just God." These two were dangerous.

Laudine squeezed his hand, demanding his attention. "Is aught the matter, my lord?"

He was saved when Arthur increased the pace so that the dancers had to skip quickly to keep up with him. They whirled in a circle, faster and faster until the ends of the chain linked. The circle spun several times before the music suddenly ended, causing the dancers to halt and give a cheer. As quickly as the first tune stopped, a second began. Laudine grabbed his hand again, and surreptitiously pressed it against her hip. As they began to dance, she looked him up and down.

"By the Lord's mercy but you're a right lovely sight. Have you heard the story about the knight, the shepherdess, and the herd dog?"

"Which story is that, Mistress Laudine?"

He shouldn't have asked, for he got a story of such

foolish bawdiness that he laughed aloud in the midst of the dance. Lucien was on the other side of Laudine and heard the tale too. Soon the whole circle had heard the story. Laughter hopped along the chain until it came back to Gray. Jesting and quips passed from one dancer to another, and Gray realized that Laudine's bawdy humor was well-known to her friends. He allowed his tight control to slacken a bit and countered the teasing and provocative enticements Laudine directed his way.

"No, mistress, I'm not going to give you a favor in return for one of yours. I fear what you may request of me."

"Mmmm, Gray de Valence, then you'll not be getting one of my sleeves for your lance tomorrow."

He leaned close to gaze into Laudine's merry blue eyes and said, "Then I'll have to steal a favor."

"Oh," she said in a low voice. "Do try."

"I will, if you do me another kind of favor."

He glanced over at the circle containing Yolande and Richard, then whispered in Laudine's ear. She giggled and nodded. The second ballad came to an end, and a farandole began. They hadn't taken two steps before Gray swung out of the chain. Laudine gripped his hand and sped after him as they darted into the circle between Yolande and Richard.

Gray snatched the girl's hand out of Richard's grasp while Laudine pulled her cousin out of the circle and shoved him into Arthur's group. A shout of laughter erupted from both chains of dancers.

Gray bent down to murmur into Yolande's ear. "I couldn't bear another moment deprived of the honor of dancing with you."

Yolande peered up at him, eyes wide, cheeks crimson. Her small bow-shaped mouth popped open in amazement, but she appeared unable to speak. It was just as well. He was beginning to realize she was one of those women who thought a childlike demeanor attractive to men. Later he would free her of that misconception. They intertwined arms and swayed from side to side. Each time he swayed in her direction, he whispered sweet compliments to her.

"Forgive me, lady, but I've never seen hair like spun clouds."

He got a smile and a giggle for that comment. When he glided in her direction again, he continued.

"Your eyes rival the azure of the sky, and I think their magnificence has slain my heart."

Yolande giggled again, but over it he heard a most unattractive snort and turned to his right to look at the other lady with whom he'd linked hands but hadn't noticed until now. He met a gaze of silver brilliance, of derision and mockery, of disbelief—and definitely not of admiration. It was the lady in sapphire and cloth of silver.

He scowled at her, then looked closer. They stared at each other. Her black brows lifted in scorn, but Gray didn't respond. Those eyes. Damascened eyes. The silver framing her face and holding her hair made her eyes glitter like a sword blade in the morning sun. He glanced at the rest of her, but the rich garb seemed to deny what his senses told him. The silver caul that gathered her hair revealed nothing, for she had wrapped her tresses in cloth of silver before donning the jeweled net. But he knew those silver eyes, that dagger stare, that insolence.

"Just God, it's the arrogant little wench with the damascened eyes."

She gawked at him for a moment as they danced into a circle, then jerked her hand. He was too quick for her and tightened his grip before she could free herself and run. Then the music ended and the circle broke. Distracted by the sudden appearance of his peasant wench in the guise of a lady, he lost his hold on Yolande. When the dance circle re-formed, Richard darted in and swept her away to join another group. Gray could only scowl as he watched them go. He heard his other partner smirk.

"Good."

Rounding on her, he found the girl gloating at him.

"I *know* you, but you can't be Mistress Welles."

Music began again, and the girl took refuge in the dance. He kept her hand imprisoned in his, but she refused to look at him or speak to him. The floor was crowded now, with many circles of dancers, musicians, and dozens of onlookers. He waited until their circle broke into a chain. As they neared a deep window embrasure, he freed his left hand, broke his tormenter's grip on the hand of the man at her other side, and pulled her into the crowd. He didn't stop until he ducked into the shadows formed by the embrasure.

Pulling her nearer, he kept a tight grip on her arm. "I crave speech with you, lady."

"Release me, or I'll call my father."

"Ah, then you are Juliana Welles."

She tried to pull her arm free, but he kept it imprisoned. He saw her mouth open to fulfill her threat even as she tried to pry his fingers open.

Leaning down, he put his lips near her ear. "Do call him. Then I can tell him about my encounter with a ragged peasant maid who wallowed in the mud with me."

Juliana stopped struggling and glared up at him. "Puling upstart knave. I heard that hog's swill you were spouting at Yolande. Spun clouds, slain heart. Thunder of heaven! You're nothing but another lying rooster knight, only prettier and richer than most."

While she ranted at him, he had been trying to see her eyes. He moved closer so that she was caught between his body and the wall of the embrasure. Now he caught the scent of violets.

"Just God but you're a wild-tempered maid."

He was vaguely aware that she'd thrust her hands between them and was pressing her palms against his chest, but he was engrossed in catching a glimpse of her eyes, which were of a gray so light that they rivaled the sheen on his most precious silver drinking goblet. She was in the midst of another tirade, but he'd missed most of it.

"I know why you're trying to suborn poor Yolande."

That got his attention. He went still and asked in a silken voice, "And why is that?"

"You've come to avenge yourself upon my cousin. Oh, don't look so amazed. Everyone knows how you ruined your liege lord's wife, and how Richard was forced to remove you from England."

"An old tale, long past and forgotten," Gray said lightly. "I'm afraid, Mistress Juliana, that you've mistaken courtly graces for something more. Perhaps it's because you've never been to court, and after all, I've recently been in France, where these matters are better understood." He lowered his voice. "Or perhaps it's because you're still a maid."

He couldn't be sure, but he thought she blushed. Then she gave him a look of indecision, as if she weren't quite so sure of her opinion of him as she let on. That look reminded him of their encounter in the mud, and of her lack of experience in matters of the flesh. He recalled her confusion, which for some reason intrigued and aroused him. He stepped so close to her that their bodies touched.

"No, you don't understand how a man banters with a woman. I should have remembered, should I not, my little black duck?"

Not the most chivalrous of remarks. She gave a cry of

outrage and at the same time stomped on his foot. He yelped, hopped backward, and clutched his foot.

"You keep away from Yolande, Sir Knave. She's a friend to me, and please you to know I'll be watching. There'll be none of your foxing and debauching or I'll see you undone."

She whirled in a cloud of sapphire silk and pushed past him. He stumbled back into the embrasure and caught himself before he fell. Straightening, he watched Juliana Welles glide out into the light to join her sisters and Yolande. She had nearly discerned his true intentions. Her interference could ruin everything.

Drawing his brows together, he contemplated this threat to his plans. He wasn't baffled for long. He had the means to control Mistress Juliana; she obviously didn't want her father to know about their encounter in the woods. No doubt she'd been out without permission. Aye, he could muzzle her, if not by threats, then by other means more pleasurable to himself.

It was only after he'd rejoined his host and the guests on the dais that Gray realized that while he was with Juliana Welles he'd completely forgotten Richard and Yolande de Say.

Wolfsbane
(Aconite or Monkshood)

The root was used to poison pests. Those who wished to get rid of rats were advised to make cakes of paste and toasted cheese and powdered wolfsbane and put them near their holes.

· Chapter 4 ·

JULIANA RAN THE LAST FEW STEPS THAT
brought her to join the group of ladies that included her
sisters and Yolande. Only when she'd put Laudine's
plump curves between herself and the Viking did she
dare glance in the direction of the embrasure to see if
he'd followed her. She was startled to find him where
she'd left him, watching her.

Clad in a black damask tunic cinched with a chain of
gold and slashed at the sleeves to reveal an undertunic of
crimson, he leaned against the embrasure. Looking directly at her across the expanse of the hall, he gave her a
slow half-smile. Everything about him, the way he cocked
his burnished head to the side, the manner in which he
crossed his soft calfskin boots at the ankles, the loose
suppleness of his lips, warned of enticing corruption.

Juliana's mouth went dry, and she tried to swallow as
their eyes remained locked. Dragging her gaze from his,
she cursed the moment of weakness when she'd allowed
Richard to persuade her to dance. He'd wanted an excuse
to be near Yolande and eventually dance with her. What
a calamity. Dancing had never brought anything but evil
to her. Not daring to look at the embrasure and this
evening's particular evil, she tried to join in the conversation going on around her.

"Where have you been?" Laudine asked her. "You
missed the great circle."

The great circle was a Wellesbrooke custom in which

the whole company of dancers joined in one large circle nearly the width of the hall.

"You know I hate dancing."

"It's your own fault," Laudine said. "If you were more pleasant to young men, they wouldn't be afraid to dance with you."

Juliana frowned at her sister, who had been blessed with a body of generous proportions that assured her plenty of young men eager to join her in dancing. Laudine was nearly seventeen, plump and full of ribald humor, and had no patience with Juliana's views on rooster knights and the unworthiness of men. Juliana risked a glance at the embrasure, but de Valence wasn't there. She jumped when Laudine and the others suddenly burst out with laughter.

"What's so amusing?"

"Yolande," Laudine said. "She just told us of the pretty words the Sieur de Valence spoke to her."

Yolande nodded and bounced on the balls of her feet while clapping her hands. "If I married him, I'd be an even greater lady than I am already."

Shaking her head, Juliana sighed to herself. Yolande had a simple view of the world due to her rarified upbringing. To Yolande, all knights were brave, all ladies gentle. And when not reminded otherwise, she tended to forget that she wasn't the most important creature in the kingdom. When Yolande was scolded for this fault, however, tragic remorse always ensued. Juliana despaired for her. What would happen to such a girl at the hands of a corrupt barbarian?

Laudine was still talking. "Mmmm, mmm, mmm, you're a lucky one, Yolande. Two cocks crowing at your chamber window, one dark and one light, but both with right pretty combs, I vow—"

"Laudine!" Bertrade put a gentle hand on her sister's arm. "Don't be so ungentle."

Her admonishment went unheard by everyone except Juliana. Laudine and several other girls shrieked and tossed jests back and forth while Juliana felt a crimson heat flood her face. Quickly she glanced around the hall, hoping that Gray de Valence hadn't been near enough to hear Laudine's comment.

There he was, by the fireplace, talking to his cousin Arthur, another of those cursed Stranges. De Valence lowered his head to hear what the younger man was saying, and a spray of moonlight hair swung across his cheek. Suddenly he straightened, his expression grave. It was then that Juliana noticed that Arthur held out a black cloak. De Valence took the garment, slung it over one shoulder, and strode for the doors. Along the way he stopped to have a word with her father; then he was gone.

Good. She was glad he was gone. Perhaps he'd quit Wellesbrooke altogether. When Richard had wheedled her into dancing, she had never thought to be coupled with Gray de Valence. Now she was glad, for she'd been there to interfere with his evil wooing of Yolande. She still couldn't forget the witless expression on her friend's face when de Valence started spewing vapid compliments at her. Thunder of God! How could women believe such muck?

And how could she herself have believed de Valence's protestations of innocence? The man was evil. Had been since he corrupted his lord's wife when he was but a youth. Juliana wet her lips as she remembered the way he'd backed her against the embrasure. He'd been so close she had felt the warmth of his body on her skin. Without touching her, he'd made her quiver inwardly with awareness—of the suppressed strength of his body, of his readiness and heat. Juliana gave her head a little shake. What was wrong with her? She was breathing rapidly, and she was hot.

Parts of her tingled that shouldn't be tingling at the thought of Gray de Valence. Not after she'd witnessed the way he preyed upon any maid who came within his reach. She glanced at Yolande, who was blushing at more frank remarks about her encounter with de Valence. Dear, credulous Yolande, who had remained her friend despite Juliana's choleric temperament.

How fortunate that she'd promised Father she would attend this tournament. It was clear poor Yolande needed a guardian. Oh, she had Mother, but Mother was busy being hostess, and her sisters were no help.

De Valence thought he'd thwarted her with his threats to tell Father of their encounter. He'd soon see that Juliana Welles wasn't cowed by mere threats. The cursed arrogant rooster knight.

"Come, Juliana, it's time for another dance." Laudine was tugging on her arm.

Juliana shrugged her off. "Not again. I'm weary of all this foolish prancing. I've got herbs to put by early tomorrow before the jousting begins."

"Oh, Juliana, you're such an old woman."

"Someone has to provide medicines for this castle, and it's certainly not going to be you, my fine mistress."

"Healing is a great virtue," Bertrade said. "The Scriptures tell us to honor the physician."

Laudine laughed. "Juliana the leech."

Juliana lifted a brow. "I've cured many a headache for you, Mistress Love-ale."

Turning on her heel, she left her sisters to form another dancing chain. As she threaded a path between the clusters of guests, Yolande touched her sleeve. Before Juliana could speak, the younger girl pulled her behind a column and began to chatter.

"What do you think of the Sieur de Valence? Is he not the most chivalrous of knights? And his eyes, so green, like spring leaves reflected in a fountain. When he smiles my bones tremble—"

"Merciful saints!"

Yolande flushed and dropped her gaze to the floor.

"Oh, forgive me," Juliana said, "but you're such a contradictory creature, Yolande. I know you're a sensible girl, but you become pigeon-witted in the presence of a comely man."

Yolande said quietly, "I know, but you forget all the time I spent in locked towers, a prisoner to my inheritance. I used to dream of having a companion. I—I prayed to God for one, and then Edmund came to deceive me as he did you, but now perhaps I've found . . ."

Yolande gave her a curious, sideways glance that reminded Juliana of one of the flat-headed cats that prowled the granaries at night. Then the girl's chin lifted in defiance.

"He's a suitor worthy of me."

Watching her friend march off to join the dancers, Juliana shook her head. Yolande had always been troublesome and changeable. She knew the complexities of her vast property and yet delighted in simple entertainments that bored Juliana. And her temper, seldom seen, could be far more frightening than Juliana's, reaching greater violence and sustaining itself when Juliana's had long ebbed. But since Juliana had cured her of a dangerous fever, they had shared a bond. Yolande gave to the older girl a respect she reserved for few others. However, Juliana was beginning to suspect she wouldn't listen to her opinions about the Sieur de Valence.

Muttering curses against arrogant Viking knights, Juliana found her maid and quit the new hall. She was on her way to the keep when Richard called her name and came running across the bailey after her. Sending Alice on ahead, she waited on the sparse grass that grew in front of the wooden keep stair.

"Juliana," Richard said as he came up to her. "I wanted to thank you for persuading Yolande to dance. Your father wants me to make better friends with her. I think he's scheming to arrange a match between us."

Richard lived at his father's barony several days' ride from Wellesbrooke and his duties rarely allowed for long visits to the family.

"It was naught."

"No, it was much. I know how you hate to dance, especially since Edmund Strange . . ." He cleared his throat and scuffed the grass with his boot. His finger stroked the eyebrow that was bisected by a thin scar, a habit that always bespoke preoccupation. "Your pardon, cousin. I also wanted to beg a favor for my lance tomorrow."

Juliana stiffened. "An unnecessary gesture, cousin, but I thank you."

"But I want to."

"Richard Welles, do you think I want my *cousin* wearing my sleeve in a tourney? I might as well give it to Tybalt if he were here."

"Oh. I didn't think."

"I know," Juliana snapped. Then she sighed and broke into a smile. "Poor cousin. I forget sometimes how much you strive to be like your namesake, but I wouldn't give even Richard Coeur de Lion a favor if he wanted it for pity's sake."

"I'm sorry."

"Good night to you, Richard."

She watched him walk back to the new hall, making his way through merrymakers and servants along the way. It was true. Richard took his knighthood far more seriously than many. He strove to be the true, perfect gentle knight. She had seen him punish vassals for lapses in behavior that other men would have ignored. The precepts of chivalry—truth, honor, valor, liberality, and courtesy—guided his every action.

Unfortunately, Richard's chivalry also made him somewhat pompous and wearisome, but his heart was good. Shaking her head, Juliana mounted the keep stairs. Richard's chivalrous standards had nearly beggared him more than once. Hugo had been forced to provide funds to his nephew when Richard's ideas about knightly generosity caused him to distribute too much largesse among his retainers.

Alice was waiting for her in her room near the top of the Maiden's Tower. Laudine and Bertrade shared a room on the floor below, while Yolande was housed along with her gentlewoman companion on the floor below them. Juliana sat quietly while Alice unwrapped her head. As she helped the maid remove her cap, she reflected on how thoroughly her disguise had failed. He'd recognized her by her eyes. She never would have thought he'd remember her damned eyes. Now, if they'd been that glittering emerald color of his own, she could have understood. But hers were plain pale gray, like half-full rain clouds.

Feeling unsettled by how he'd teased and taunted her, Juliana crawled beneath the covers of her bed. She pulled her knees up to her chest and wrapped her arms around them as Alice put away her clothing. The room was lit only by a few tallow candles, but its white plaster walls were painted with murals of her own choosing.

One showed the myth of the unicorn, while another

pictured Francis of Assisi among the creatures of the forest. She loved this image in particular, for she'd come to believe in Francis's teachings. His precepts of simplicity, the oneness of nature and mankind, peace, humility, and love for the meanest creatures, these appealed to her. Friar Clement, the Franciscan who lived in a cave in the hills above Wellesbrooke, was her friend. He spoke continually of how people were flesh and blood, not pure spirits, and that they should practice kindness and courtesy.

Thinking of the teachings of Francis of Assisi and Friar Clement eased the tumult within her and made her happy. On their long walks in the hills, Friar Clement had pointed out how the beauties of the earth were a sign of the presence of God—the birds, the flowers, the animals, the sky. Peace descended upon Juliana as she thought about the view from the hills of the glittering Clare and the dark green of the forest beyond.

Friar Clement never spoke about human beauty, though. What would he say about the exquisite Gray de Valence? Was his beauty more evidence of the presence of the Lord, or was that soft moonlight hair and powerful body but lures, the disguise of Satan? Juliana was musing upon this question when Alice answered a knock at the door.

The maid engaged in a whispered conversation with a page. "Mistress, a servant of one of the guests has taken ill. A man-at-arms has come for the leech your father hired for the tournament, but the fool has gotten himself drunk."

"Very well." Juliana threw back the covers. "Fetch my healing box, and you'd better bring my casket as well."

The call to attend a sickbed late at night was one to which she'd grown accustomed. At one time, Mother had despaired of weaning her from her love of practicing at knife-throwing and other arts of weaponry with her brothers. Then she had introduced Juliana to the mysteries of herbs.

Dressing quickly in a plain linen gown and mantle, Juliana took her healing box from Alice. The maid and the page led the way down the spiral stair holding tapers. In the arcade of the old hall the man-at-arms was waiting, and soon she was following him out of the castle by the landward gate.

The stretch of land between the spiked palisade and the moat was covered with encampments, and the group wove its way through the multihued tents of the knights and barons who had answered the call to tournament. Juliana walked around a line of tethered horses, passed squires giving chain mail a final polish before retiring, held her skirts as she eased by campfires. Then her steps slowed, for the man-at-arms was heading for tents of green and white trimmed with gold.

A pennant flew in the breeze, and she could see the dragon writhing on it as its golden wings caught the light of torches set beside the tent entrance. She hesitated, realizing that the guard's cloak had concealed the colors that would have identified him as a de Valence man. The escort stopped at a small tent beside the pavilion reserved for the Sieur de Valence. Juliana nearly sighed her relief.

The man held open the tent flap for her. Holding her healing box in one hand, she pressed the other against her skirt as she stepped through the narrow opening. She stopped just inside and allowed her eyes to adjust to the dim candlelight. Silk hangings of crimson and gold in abstract designs dazzled her vision, and she glimpsed a rarity, an ostrich-feather fan. A dark figure was kneeling beside someone on a cot draped with more silk and furs.

The figure rose up, higher and higher. Juliana craned her neck back. The man turned toward her as he spoke.

"What took you so long, you flea-ridden—"

Juliana felt her jaw drop as Gray de Valence loomed over her, scowling, his arm drawn back to deal a lazy underling a blow of chastisement. He froze as they beheld each other, his arm still drawn back. Slowly it lowered until it came to rest at his side. His gaze never left hers.

"Just God, if it isn't the insolent maid with the damascened eyes—again." He almost smiled, but a cough from the patient on the cot rid him of all amusement. He glared at her. "Where's the leech?"

Juliana recovered her senses, blinked, and said, "He's drunk. They sent for me."

He did smile then, as he raked her body with a glance.

"This is no matter for maids, Juliana mine. My servant is quite ill, and there's no time for unskilled dabbling."

There was a long, racking cough from the patient that ended on a moan. Juliana looked around de Valence and saw a black-haired youth toss his head from side to side.

"You, my lord, will call me Mistress Juliana." The patient groaned, and she nodded at him. "Do you want me to help him or not? Speak quickly, my lord, for I've no patience with men who think women healers are naught but charlatans or witches. From the sound of that cough, your intolerance and ignorance could cost your servant his life."

He scowled at her, but said nothing as he turned back to the patient. Kneeling beside the cot, he said roughly, "This is Imad, my servant. Help him if you can, but be careful."

Ignoring de Valence's rudeness, Juliana set her healing box on the ground and joined him. Briefly she wondered about the luxury de Valence had provided for a mere servant. On the cot lay a youth unlike any she'd ever seen. His skin was a warm brown, his hair obsidian black. Slight, with a sharp, straight nose and date-shaped eyes, he muttered to himself in a guttural foreign language. He had been propped up on pillows of costly samite to ease his breathing, but he still wheezed. Juliana put her hand to his head and felt the heat of fever.

As she bent over Imad, he began to cough again. His body shook with the violence of the spasms. Suddenly de Valence leaned close and gripped the boy's shoulders. His arms came down over hers, and he held Imad steady. Trapped with her hands on the boy's forehead and neck, Juliana pursed her lips and waited for the coughing to subside. Her arms were on either side of his left one. De Valence moved, and his shoulder pressed into her breast. Juliana started, then pulled away, causing de Valence to turn his head.

She went still, for he had fastened a tortured look upon her. This time when she stared into his eyes, she found no derision, no cool iniquity, only fear, and beneath that, something disturbingly intense.

She stuttered, "H-he has a catarrh."

"I know that, woman," de Valence snapped. "Do something about it."

His sharpness destroyed her fear, and she straightened up to glare at him. "You'll address me with courtesy, or I'll not lift my hand to him."

"Arrogant little—"

Juliana rose, but he caught her wrist.

"No, don't leave. Forgive me. Imad is dear to me, and I'm worried."

Juliana stared at the hand holding her wrist, and he quickly released her. A small victory, and one she dared not test. She would have treated the boy despite his master's rudeness, but de Valence needn't know it. Calling to

Alice, who was waiting outside, she ordered the maid to set water to boil on several braziers.

While Alice and the man-at-arms were busy complying, Juliana delved beneath the neck of her gown to find the chain from which the key to her healing box was suspended. Unlocking the box, she searched among dozens of small vials, tubes, jars, and bundles. At last she retrieved a small black tube sealed with a cork and wax. Breaking the wax, she went back to the cot where de Valence was still kneeling. "I'll need wine."

A word from de Valence sent the man-at-arms scurrying from the tent. In but a few moments he was back with a flagon and a cup. De Valence filled the cup and held it out to her.

"Hold it quite still," she said as she uncorked the tube. "This is wolfsbane—"

De Valence cried out and jerked the cup out of her reach. "Wolfsbane! You're going to poison him. Are you witless, or simply mad?"

"Enough!" Juliana's booming command caught de Valence off guard. He blinked, then stared at her. "You listen to me, my lord Know-all. That boy's cough is dangerous."

Turning to Imad, Juliana pulled down the covers over the boy and pointed to his chest. "Listen to his breathing. Go on. Put your ear to his chest."

De Valence complied, lowering his head to the boy's chest. After a short space, he closed his eyes.

"Mercy of God."

"His chest is filled with liquid," Juliana said. She pointed to the pots of water Alice had set to boil on the braziers. "He must breathe warm air. The water must be kept boiling, and I'll put herbs in it to ease his chest. But the catarrh has advanced to a dangerous strength and must be fought with the wolfsbane. Without it, he will get worse."

"Worse?" De Valence whirled around, the wine cup still in his hand, and cast a glance of anguish at Imad.

Juliana pursed her lips and surveyed the boy as well. He was flushed with fever and every breath sounded rough and liquid. "I'm not accustomed to justifying my remedies, but you're a stranger, so I'll tell you that I've helped others with wolfsbane, including the Countess of Chessmore."

Running his hand through his hair, de Valence looked from Imad to Juliana. He caught his lower lip between his teeth, then swore and held out the cup. Juliana took it, emptied a minute portion of dark powder into the wine, and swirled it around.

"Hold him upright," she said.

De Valence did as she requested, and Juliana held the wine to Imad's lips. The boy protested, but at de Valence's command, drank. Stepping back, she watched de Valence settle Imad under the covers, but soon grew annoyed at the way he stared at the boy as if he expected him to expire at any moment. She turned her back to them, put away the wolfsbane, and retrieved her small jar of cinquefoil.

Alice had anticipated her, and brought the cooking pot used to heat tisanes and other remedies. In it was simmering watered wine laced with honey. Juliana put several pinches of cinquefoil into the brew along with hyssop and a little valerian. Alice returned the pot to a brazier and stirred it.

Looking up from replacing the herbs in her healing box, Juliana found de Valence staring at her. Under that assessing, speculative perusal, she grew uneasy. She shut the lid of the healing box, found the key and fumbled with it as she tried to turn it in the lock. He was still staring at her when she chanced a look, but his gaze was filled with surprise, and he nodded at Imad.

"His coughing has eased a bit."

Juliana heard the note of astonishment in his voice and sniffed. "You mean he's not dead?"

De Valence swiftly turned back to her. "You take offense easily, Mistress Juliana. Please understand that I wasn't aware of your skills, and to find so lovely a maid gifted with such an art is unusual."

Thunder of heaven, the man uttered compliments as easily as he snapped orders. Did he know how unaccustomed to flattery she was? Juliana eyed him with distrust, but he only met her glance with an easy, composed smile. Then he alarmed her by rising abruptly and approaching her.

She clutched the healing box in front of her and tried not to skitter backward. After all, Alice was with her. Still, she couldn't help the tiny jump she gave when he took the box from her, set it aside, and clasped her hand. Bending over it, he brushed his lips against the skin on the back of it. She felt the soft pliancy of his mouth as it skimmed over the surface of her skin once, twice, a third time, in a caress of such intimacy that she found herself short of breath and unable to do more than stare at his bent head in astonishment. Then alarm descended upon her. He straightened, still holding her hand, and drew her close so that she felt his hip brush hers.

Using a vibrant and yet low tone only she could hear, he said, "I'm in your debt, fair Juliana. Tell me, damascened love, how may I repay you?"

She felt surrounded by heat and muscle, and transfixed by the memory of supple lips molding themselves to her flesh. Never had a man approached her so boldly or so intimately; the last of her courage deserted her. Ducking low to retrieve the healing box, she slipped out of his grip and put the container between them. She tried to speak, but her voice cracked, and she was forced to start again.

"I—I'll leave Alice with the boy tonight." She skittered backward toward the tent entrance, but he followed her. "She'll keep the water boiling and give him a healing tea I've made."

De Valence stepped around her and blocked the entrance. She collided with the arm he put out to stop her.

"You haven't said how I may repay you."

Juliana swallowed hard. "That's unwarranted, my lord."

"Look at me, Mistress Juliana, or are you afraid to?"

At this, she lifted her gaze to scowl at him.

"Ha! I knew it. The insolent little black duck."

Eyes growing round with dismay, irritated that he could fluster her so easily, Juliana lifted her chin. She knocked his arm aside and marched out of the tent.

"Arrogant Viking," she muttered to herself. She nearly stumbled when he called after her.

"Very well, Juliana mine. I'll think of a way to recompense you in some fitting manner at the tournament. I'll devote myself to the task, and to making you blush and quiver again as you did when I kissed your hand."

Hyssop

This herb healed all manner of evils of the mouth and slew worms in a man. If it was drunk green or in powder, it made a man well colored.

• Chapter 5 •

WATCHING JULIANA WELLES MARCH BETWEEN the campfires and tents in front of the castle, Gray de Valence found himself unable to look away from the sway of her hips. She'd forgotten her cloak in her haste to get away from him. He noticed that she'd worn another of those old gowns that made her look like a peasant. It hung loosely over a plain undertunic, and a leather girdle clung low on her hips. He watched the band of leather undulate as she walked and suddenly felt himself rouse at the sight. Just God! How had she captured his desire so easily?

He deliberately turned his back and went to Imad. He ran his hand through his hair, impatiently thrusting the heavy locks back from his face as he studied the boy. Saladin had given Imad to him when he left Egypt, and he felt responsible for the youth, troublesome as he was. Imad had insisted upon jumping into that icy stream to help him bathe this morning even though he was already sickening, and this was the result.

Gray listened to Imad's breathing as the maid Alice moved a steaming pot closer to the patient. He took the cup of herbal brew from her and fed it to the boy himself. Imad coughed a little, but not as violently as before Juliana had treated him. The churning anxiety that had sent him rushing from the hall faded as Imad began to breathe more easily.

"Master, you should be abed." Imad was looking at him through heavy jet eyelashes.

"You've worried us all, you stubborn whelp."

"It's this cursed chilly land of yours, master. The noble Saladin has condemned me to suffer great tribulations by sending me to this kingdom of ice and barbarity."

Gray looked down at his servant through half-closed eyes and smiled. "You're free to leave."

"I'm a true believer, master, and I'll not be free until I've repaid my debt to you. Please, take to your bed. I know how important this tournament is to you." Imad paused to cough again. "How will you—"

Gray held up a hand to silence the boy. He waved the maid out of the tent, then came to sit on a stool beside Imad.

"How will you practice your vengeance, master?"

"I'm going to make him wait for it," Gray said.

Imad coughed and smiled at the same time. When the spasm was over, he said, "You mean you're going to make him watch you destroy man after man until he near pisses himself with fear."

"It's the only way I can draw out his suffering."

Gray held the cup full of herbed wine to Imad's lips. Imad finished the drink and sighed. He closed his eyes. "The lady works great magic with her herbs, praise be to Allah." He opened his eyes to slits and looked at Gray. "A most spirited woman."

"Go to sleep, Imad."

"Allah is merciful to bring such a healer to me in this land of savagery."

Gray slanted a distrustful look at his servant. "I'll have none of your meddling. Mistress Juliana isn't—she plays no part in my plans. Do you hear?"

"I hear, master."

"But do you obey?"

"Is it not the will of Allah that I obey my master?"

Leaning over the boy, Gray fixed him with a viper's stare. "Don't give me that Eastern answer that is no answer, you little catamite. If you interfere I'll send you back to Saladin. I swear it."

He got no answer, and his attempt at intimidation failed, for Imad had fallen asleep, either from exhaustion, the medicine, or guile. Leaving the tent, Gray signaled for Alice to return to her vigil. He went to his pavilion where he lay on the folding bed one of his squires, Simon, had prepared. As Simon put away clothing and extinguished candles, he threw an arm over his eyes and tried to rest.

He was so impatient for dawn. With it would come his opportunity to torment Richard Welles. At the same time he was going to win the regard of Yolande de Say. Once he'd gained victory in the tournament, to him would fall the honor of choosing the Queen of Love and Beauty. And he'd choose Yolande of course. A simple way to win her regard and persuade her to a betrothal. She was a sweet innocent; winning her would be effortless. Not at all the challenge that seducing the willful Juliana would be.

Gray shifted uneasily as the thought called up the image of Juliana Welles. Her hair had been unbound this time. Long, softly curling black skeins had fallen down her shoulders and wound over her breast. He'd turned to see her enter the tent, and a vision had flashed in his mind of her standing there with her hair unbound, but without clothing. The picture teased him, as those curls teased his imagination by concealing the tips of her bare breasts. The vision had taunted him the whole time she'd been in the tent.

What was he thinking? He couldn't distract himself with lust for this girl. He was close to bringing to fruition the plan that had kept him alive since he was nineteen. But those damascened eyes . . . And he couldn't keep that vision out of his mind—black curls winding around white breasts. He groaned and turned on his stomach. Bending one leg, he pressed his swelling flesh into the mattress and clenched his teeth.

He couldn't continue like this, or he'd get no sleep. Ruthlessly he forced himself to think of the only thing he was sure would banish Mistress Juliana from his mind. He called forth the memory of the branding.

The Muslim pirates had attacked the ship on which he'd been a prisoner of Welles and the other knights Baron Etienne had set upon him. He'd been freed and given a sword to fight with, and soon had pursued the leader of the pirates across the deck, only to run into a group of the thieves jumping from the pirate ship to his. Surrounded, he stabbed and slashed desperately but was felled by a blow from behind. When he regained his senses, the Christian ship was gone, and he was a prisoner.

He spent countless days in the foul, dank hold of that ship, chained, beaten, starved. Then, without warning he was hauled up to the deck, across a gangplank to a dock swarming with people. Two sailors threw him to the ground at the sandaled feet of a man in a turban and greasy robe. Before he could summon the strength to lift his head, he'd been sold. Nearly delirious, the next memory he conjured up was of being forced to eat and drink, and the next of burning heat, high limestone cliffs, and a quarry.

After that, the next clear remembrance was burned into his soul. He woke because they shook him and cuffed him. Four guards grabbed him and propelled him from darkness into the glaring heat and sunlight. They threw him down before a fire where another guard stood holding a long rod with a white-hot tip. Before he could get up, two of them pressed their knees into his back. He struggled, but they shoved his face in the dirt while two more sat on his legs.

He saw dusty boots as the fifth guard knelt. Then he saw the brand. He shouted and bucked, but they held him down. The brand darted at him. It pressed into his shoulder, high on his biceps, and withdrew. In that first instant, he felt little, only a vague heat. Then his flesh burst into agony.

His body jerked, and he screamed. Pain clawed its way through his arm to the rest of his body. His back arched, and he went stiff with the effort to escape his own body and the pain. Then he fainted.

He woke later to pain and the shame of having been defiled and treated like an animal. As days passed, the brand faded from bright red to white, and revealed itself to be a stylized symbol he later learned was a reed leaf used to distinguish slaves belonging to the quarry.

He didn't know how long he spent in the quarry among other condemned men and guards with scimitars and whips. He didn't even know where it was, except that there was nothing around it, no towns, no rivers, nothing. Then one day he'd been hauling waste stone in a cart. A wealthy visitor had come to the quarry to choose stone for his house. Gray had seen the man at a distance, noted without interest the azure silk of his robes.

He was hauling his cart along the base of a cliff when the visitor and his entourage walked past. He heard a shout from above where a block of limestone was being cut from the cliff, and saw the block shift. A piece of the cliff dislodged and fell. The man in the azure robe walked into its path. Gray cried out, but he spoke in English. Lunging over the cart, he sprang at the visitor.

His body smashed into the man, and they plunged down a small incline a moment before the boulder landed.

Gray ended up on top of the visitor. He was still breathless from the jolt of the landing when the guards set upon him, throwing him from the visitor, kicking him. He doubled over, then lost his temper and kicked back. A foot jammed into his back and a fist cracked into his jaw. He collapsed on his stomach, and heard the crack of a whip.

The lash bit into his back, but he refused to cry out. The lash cut again, drawing blood. It withdrew, and he braced himself for another cut. It never came. He heard a voice snapping with authority, but he hadn't been in this place long enough to understand more than a word or two.

A shadow blocked out the burning sun. Gray lifted his head. Through vision blurred by drops of sweat, he looked into the face of the man in the azure robe. It was Saladin, who had been named for the great warrior, conqueror, and ruler.

Saladin spoke to him. He hadn't understood, but his understanding wasn't required. Saladin waved a hand. Gray was picked up and dragged after the nobleman. An animated conversation took place between the overseer of the quarry and the man whose life he'd saved.

Weak from maltreatment and the beating, and unaccustomed to the heat, Gray lost the battle to remain conscious. His last sight was of the azure robe and a spray of gold coins Saladin threw at the feet of the overseer. He'd been sold like a horse, to Saladin, prince of a noble house, warrior, commander of armies in the fight against the Christian invaders of Egypt and the Holy Land.

Gray cursed and sat up, more awake than ever with the memories of his years in the hands of Saladin. He lay back down and covered his eyes again. Better to surrender to lustful reverie about Mistress Juliana than to lie awake remembering Saladin. Remembering how he'd been slowly seduced into accepting his fate, accepting corruption made palatable by villas of polished stone and gold, fountains of cool water, beds of silk and down, and relentless, manipulative persuasion.

Gray bit his lip and turned away from those memories. He sought refuge in the image of damascened eyes and the tantalizing vision of Juliana's hips. He remembered how they moved in a gentle arc—up and down, up and down, their path marked by the movement of that leather girdle. How would she look clad only in that braided leather? A picture of her bare, smooth curves bound by the girdle teased him, and he fell asleep trying to complete every detail of her body above and below that band of leather.

Leaning out the north window of her chamber, Juliana searched the morning sky for clouds and found none. It was one of those mornings when the sharp, cool wind put a snap in her step and color in her cheeks and made the world seem cleaner and brighter. Or was the day's beauty only a result of her mood? She shivered as the breeze penetrated her shift and tossed black curls about her face. Even to herself she was reluctant to admit that the shiver was more from anticipation than the cold.

Not until she'd regained her chamber last night had she realized what Gray de Valence had meant by promising to recompense her today for helping his servant. Then she'd remembered that today was the first day of the tournament. He had said he'd repay her at the tournament. De Valence would be occupied with ceremonies and contests. How could he repay her? The obvious answer had risen up to smack her in the face—he was going to ask for her favor when he rode into the lists.

At first she'd rejected the idea, but its logic demanded her consideration. Begging a lady's favor was the courtly tradition, and she'd seen for herself how well versed in courtly love was Gray de Valence. For a few moments her fancy expanded so that she even contemplated the possibility that, if he was victorious in the jousting, Gray de Valence might choose her as the Queen of Love and Beauty. That unlikely occurrence she rejected, only to return to it in her dreams later.

She was angry with herself over her dreams. As she gazed out at the river Clare, the memory of them brought added color to her cheeks. Never had she had such dreams. Dreams of dark, seething passion that brought a response from her body when de Valence appeared in them. Was she evil to dream of this man? Surely Satan had made her envision his naked body and how it would feel against her own. Juliana put her palms to her hot cheeks as she recalled the dream. Oh, but what of Yolande? Remorse warred with desire, a new kind of battle for Juliana. Desire won. After all, Yolande couldn't be in love with a man to whom she'd hardly spoken.

Alice distracted her by entering the chamber, arms loaded with clothing Juliana was to wear. Earlier this morning, Juliana had earned a long look of consternation when she told Alice she'd changed her mind about her garments.

Instead of the ordinary wool gown she'd planned to wear, she'd requested one she'd never worn. It was a sleeveless overgown of dark forest-green samite—silk interwoven with silver thread. The side lacing was of silver while the undertunic was of the finest Persian silk of a much lighter pale green. It clung to her body in a way that hitherto had made her reluctant to wear it, until today.

Juliana noticed Alice yawning as she helped her bathe and don the fragile undertunic. "You're weary from nursing that boy, Alice. After you've helped me, you must rest."

"But I don't want to miss the tournament, mistress!"

"Can you stay awake for it?"

Alice eyed Juliana while she slipped her arms through the slits in the overgown. "I can stay awake to see why you've suddenly taken to dressing as you should after vowing never to—"

"Hold you tongue!" Juliana knew how odd her behavior must appear to Alice. After all, she'd vowed never to bother with fine clothes and courting after Edmund Strange. "I'm going to wear the silver veil and filet."

Alice gawked at her, causing Juliana to flush and stamp her foot.

"Fetch the veil, Alice, and—" She caught her lower lip between her teeth before continuing. "And bring my ivory casket."

"Have you taken ill, mistress?"

Alice was saved from a scolding when Laudine and Yolande burst into the chamber. Her plump and inviting curves clad in crimson damask, Laudine managed to look like an exotic rose from some caliph's pleasure garden. Her features were dominated by round blue eyes the color of the sky after a spring rain. Her perpetually knowing expression was absent at the moment, banished by sheer excitement. In contrast, Yolande appeared a dancing miniature who hopped from one foot to the other with the force of her gaiety.

"Here it is, Jule," Laudine said. "My maid finished it last night." She tossed a gown onto Juliana's bed. Yards of sendal billowed out and fell to the mattress in cascades of white shot with gold and sewn with pearls. "You're Virtue."

Juliana's hands froze in the midst of settling a transparent veil over her unbound hair. "What?"

"You're Virtue." Yolande set a caul of gold and pearls on top of the gown.

"What are you two babbling about, Laudine?"

Yolande cast a glance of dismay at Laudine. "I told you she'd be like this."

"The siege. Praise be to Our Lady of Mercies. Do you purpose to tell me you've forgotten the siege?" Laudine folded her arms under her generous chest and shook her head. "The order of the tournament. Remember? I reminded you yestere'en. First the jousts, then the mêlée, and on the third day, the siege of the Castle of Love and Beauty." Laudine patted the golden braids looped over her ears. "No doubt I'll be the Queen of Love and Beauty and thus command the castle."

Juliana groaned as she bent to allow Alice to set a silver filet on her head over the veil. "I'd forgotten."

"Now don't say you're going to Vyne Hill," Laudine said. "You promised you'd attend all three days of the tournament, and we've already chosen our guises. If you don't play Virtue, I might have to, and I have my heart set on being Desire." Laudine's eyes sparkled with anticipation. "My gown is the color of rubies."

"Don't you ever think of anything but how to torture men by arousing their lust?"

"Of course I do, but nothing else is so entertaining." Laudine grinned at Juliana and waggled her eyebrows up and down. Juliana tried to look severe, but ended up giggling, which caused Laudine to pause and stare. She surveyed the rich gown, the filet of silver, and raised her brows. "Mmm, mmm, mmm. Someone's going hunting today. How unlike you, sister."

Making haste to distract, Juliana said, "What of this siege?"

"Ah!" Yolande clapped her hands. "Your father has caused a mock castle to be built, and we ladies are to defend it. Now do you recall? Bertrade will portray Chastity, I am Honor. Then there are Humility and Pride and, oh, many others. The winner of the tournament will lead the knights in siege and try to take the castle." Yolande put her fingertips to her lips and giggled. "We're going to pelt them with cakes and flowers, and try to defend against them. But not too well, of course, or my lord de Val—er—the men won't be able to get to us."

"Of course," Juliana said faintly. For a moment she'd forgotten the mock siege, and about Yolande. Yolande didn't know what had happened last night between her and Gray. She didn't know about his promise. If Juliana took part in the siege, Gray de Valence might besiege *her*. Ignoring the tingle of excitement that shot through her, she listened to Laudine continue to scold.

"Now, Jule, you've already embarrassed Father and Mother by vanishing last night. You missed the viewing of the great helms."

Before a tournament, the helms of the participants were placed on display with all their fanciful headdresses. Everyone inspected them, and any lady who wished could stand before that of a particular knight and denounce him for an unchivalrous act. Laudine was in the habit of making up fantastical tales about some poor knight and forcing him to go on his knees before her and beg forgiveness.

"At least you've kept your promise to come today," Laudine said. "What are you doing?"

Ignoring Laudine's and Yolande's stares, Juliana

opened the ivory casket Alice had brought to her. Removing a top tray, she sorted through jewelry until she found her silver girdle. She hesitated, then drew out a heavy silver brooch in the shape of a garland and studded with amethysts. The dark green overgown scooped at the neck and then cut down the center of her chest to reveal the pale green garment beneath. She used the brooch to pin the edges of her undertunic at the neck where it slit into a vee just over her breasts. Looking up, she found Laudine staring at her.

"Holy saints!"

Juliana reddened. "What?"

"You've a lover." Laudine covered her mouth with her hands and giggled. "At last, Juliana has a lover."

"She has?" said Yolande, aghast.

Juliana drew herself up and looked down her nose at the two. "I do not."

"But you're coming to the tournament," Yolande said.

"I have promised."

Laudine laughed. "And you're coming to the siege. I know it."

"Verily," Juliana said through stiff lips and with stilted dignity. "I have promised it, and I always fulfill my promises."

Laudine scampered around the bed and grabbed Juliana's arm while she danced a little step of excitement.

"Who is he? Who is he?"

It was impossible to remain quietly dignified when one's sister was tugging one's arm and Yolande was hopping in front of one. Juliana's body jerked with each tug until she yanked free and scurried out of Laudine's reach and bellowed.

"Thunder of God!"

Laudine stopped giggling. Yolande thrust her hands

behind her back and gawked at her, lips twitching with merriment.

Juliana refused to look at her boisterous and irritating sister or her small minion. She went to a chest and began sorting through kerchiefs.

"There is no lover."

"Then why are you searching for a kerchief to give as a favor?" Laudine asked.

"Just because I carry a kerchief—"

"You never carry kerchiefs," Yolande said. "You always forget them."

She found her best cloth-of-silver kerchief and slammed the lid of the chest. "I do not."

"Do too," Laudine said.

"Do not—aaarrgh! Laudine, enough of this madness. We'll be late."

"Oh, I've forgotten my own kerchief," Yolande said. "I must fetch it quickly."

She rushed out of the chamber, much to Juliana's relief. She still felt guilty for having gained de Valence's interest even if she hadn't intended to do it. Laudine snickered at her as Alice came forward to offer a light mantle of green that matched her gown. Juliana took it and stalked to her chamber door.

Laudine hurried to her side and gave her a sidelong glance. "You'll be sitting with us in the lodges this time, then?"

"Of course."

"Certes, you do have a lover," said Laudine.

Throwing up her hands, Juliana noticed the silver kerchief and concealed it in the folds of her cloak. "Why do you say so?"

"Because, sweet sister, when you promised to come to this tournament, you vowed before the whole family that you'd stand behind the palisade with the farmers, shepherds, and vendors, and that it would be the Last Judgment before you'd sit among us gaudy, simpering pigeons and flutter and coo at every knight who rode by."

Juliana lifted her skirts as she preceded her sister down the tower stair. In a faint voice she said, "Verily, I don't remember saying such a thing, and anyway, someone has to sit with you and prevent you from casting your pelisson and undertunic at some pretty man."

"Good," Laudine replied. "If you're by my side, I'll be sure to see which brave and fearless knight has dared to beg for your favor, Juliana Welles. He must be valiant, full of courage, and right beauteous to set your heart aquiver."

"I am not aquiver."

"Now who could that be? Most of the knights here never impressed you before. Who is new and pretty among them?"

"By God's mercy, you've turned fanciful. You're the one who gives favors to every knight who looks your way. How many have you given this time?"

Juliana held her breath, hoping that she'd distracted her sister.

"Five," Laudine said with pride.

"Thunder of God. Five? Who are they?"

As Laudine named her suitors, Juliana felt a wave of relief. After her rejection at the hands of Edmund Strange, she'd vowed never to chance another humiliating rejection. But she hadn't ever imagined encountering someone like Gray de Valence.

He had stirred her, and what was wondrous was that she knew she'd stirred him. Such a thing had never happened to her. She was unsure, but the warmth that had burst in her heart at the thought of his promise wouldn't leave her. She had tried to reject what she felt and the timorous hope she still refused to put into words. No, she couldn't admit it to herself. So how could she speak of it, even to Laudine?

Better to wait until Gray de Valence stopped before her in the lists and dropped his lance for her favor. Then she would admit hope. Then she would smile openly. And then she would speak his name.

Dittany

It had the property of drawing a thorn or iron out of a man's body.

• *Chapter 6* •

JULIANA WALKED BETWEEN YOLANDE AND Laudine and behind her mother in the parade of ladies headed for the lists. Bertrade trailed behind with several of her friends while more visiting ladies followed. Havisia was too burdened with playing hostess to the Countess of Uvedale and other senior noblewomen to pay attention to her daughters. Thus Laudine could make free with earthy jests without fear of censure. Smiles and laughter issued from the group surrounding Laudine and washed down the line of women in ripples and waves of humor. In spite of her slight feeling of guilt, Juliana's spirits were as high as the pointed tops of the Wellesbrooke towers.

They progressed over the drawbridge at a stately pace past crowds of lesser folk who had gathered for the spectacle. Cheers went up at the sight of the ladies adorned in their richest garments. Every peasant within walking distance of Wellesbrooke had come to see the display their lord and his family and guests provided and partake of their generosity—both of food and largesse.

At first Juliana was too engrossed in anticipation of the form of Gray de Valence's repayment to pay attention to her surroundings, but as they neared the exercise ground that had been transformed for the tournament, she began to take note of the scene. A double wooden palisade marked the perimeter of the lists, the outer of which was shoulder-high. The inner contained many gaps, and between the two was the space where squires, spare horses and armor, attendants and heralds stayed. Already a noisy multitude of humbler tournament onlookers had surrounded the outer palisade.

Along one side of the rectangle formed by the palisades a series of lodges had been erected. Shaded by brilliant canopies, with carpets on the flooring and dazzling with multihued pennants, these were the destination of the ladies. The Welles family and their ranking guests would occupy the central lodge.

In the distance, Juliana could hear her father's heralds calling out among the avenues of tents, "Jousters make ready!"

As she mounted the steps to the central lodge, she saw dozens of squires and other servants racing back and forth carrying chain mail, lances, even hourts, the protective padding worn around the neck of a destrier. As the eldest daughter, she followed the Countess of Uvedale and other highborn ladies and took her seat on the front bench set beside the chairs provided for the older women. Yolande sat beside her while Laudine sat next to the heiress.

Her mother happened to glance her way and gave her a look of wild surmise. Juliana avoided her mother's eyes. Only a few days ago she'd ranted about having to be in the lodges and threatened to sit in the back row of benches with the youngest demoiselles and the maids.

A stir went up from the lodges when the six camp marshals appeared in the lists with Hugo at their head. Dressed in surcoats of fine damask and silk, they were followed by heralds and pursuivants who would assist them in judging the tournament. Behind them came the lower sergeants and varlets whose task it was to keep order, bring new weapons and clear away broken ones, and to rescue fallen knights.

For the first time in years Juliana's excitement almost made her wriggle in her seat. She could barely contain her impatience for the beginning ceremonies, and didn't listen to her father's speech at all. She did hear the blare of trumpets that announced the procession of contestants. Her spirits soared with the strength of the cheers from the onlookers.

A forest of lances appeared—marching two by two—decorated with ladies' sleeves, kerchiefs, scarves, ribbons, and stockings. At the head of the procession rode the knights of highest rank, Javain de Marlow, Earl of Ravensford, and the Sieur de Valence. Next came Vail D'evereux, Baron of Durance Garde, and Sir Robert Beckington, followed by Richard Welles and Simon Reynolds, Baron of Green Rising.

Juliana saw none of them, only Gray de Valence. Resplendent in an emerald-green surcoat emblazoned with the de Valence dragon in gold, he rode with his helmet under his arm and his lance aloft. From it streamed a sleeve of azure silk, several scarves, and a stocking. Juliana scowled momentarily, for she recognized that stocking. It was Laudine's. She cast a glance of concupiscent irritation at Laudine, but her sister was leering at another of her suitors.

The procession was nearing the central lodge. Already the ladies were calling out to the knights, draping favors across lance tips, urging their favorites on to victory. Juliana's palms grew damp, and her skin felt as if a multitude of ants scurried beneath its surface. De Valence and the Earl of Ravensford approached. They paused to salute the countess and Havisia.

Laudine startled her by calling out to that French knight with the mocking blue eyes, Lucien, but Juliana managed to remain still. A welcoming smile flitted over her lips. That great black destrier began to walk again.

Her vision filled with wide shoulders clad in chain mail and emerald silk. She curled her fingers around the cloth of silver kerchief. Yolande would be hurt, but she was young and would forget.

Watching the tip of that favor-shrouded lance, she was ready when it began to dip. Her body craned forward toward the railing that separated her from him. She let her hand edge forward, holding the gossamer silver. The tip of the lance sailed gently down, past her shoulder, slightly out of reach. In that brief space of time, she caught herself before her hand could reach out to pursue the weapon. Jerking it back, she thrust it into her lap and watched the lance tip point at the girl beside her, Yolande.

Had all the blood drained from her face? Her mouth had frozen into a smile; of this she was certain. Drawing her shoulders up, she scooted back, as if she had been changing to a more comfortable position. Her gaze shifted so that she stared ahead. Out of the corner of her eye she watched Yolande blush and let her finest embroidered sleeve fall over the lance of Gray de Valence.

The procession moved on. Lances saluted, dipped, sailed up draped with colorful prizes. Juliana smiled and offered her congratulations to Yolande and her sisters for the number of favors requested of them. She laughed at Laudine's jests, whispered judgments of the prowess of various knights. It was the most difficult thing she'd ever done—harder even than surviving Edmund Strange's repudiation of her.

De Valence hadn't wanted her favor. He'd never intended anything so honest as an open tribute. Why had he spoken to her as he had if he didn't want her favor? *Fool, for a base reason even you should have suspected, though you're unaccustomed to such attentions being directed your way.* No, she wouldn't think of it. She had to survive this hell-spawned tournament with her pride intact. She hadn't betrayed herself, had she?

Even as she affected her pretense, mortification and pain suffused her, then gathered and settled in her chest somewhere. Was it in her heart? Her throat ached from the effort to stifle a sob, but she would rather suffocate than shame herself by bursting into tears. Later, when she was alone, she would flay herself with rebukes for believing the lies of another rooster knight. Then she would let the hurt out in tears. Now she would save her pride.

No one, especially not de Valence, would suspect she'd been so foolish as to hope for a suitor. The tournament progressed around her, although she paid no real heed to any of the jousts. Hugo had declared that arms of peace be used, so lances and sword points were blunted. Sword blades were dull, and lances were light and made of brittle wood. This she regretted, for it lessened the chance that Gray de Valence would be killed.

Still, some mischance might occur. Perhaps there was something to look forward to in this tournament after all. Juliana settled down to wait, for during the time in which she'd been sitting here dazed, de Valence's herald had issued a challenge to Richard. The announcement had created a great stir among the crowd; everyone knew of the unspoken enmity between the two men. Richard had one more joust before he met de Valence.

There was hope yet. She had seen Richard fight, and he was formidable, especially with a sword. If she was patient, she might be granted the pleasure of seeing Gray de Valence skewered right between the golden wings of that dragon on his chest.

He was furious. Years of anticipation were to have culminated in Richard Welles's disgrace, and now that bastard had ruined everything by coming to him with the truth. Stunned by what Welles had told him just as the tournament began, Gray de Valence had been performing his part in the contest through a haze of confusion. He'd been so preoccupied that he'd forgotten his instructions to the herald to challenge his enemy. Too late now to withdraw it.

Standing in the lists behind the inner palisade, he allowed his squire to relace his chain mail while he lapsed into agitated thought. Welles had come to his tent as he was arming, surprising him and his entire household. Neither of the other two men he'd sought out in revenge had wanted to talk to him. That is, except Garnier de Moselle, who had talked after he'd attacked Gray when his back was turned. Then he'd begged for mercy when he lost anyway. The begging had been a delay while the whoreson got his hand on a concealed knife. Garnier was dead.

But Welles had come openly to his tent. He'd come openly and had the temerity to chastise Gray for his quest for vengeance. He had stood there in all his majestic, black-haired bulk and shaken his head at Gray. Shaken his head!

"I knew you were but pretending to be the reformed and gentle knight for my uncle's benefit. This farce in which you're engaged does you no good, de Valence. Avenging yourself upon innocent men won't take away the stain on your honor."

Gray pulled a mailed glove onto his right hand and worked the fingers. "Haven't you ever heard of trial by arms? God is my judge, and my witness, and he's seen me defeat William Lawrence and your friend Garnier de Moselle." Gray left off studying his glove and fixed Welles with a frost-ridden stare.

"And he told me the truth at last. Before he died, that

is. He told me it was you who had seduced Baron Etienne's wife, that you feared discovery after being caught with her by a maid. That's why you cast blame upon me. To avoid being exposed for the deceiving spawn of Satan that you are. Once, I thought you were my friend, Welles. I can forgive much, but not the betrayal of a knight who said he was my friend."

Instead of loud refutations or defiant laughter, all he got was a gaze of bewilderment.

"Garnier said *I* was the lover?"

"Very good, Welles. Such honest confusion. You'd do well in the Egyptian caliph's court."

Welles was frowning, distracted. "Why would he tell such a lie? He knew I didn't—"

"This farce is useless. I don't believe you, and I will kill you."

He grew more annoyed than ever when it became apparent that his enemy wasn't listening to him. Welles wasn't even looking at him. He walked back and forth in Gray's pavilion, head down, rubbing his chin. He stopped suddenly to contemplate a clothing chest and mused.

"He must have feared for his life."

"True," Gray said lightly. "And he wouldn't risk dying with the stain of a lie upon his soul."

"But he did."

"What do you mean?" Gray snapped.

"He did go to God with that sin upon his soul, for I never touched the baron's wife. We all thought you did."

"We?"

"Everyone in the household," Welles said. "I remember the day the baron found out. Garnier and William Lawrence came from his chamber, told the rest of us knights the truth and swore us to silence."

"While I was hunting."

"Yes, but then why would he lie all these years later

when . . ." Welles suddenly looked up at Gray. "Dear God and the Blessed Virgin, Garnier and William."

Gray was growing uneasy. "You're the one who took me prisoner. You're the one who accused me and threw me on that ship."

"At Baron Etienne's request. But—"

"Damn you, what's wrong?"

"I never thought about it, but Baron Etienne gave no sign that he knew until after Garnier and William sought private words with him. And it was Garnier who suggested abducting you and taking you abroad. He always was jealous of you. His jealousy was the talk of the demesne." Welles approached Gray and lowered his voice. "And if he told you such a lie after all these years, then I think he may have been lying all along."

Gray turned away from Welles and picked up another gauntlet. "I didn't know you were so afraid of me."

"Afraid?"

"Why else would you make up such a tale?"

Welles's eyes widened and he turned crimson. "Are you accusing me of lying?"

"No doubt you've heard of the craven way Garnier died."

"I, Gray de Valence, do not lie."

"Ha!"

"You've been too long among heathens, de Valence. Slavery must have made you feeble-witted, or you would have remembered one small thing."

"What is that?"

"During the weeks in which the baron's lady was supposed to have strayed, I was recovering from a wound near the groin I got while training with the new squires. I'm surprised you don't remember since you dragged me from the practice yard yourself. You saw the wound, so tell me how I could have bedded the baron's wife in such a condition."

Gray shook his head, his thoughts confused.

"I beg your forgiveness, de Valence, though I don't blame you if you withhold it. I was your friend, and I never came to you and asked you for your side of the quarrel. I should have, and I deserve whatever punishment God ordains for me."

All Gray could do was mutter, "You were wounded— just God, you were wounded, and all this time I—"

The noise and confusion of the tourney battle rose around him as Gray remembered Richard Welles's revelations. It was true; Welles had been wounded. And even so brawny a man as he couldn't have performed with a woman before the injury healed. The news hurled him into chaos. Of the precepts and grudges that had ruled his life since his disgrace, the most powerful had been Richard Welles's guilt. Now that was gone. And he had killed the real culprit without knowing it. Garnier, the cur, had robbed him of the sweetest of revenges—knowing the truth and avenging it.

Simon wrapped his sword belt around Gray's waist. It hung low on his left side where his scabbard waited to hold his sword, but Gray made no move to sheathe it. Since recognition of the truth had burst upon him, he'd carried out his duties at the tournament with but half his attention. He was fortunate not to have been trounced, so far had his attention been from the three jousts he'd won. The squire lowered the great helm onto his head and attached it.

Gray shook his head. He had to put aside his frustration and the disorder of his mind. Simon was leading his destrier forward. The animal bobbed his head and jerked at the bridle. Gray sheathed his sword, checked that his two-handed battle sword was in place on the saddle, and mounted. Taking up lance and shield, he turned his horse into the lists as trumpets sounded the call to arms.

An abrupt silence descended upon the tournament grounds. Neither the de Valence nor the Welles pursuivants indulged in the customary exchange of shouted insults. Gray faced Richard Welles across the expanse of the lists, both of them rigid on their tall destriers.

A marshal waved his white baton and called, "In the name of God and Saint Michael, do battle!"

Gray saw his opponent mirror his sudden kick to his stallion. A shout went up from the lodges. The ground quaked beneath him, and sod flew as he hurtled across the lists. As the stallion reached a gallop, he bent low in the saddle, swung his shield to cover his body, and lowered his helm almost to the top of his shield. Through the slits in the helm he could see Welles doing the same. Years of training urged him forward. He was committed to the attack.

Swerving his horse so that he passed his opponent on the right, he dropped his lance point, his aim deadly. At the last moment, almost against his will, he shifted his aim. Not much, just enough. The crash jolted his whole body. His lance splintered, and he dropped it as his horse swung back on his haunches. Hooves cast great clods of dirt. Quickly he swerved to look at Welles. A long jagged mark on his enemy's shield told him he'd struck true. A cheer rose up from the crowd.

They rode at each other a second time with the same results. Again that tense silence marked the charge. Again both men came away still in the saddle. Now his arm vibrated with the shock of the clashes. For the third time Gray's destrier surged forward. Through flying dirt and the thunder of hooves he galloped. His lance dropped. This time he forced himself to keep it straight. The jolt rammed through him and sent him sailing through the air. He hit the ground hard and sprawled there. A great clatter of armor told him Welles had been flung from the saddle too.

Gray shoved himself to his feet beside his snorting, plunging destrier and drew his sword. He barely managed to pick up his shield before Welles was upon him. He countered an overhand blow. The force of it dented his blade. He feinted, lifted his shield to a second blow, then lunged.

His sword caught Welles in the ribs, and he heard a muffled cry. It was a sound he'd imagined hearing for what seemed like centuries, the sound of his betrayer's pain. And there was no fulfillment. Instead, the sound left him feeling empty. There was no exultation, no vindication, no triumph. He was fighting an innocent man because he hadn't wanted to give up his desire for revenge. He was a fool.

With that thought, Gray dodged a brutal blow that would have dislocated his shoulder. As Welles hurtled at him with the impetus of the strike, Gray swung his sword. As he swung, he turned the weapon so that the flat of the blade struck his opponent in the stomach. Welles cried out, doubled over, and fell on his face. He rolled, but Gray was too quick for him.

Gray stopped the roll with his boot and shoved Welles back to the ground. The tip of his sword descended to rest over his enemy's heart. Welles froze.

Something was wrong. Gray hesitated for a moment, then realized that the crowd had gone silent again. He looked up at the lodges for the first time, and saw Hugo staring at him, white-faced. His gaze dropped to a smaller figure with wide gray eyes. He almost smiled. The little black duck who haunted his dreams thought he was going to kill her cousin.

He'd had enough of killing. Stepping back, he lifted

his sword with a flourishing salute and offered his hand to Richard Welles.

"Garnier is dead, and I don't want to kill you for having been deceived by him."

He could see nothing but the black slits of Welles's great helm, but he heard a guffaw.

"It took you long enough to decide."

Welles took his hand, and Gray pulled the man to his feet to the accompaniment of a roar from the crowd. He looked across the field expecting to find Juliana Welles cheering along with the rest and casting grateful looks in his direction. She didn't. She sat while everyone else stood and cheered. She sat and glared at him across the lists, mouth set in a line as thin as twine, gaze chilly.

He removed his helmet to get a better look at her as he and Welles walked toward the lodges. Thrusting back the padded cap that protected his head, he sought her out again. All he saw was a swirl of forest-green silk as she turned her back on him. By the time he reached the Welles lodge, she was gone.

Houseleek

The juice of houseleeks laid on hot ulcers drove away infection. They were often planted on roofs to ward off lightning.

• Chapter 7 •

JULIANA HIKED HER SILKEN SKIRTS UP PAST HER
ankles and stomped down the lodge stairs muttering.
"Where there's patience and humility there is no anger
or vexation. Where there's patience and humility, there
is no anger or vexation. Thunder of God! Where there's
patience and humility, there is no anger or vexation."

Father Clement had recommended that she repeat
these phrases, based upon the teachings of Francis of
Assisi, whenever she grew so vexed as to contemplate
violence. She ground her teeth and forced herself to continue as she tramped through crowds of merry farmers
and retainers.

"Where there's patience and humility, there is NO anger or vexation. None. Arrogant, lascivious Viking. Spawn
of a demon. Where there's patience and humil—"

"Mistress! Mistress Welles, God save you, mistress."

Juliana growled under her breath and turned to find a
page calling her name and trundling after her. He wore
the de Valence colors. She whirled around and stalked off
through the forest of tents and pavilions, but the boy
caught up with her anyway.

"Mistress Welles, your pardon, but I've come from
Imad."

With reluctance Juliana stopped, causing a squire
bearing a ruined hauberk to dodge around her. "Yes?"

"The paynim Imad begs a visit from you, mistress."

"Is he worse?"

"I don't know, lady. It's this way."

The boy trotted off without waiting for her consent. Juliana sighed and followed him to Imad's tent amidst the azure and crimson carpets and clouds of silk. Better to go now than to risk meeting de Valence later. Imad was sitting up on his luxurious cot breathing her medicinal steam when she entered his tent. He made a graceful gesture with his hand as he bowed and whispered a greeting in Arabic. The violence of his cough had ebbed.

"The blessings of Allah be with you, mistress."

"Yes, well, what's wrong?" She bent and touched her palm to his forehead. He started. "Hold still so I can see if you've a fever, for God's pity."

"Forgive me, mistress, but in my land, a lady would not touch me."

"If I hadn't touched you, you'd be right evilly disposed today." Juliana released him and stood back. "You're much better."

"Yes, mistress, and my master has allowed me the honor of presenting a gift as a token of our gratitude. He says I owe you my life."

Imad gestured to the page, who was standing at the tent entrance. The boy picked up a casket and approached her. Impatient to be gone, still furious and in no mood to receive anything from Gray de Valence, Juliana barely glanced at it. Imad took the box from the page and held it out to Juliana, who then stared at it as if it were cow entrails. It was of ivory carved with scenes of the story of Tristan and Iseult. It had a gold lock and gold legs and corner reinforcements. When she didn't take it from him, Imad set it on his lap and lifted the lid.

Inside sat almost a dozen of the small pots and herb jars she had lost in the mud yesterday. Juliana gaped at them. Then Imad removed the tray in which the pots sat to reveal the bottom of the casket. There lay dozens of phials, tubes, and jars of brilliant and delicate glass protected by cambric.

Juliana blinked, then scowled as she realized de Valence was giving her pots when she had expected . . . Juliana flushed with renewed humiliation. She didn't want clandestine gifts, and he didn't think her deserving of courtly gestures made freely before their equals.

Imad bowed over the casket. "O, divine lady of light, my master is indebted beyond his ability to repay. This unworthy one as well. I owe the mistress my life, as I owe the master my life. I will serve her forever."

Drawing herself erect, Juliana adopted her most haughty expression.

"This gesture is unnecessary. I was but conducting my duties as healer to all the folk in Wellesbrooke, and I desire no payment. I'm pleased you're delivered out of danger. You should continue to rest for at least three days. God speed your recovery." She turned from him.

"But, mistress, what shall I tell the master?"

Juliana rounded on him, eyes glittering. "Nothing! You were ill. I am a healer; I healed you. That is the end of the matter, and there's naught to be said by me to your cursed master. God rest you, Imad."

Marching out of the tent, she heard a sneeze and turned to find Alice waiting for her.

"Oh, mistress, your mother sent me to find you. The tournament's not half over, and she commands you to return."

The maid buried her nose in a kerchief. Juliana ignored her and headed for the castle. Alice scrambled after her, breathless and urgent.

"Mistress, you mother has sent for you."

Sweeping across the drawbridge beneath the gleaming whitewashed walls of the castle, Juliana tossed a comment over her shoulder. "Go back and say I've taken ill of an ache in my head and am in search of houseleeks to assuage it."

Alice gasped and shook her head.

"I can't do that. Why, she'd box my ears."

"Nonsense." Juliana stopped to lift her skirts out of the dust before speeding across the nearly deserted bailey. "Tell her you found me faint and that you helped me to my room. Then send a page to find Bogo, Eadmer, Warin, and Lambert."

Alice hurried around Juliana to stand in front of her and stare in dismay. "Oh, no. I thought you'd forgotten about that."

"You do as I say, Alice, and be quick, because I'm going to Vyne Hill at once. There's time to make the trip with a few hours to spare before dark."

Groaning, Alice rubbed her forehead. "Oh, now I be the one with an ache in the head."

Paying no attention to the maid's protests, Juliana marched past haystacks, stables, the board pit, and the mews to enter the keep. Up in her room, she slammed her door closed and stood glowering at the painted unicorn scene on her wall. Finally she gave vent to her rage at de Valence in a stream of inventive curses. She had feared it would erupt before she could gain her chamber.

But cursing wasn't enough. She raised her voice, shouted, threw cushions, and tore the filet and veil from her head. Gradually her rage faded, giving way to remorse, shame, and a fierce anger directed at herself. She hated herself for being so witless as to succumb to the blandishments of a man known for his skill in dalliance.

By the time Alice returned, she had spent her fury. Now it had congealed into a hard mass that sat in her chest, growing heavier and heavier. Her mouth settled into a distracted frown. Urging the maid to hurry the packing, she vowed to deliver a fitting answer to the Viking's disdain of her.

He thought to make free with her while giving his honorable attentions to little Yolande. What presumptuousness. Stuffed full of male pride, that's what he was. The worst of all the rooster knights she'd ever confronted.

Thinking about him made her furious all over again. She had to get away from Wellesbrooke before she was forced to endure his presence. If she didn't, she would do something terrible to him in front of everyone and disgrace her family. Much better to spend the night at Vyne Hill. She had to check on the progress of repairs to the manor roof and to the mill. Such tasks would distract her from her rage. Also, the trip would enable her to give certain instructions to Eadmer and the others. If she was to accomplish her revenge, she would need their help, and perhaps Richard's as well, although he wouldn't suspect he was helping.

Late afternoon saw Juliana riding at the head of her little group of travelers out of Hawksmere Forest into the village of Vyne Hill. She walked her horse over the ford in the stream that skirted the settlement. Before her lay thatched houses interspersed with animal pens, garden plots, and fruit trees. Wheat, barley, and fallow fields surrounded Vyne Hill in a crisscrossing patchwork. At the center of the village lay the old Norman church, its graveyard and the village green. Between the forest and the stream on the west peasants grazed their animals on pastureland.

Vyne Hill manor lay on a rise beyond the village. The stream skirted behind the house and wound its way past the settlement. One of Juliana's greatest tasks had been to set men to repairing the old moat that surrounded the manor and rechannel water from the stream so that it filled the dry ditch once more.

Her progress through the village was slowed as farmers and their wives and children left work to greet her. When she had first come to Vyne Hill, they'd been distrustful. The old countess had neglected both the manor and the village. The mill had ceased to work, and they suffered from banditry since no one undertook their defense. It had taken her months to win their trust. Fixing the mill and grinding their grain at no fee had finally convinced them of her serious intentions. Hugo had been annoyed at the cost, but he lent her the laborers anyway.

Hiring Piers Strong Arm, the old blacksmith, as her steward had further endeared her to the villagers. He was waiting for her on the rickety old drawbridge that stretched across the still-dry moat. In the distance she could see men clearing debris from the channel that connected the moat to the stream.

After receiving Piers's greeting, she rode into the courtyard formed by the conglomeration of buildings that had been added to the manor over the years since its owner had been murdered by Norman invaders. The villagers believed Vyne Hill to be haunted by the old Saxon lord. At night they especially avoided the oldest chamber in the house and its undercroft, for these sat on the site of the ruined Saxon hall.

Juliana dismounted in the courtyard with the help of Eadmer, the youngest son of Hugo's armorer. Eadmer's watery blue eyes glinted with excitement, for he and his other young friends had accompanied Juliana on certain adventures before and had missed the outings of late. She'd promised each of them good marriages and land to farm. When she moved to Vyne Hill, they would move with her.

Wading through a flock of geese pecking at grain near

the stable, Juliana listened to Piers's reports on the progress of repairs to the larder, to the roof of the hall and the walls in the buttery and servery. The yard was noisy with the sound of carts arriving with grain, of pigs and geese fighting and horses clattering to the stable. Juliana issued orders for more repairs and doled out payments from her modest store of coin. The afternoon waned as she inspected the work going on in the buttery, the servery, and the hall.

"Yes, Piers. I know how wonderful it would be to have a leaded roof, but other things are more important. We have to see that all the houses in the village have adequate roofs before next winter. You said several families lost sheep and pigs and can't replace them. And we must purchase more draft horses. Plowing is more important than a fancy roof."

"Yes, mistress."

"And you're sure little Jacoba has been given that remedy I sent?"

"Oh, yes, mistress. She be right well disposed now. Her mother wanted to come to thank you, but I said she had to wait because you were sore busy this afternoon."

"As long as Jacoba is better. I'll visit her later tonight. Now I want to see Eadmer, Lambert, and the others before I inspect the orchards."

The day fled as she tried to make up for the time she'd been away. She was glad of the occupation, for it kept her from reliving her stupidity at the tournament this morning. In the haunted chamber, where she was certain there would be no one to overhear, she gave instructions to her four young minions. Then she toured the orchards.

By the time she finished, the sun was waning. She, Piers, and Alice walked back over the drawbridge and past the gatehouse that pierced the low defensive wall that made a stone square around the manor. She was walking across the yard, one of the manor puppies at her heels, when she heard the thud of hooves over the bridge. Turning, she beheld her cousin Richard cantering toward her on his favorite palfrey—and beside him rode her nemesis, Gray de Valence.

Astounded at the appearance of the very man she most wanted to avoid, Juliana stood like a crossroads marker in the middle of the yard as they slowed their horses to a walk and stopped in front of her.

"I told your father you'd be here," Richard growled.

Juliana looked from her cousin to Gray de Valence, who said nothing but smiled at her in a way that convinced her he'd learned it in some heathen harem. She flushed and turned back to Richard.

"Thunder of heaven! What are you doing here?"

Richard scowled down at her. "My lord, your father, sent me to fetch you."

"Fetch? Fetch? Are you a hound to be set upon hapless creatures, sniffing and baying? I've work to do, Richard. God speed you back to Wellesbrooke."

She was mortified, furious at her father for embarrassing her by setting Richard and the Sieur de Valence, of all men, to catch her and bring her home like some runaway cow. Juliana turned her back on the men, not daring to look at Gray de Valence again. She hadn't gone three steps when she heard a voice of commanding timbre speak.

"We would fain escort you home, mistress."

She stopped in mid-stride and rounded on de Valence. He was still astride his horse. Not the black monster, but a calmer bay of equal girth. He rested his forearms loosely on his saddle and smiled that same smile of barely disguised seduction. This morning she might have responded to that smile, had it been accompanied by the tipping of a lance in search of her favor. At this thought, Juliana's rage burst into life again.

"I am home, my lord." She walked away.

"I told you she was stubborn," Richard said. "Wait, Juliana. You must come back with us. Your mother is distraught, and your lord father nearly had convulsions when he realized you'd gone."

Juliana paused in the hall doorway. "So he sent you chasing after me as if I were a lost puppy? And what madness possessed you that you dragged a stranger here to witness this folly?" De Valence threw back his head and laughed. Juliana flushed and bit her inner cheek.

"Gray came so that we might have time to discuss certain . . . private matters," Richard said. "If you're embarrassed at his presence, you've only yourself to blame for it, running off to this ruin in the midst of nowhere when you should be at your mother's side."

"Don't you chastise me, Richard Welles." All she had to do was hold her ground. Richard was too much the perfect gentle knight to win against her. She folded her arms and raised her voice. "Go away, both of you. I'm not coming back, so you might as well leave."

Shaking his head, Richard threw up his hands and glanced at de Valence. "You see? It's useless when she sets her mind."

Gratified, Juliana had her hand on the door latch when de Valence laughed again and dismounted. Her eyes grew wide as he began to stride toward her.

"You're too much steeped in chivalry and courtesy to deal with this unruly little black duck, Richard."

Her hand shoved open the door as he neared, and she prepared to flee.

De Valence slowed as he reached her and murmured, "Mistress Juliana, by your leave."

She thought he was bowing to her, but suddenly he

stooped, wrapped his arms around her thighs, and tossed her over his shoulder. Juliana shrieked as her head went down and her bottom went up. Blood rushed to her face. The net holding her hair came loose and black curls brushed the packed earth of the yard. She arched her back and tried to twist out of his grip, but he bounced her on his shoulder. Jolted, the air rushed from her lungs, and she gasped.

With warning she was tossed in the air and landed on his saddle. She nearly overbalanced, but de Valence swung up behind her, grabbed her shoulders, and planted her between his thighs. Juliana writhed and jabbed her elbows into his ribs.

"Let me go, vile caitiff whoreson! Son of a crow, damnèd whelp of Satan, sodding beast-lover!" She twisted in his arms and tried to scratch his eyes.

De Valence let out a curse as she nearly struck his face, then pinned her arms to her sides with a grip that almost suffocated her. Juliana squirmed, breathless and red-faced, her hair streaming about her shoulders. Finally comprehension penetrated rage—she wasn't going to win.

Breathing hard, she went still and scowled at her cousin through tousled hair. "Richard, how can you let this evil knave treat me so? Where is my courteous and gentle knight?"

Richard had watched the spectacle openmouthed. Now his lashes fluttered as he seemed to wake from a daze, and he let out a guffaw that echoed off the walls of Vyne Hill manor. Around them her retainers had stopped in their duties to form a ring around their betters and watch in horrified awe as the richly garbed, silver-haired stranger bested their mistress.

Juliana caught sight of Eadmer and Warin. Each held a rake and an axe. They hovered nearby, but it was clear to her that they had no thought of confronting these two noblemen. Nor would she have ordered them to, for it would have meant their deaths.

De Valence's grip on her arms was beginning to hurt. Juliana made another desperate attempt to free herself. She kicked backward, hitting de Valence in the shin. He yelped and swore. Suddenly she was loose, but only for a moment. Then the world tilted as he lifted her in the air. She came down with a thud on her stomach across his legs, her head and legs dangling and her bottom up. His hand came down on the small of her back and easily held her in place.

Juliana shrieked and wriggled, but a few moments' struggle left her out of breath and exhausted. She stilled and tried to fill her lungs. Hot and humiliated, she indulged in the most lurid of her abundant store of curses. Through the stream of invective, she heard de Valence chuckle.

"I do believe she's growing weary, Richard."

He shifted so that his thigh supported Juliana's breasts. If she could have, she would have taken a knife to him then. She had to settle for pounding his boot. Her blows made no impression on him, and she finally stopped.

"Ah, the little sparrowhawk has lost the strength to screech and claw."

Juliana contemplated sinking her teeth into his leg, but decided she didn't like what he might do to her in return. "You're going to pay for this, you foul scourge."

"You're a right insolent and careless maid, Mistress Welles, and a trial to your poor cousin here. No doubt you've never been sharply punished for your waywardness, therefore we must have an understanding. You're going back with us. You can make the journey upright, or over my saddle. Make your choice quickly." He pressed down on her back, thrusting her against his thighs. His voice roughened slightly as he went on. "I myself would enjoy bearing you home as you are now."

The effort to dampen her rage drained Juliana of the last of her strength. She would have to wait for her revenge.

"Let me up, damn you."

"Are you going to come meekly, like a proper, biddable maiden?"

"I'll come," she muttered.

The hand on her back shifted, and she was whipped upright. With a bump she landed between his legs again. Swiping at her hair, she thrust it back from her damp, pink face.

"I'll ride with Richard."

"You'll ride with me. Richard is too accustomed to bowing to your temper."

Juliana cast another glance of appeal at her cousin, but he had turned away to give instructions to Piers and his own men. She started when hands encircled her waist and lips whispered near her ear.

"Why did you run away, my sweet lark?"

At the endearment, Juliana lost her hard-won control and jabbed her elbow into his ribs. She smiled at his cry of pain, but her smile vanished when he snaked his arms around her and beneath her breasts. He pressed his lips to her ear again.

"Another such attack, lady, and I'll tie you to a pack horse for the journey."

"You wouldn't—"

"I have before, and I will, though it costs me the feel of your body against mine. Someone has to tame that evil disposition of yours, Juliana Welles, and since your family can't, I will." He paused for a moment. "And I'm bound to thank God for setting me the task."

"Tame? Tame? Speak not of taming, Sir Knave. When I see my father, he'll have your head on a spit for what you've done."

"More likely he'll hold a feast in my honor. Now be quiet, your strident voice is unsettling my horse."

Juliana clamped her mouth closed while she watched Richard walk his horse back across the courtyard. De Valence nudged his own mount with his knees. The movement caused his thighs to surge against her, and Juliana felt a strange disturbance within her body. She tried to lift herself away from him, but de Valence tightened his grip and drew her closer. Feeling at once enraged, thwarted, and oddly stirred in some unnameable way, Juliana distracted herself by planning exactly how she was going to make Gray de Valence pay for humiliating her in front of her servants and the entire village of Vyne Hill.

Spurge

Used to purge the belly, as a cure for choler and melancholia. It was said to be a laxative that prevented bad dreams.

• Chapter 8 •

WHEN HE HAD FORCED JULIANA TO RIDE WITH him, he'd been pleased with the idea of being able to hold her for the entire journey. Too late he had realized he'd condemned himself to purgatory and torture. Every step his horse took caused her bottom to surge against him. He could smell the scent of violets in her hair. And his hands . . . his hands . . . It took all his considerable will to keep them from sliding up her body to touch her breasts.

By the time the full moon appeared, he was so uncomfortable he relinquished his burden to Richard. All he could do was hope no one had noticed the sweat on his upper lip or the way he strangled the reins to keep from bellowing his frustration. He spent the rest of the journey willing away the effects of touching Juliana Welles.

She was furious with him, but then, she seemed to spend a good deal of her waking hours in a state of irritation. He suspected she was angry at him for some obscure, Julianaish reason, which was why he had tried to find her after the tournament. It was during his search that Arthur had reminded him of the disaster of her near-marriage to Edmund. He'd forgotten it, but now he could understand some of her aversion to knights and barons.

Edmund was the ambitious eldest son of his father's sister. He'd made a good match with Juliana only to decide on his wedding day that Yolande was a far richer prize. Guileless and young, the de Say girl had been unable to hide her infatuation with him. Knowing that the path to greatness lay in accumulating land such as that held by Yolande, Edmund had conceived an ingenious way to rid himself of Juliana. He pretended not to have known of her slight impairment, called attention to it at the bedding ceremony, and cried foul. A furor ensued during which the church intervened. The marriage had been annulled.

Gray shook his head as he guided his horse along the track that would lead to the east bridge of Wellesbrooke castle. Edmund had always been a selfish fool, and mean. One of the reasons Arthur was with Gray was that from boyhood Edmund had amused himself by beating and tormenting his younger brother. Once he'd picked Arthur up and thrown him into a beehive. And when they were youths, Edmund had introduced Arthur to a whore without revealing that she had the pox. Luckily Arthur had been too shy to do more than kiss the woman. Now the two brothers rarely saw each other. If they did, chances were they would end up in a deadly fight.

Thus Gray had no illusions about Edmund, his meanness, or his plotting. God be thanked, his schemes usually failed, as did the one concerning Yolande. After ridding himself of Juliana, he'd abandoned the heiress for a richer one, never realizing that neither the king nor his regent had any intention of bestowing either girl on so unimportant a knight as Edmund Strange. And he'd given up Juliana. Wild, ungovernable, exciting Juliana. No, *don't think about her*. If he thought about her, he'd begin to lust again.

The ride had given him the opportunity to mend their friendship and to query Welles about his feelings for Yolande. To his relief, Richard seemed uninterested in the girl. Still, what had possessed him to accompany Richard

in his chase after Juliana? He should be at Wellesbrooke
wooing little Yolande instead of chasing after a spoiled,
unruly black-haired witch. Now that his plans for vengeance had been wrecked, he needed to pursue his second aim, which was equally as important.

He was heir to Stratfield, and his father was in ill
health. It was imperative that he make a good marriage,
an alliance that would bolster Stratfield against any ma-
rauding barons who might cast their greedy glances at
the family possessions. In addition, he had two sisters,
one barely thirteen, the other at the marriageable age of
fifteen. They and his ailing father had to be protected,
for a family without an heir was at the mercy of preda-
tory relatives as well as barons who wouldn't hesitate to
attack and take Stratfield upon some flimsy pretext.

Yes, it was his duty to make a powerful and fruitful
marriage. He needed sons. Yolande was young enough to
bear many children, some of whom would survive.

And he had other reasons for having chosen Yolande.
Ones he didn't like to admit to anyone. He wanted a girl
young enough to be guided, who would look up to him
without asking questions about his past. The difference
in their ages would provide a certain distance between
them. After what had happened to him, what he'd done,
he needed that distance.

There was another reason. In that Egyptian quarry,
when he'd been desperate, worn down with shame and
hopelessness, he had imagined himself back in England.
In those dreams, he was untouched by scandal, a knight
worthy of the greatest prize a man could win—a pure and
noble bride.

During that time of beatings and hunger, he'd promised himself such a prize, an ideal woman of ideal beauty
of the *amour courtois*, with pale skin, golden hair, and
sky-blue eyes. A girl like Yolande who through her purity

and excellence would banish corruption and shame from his soul. With a wife like that, people would forget the lies that had been spread about him.

Thus he'd chosen Yolande. Not that he would have been allowed to select anyone of lesser rank. An heir had a duty to safeguard the family rank.

Gray sighed. What had seemed a most pleasant obligation was growing into a chore. Yolande was a sweet girl, but increasingly he realized that her delight in childlike things wasn't affected. She liked blindman's buff and hide and seek, pastimes too simple for Gray, who had sampled far more complex pursuits. And Yolande was young, too young to have gained that fascinating patina that comes with experience of life. No, he was beginning to fear that poor Yolande was—uninteresting.

It was Juliana's fault. He hadn't been able to forget her since that first meeting in the mud. When he should have been planning trysts with Yolande, he was thinking about black curls intertwining around Juliana's breasts. When he should have been dining with Yolande, he'd gone chasing after Juliana, burning with curiosity about where and why she'd vanished from the tournament.

He was vowing to forget Juliana's damascened eyes and to keep himself away from the wench as he followed Richard and the object of his desire over the east bridge to Castle Wellesbrooke. Torches lighted their way, and the drawbridge had been lowered when a shout came from the riverbank. Another party was riding in behind them. He rode back to meet them, and found his cousin Edmund at the head of the party.

"By Our Lady of Mercy," Gray said as he pulled up alongside Edmund. "What addled folly is this?"

Edmund was grinding his teeth. His dark blond hair was plastered to his head with sweat. Long-limbed and wide-shouldered like Gray, he was more round of shoulder. His nose was long, which gave him the appearance of an intelligent fox. He had the habit of looking at people as if he were a gold merchant and they ingots of gold he suspected of impurity. Arthur said his soul was part demon, part counting clerk. Edmund bent to rub his leg, and Gray noticed that he wore no boot on his left foot. His ankle was swollen.

"Just God, Edmund, how can you show your face here?"

"God's greeting to you, cousin. I'm not here apurpose. I was on my way to London and my horse threw me. My ankle caught in the stirrup, and I can't ride much farther."

"You should have camped in the forest. Even if this weren't Wellesbrooke, Arthur won't welcome you, and I'll not have you snarling and snapping at him."

He would have gone on, but Edmund suddenly bent over his mount's neck and would have fallen if Gray hadn't caught him. A squire ran to help, and soon they had the injured man draped over his saddle. Gray found a lump on Edmund's head and realized his cousin was in worse condition than he appeared. There was no help for it. He would have to take Edmund to the castle.

Leading his cousin's horse, Gray rode back over the east bridge to find Richard and Juliana waiting for him. They hadn't moved from their position before the portcullis.

"Richard, it's my cousin Edmund. He's been hurt in a fall while traveling to London, and I must beg refuge for him."

He barely heard Richard's reply, because he was looking at Juliana. For most of the trip her face had sported varying shades of pink and red due to thwarted fury. As he watched, color faded from her skin until it resembled bleached parchment. For a moment, the briefness of a candle's flicker, her eyes widened, and he glimpsed a well of pain. Then she narrowed those damascened eyes, and the pain was gone.

"Another craven succubus. I'll not have him in the castle."

Richard stared down at the girl sitting before him in the saddle. "Juliana!"

"Forsworn cheating cur. Let him go with de Valence."

Shaking his head, Richard said, "Your father would never approve of sending an injured knight away from his hall, even Edmund Strange."

As if in answer to this, Hugo himself bellowed at his daughter as he barreled toward them. At the sound of her father's voice Juliana clamped her mouth shut. Hugo arrived and would have berated his daughter had he not been distracted by the sight of Edmund Strange facedown over his saddle.

Everyone dismounted, and the men discussed what was to be done with Edmund. As expected, Hugo extended his hospitality to the injured man. Juliana snorted and would have walked away in disgust if Gray hadn't blocked her path.

"Where are you going?"

"To my chamber. Now get out of the way, Sir Barbarian Heathen."

She tried to step aside, but he moved with her.

"You never told me why you left the tournament. Imad said you refused my gift—"

"Thunder of God! Let me pass."

They both jumped when Hugo bawled her name and strode over to join them.

"For God's pity, what madness made you vanish in the midst of the tourney? No, don't tell me. There's no use listening to your foolish reasoning. You're an ungrateful daughter and should be taught a lesson." Hugo paused while Edmund was carried past on a litter. A gleam entered his eye. "The leech is busy treating wounds gained in the tournament. Therefore you'll have to care for our new guest. See to it at once."

Gray saw that well of pain open in Juliana's eyes and vanish again. "Lord Welles, I'm certain my squire can attend to him."

"Juliana will do it, my lord."

"I will not!"

Gray winced at the bellow that issued from Hugo's lungs, but Juliana stuck out her chin and crossed her arms. Hugo pointed a thick finger at his daughter.

"You'll tend to him or you'll get no more help from me for your rat-ridden old manor. Do you hear?"

Juliana growled, "Faaahther."

"No, I'm adamant."

Gray was startled when she turned on him. "You. You're to blame for this, and I'll see you sharply punished for it, Viking."

Uttering a wordless snarl, Juliana whirled around and stalked after the litter. Gray stared at her back with his mouth open. Hugo came to join him in watching Juliana's retreat.

"Watch yourself, boy."

"My lord?"

"I don't know what you've done, but she's right evilly disposed toward you, and foul things happen to men who cross Juliana." Hugo brightened. "At least she won't be coming after me as long as she's pointing her sword at you. Good e'en, my lord."

Hugo left him then, and as he went, Gray heard him begin to whistle. So, Mistress Juliana was going to try to punish him, was she? Gray chuckled at the thought. There was little she could do to him, but he was going to enjoy showing her what happened to impudent maidens who tried.

The night passed with no more upsets. The next day was the one chosen for the mêlée. As he expected, Juliana was in her proper place in one of the lodges set up in a meadow near the castle, where she was forced to watch the contest from beginning to end. Gray had been asked to lead one of the two opposing forces. Throughout the day he engaged the enemy in a pitched battle along with friendly knights, including Richard.

In the great rush of men and horses, he was nearly trampled several times. Richard was wounded slightly in the arm after lances had been broken and the battle progressed to swords and maces. Great clouds of dust rose, blinding him, his allies, and the enemy as well. At last a breeze cleared the air for a moment, and Gray was able to muster his men for a final onslaught. He caught sight of the enemy banner, swooped down on the knight holding it, and knocked him to the ground. His men rushed forward, swamping their rivals, and the mêlée was over.

He rode back to the lodges bearing the captured banner to Hugo and lowered it in salute. Face smudged with sweaty dust, he wiped his brow and listened to his host proclaim him the victor and ask him to choose the Queen of Love and Beauty. He glanced aside at Juliana, but she wasn't at her mother's side as she had been earlier.

Searching the onlookers, he finally found her sitting in the back row of benches with the waiting women. She was whispering something under her breath. The maids giggled. She lifted a mocking brow at him, and he scowled. What was she saying about him?

He heard his name again, and looked at Hugo. The

older knight was holding out a circlet of gilded vines and flowers.

"To the victor goes the honor of choosing the Queen of Love and Beauty."

Ah, yes. Duty. He lowered his lance and snagged the golden filet. The sooner he dispensed with this folly, the sooner he could corner Juliana. Holding the circlet on the tip of his lance, he nudged his horse until he came to Yolande. Bowing to her, he let the circlet slip into her hands.

"There can be but one choice, a lady of unsurpassed beauty whose grace has pierced me like a dart."

Through the cheers, he heard another sound. Was it a contemptuous snort? He slid his gaze up to find Juliana Welles looking down her nose at him. Everyone else was cheering him; she sneered. His brows drew together. Had she not seen his prowess? Did she think it easy to fight off a hoard of charging knights whose whole business in life was war? The girl knew nothing of valor and knightly skill.

No doubt she thought she was punishing him as she had vowed to do by withholding her admiration. But he could do without her praise. She whispered something to the maids again, and he was drenched in a shower of giggles. She was making a jest at his expense again, the wretched little wight.

Before he could think of a suitable response to this mockery, a trumpet signaled the end of the day's contest. Hauling on his reins, he turned his horse and rode with the other knights back to the castle. He accepted congratulations from all and sundry, but his mood was foul. At last he was free to go to his pavilion where Simon began to disarm him while he fumed.

He hadn't expected Juliana's mockery to goad him so. What cared he for the approval of an evil-tempered little black duck? He'd been schooled in courtesy and chivalry at the courts of Poitiers and Troyes, in the French heartland of grace and manners. He had shown himself to be a skilled and lethal warrior. Every lady at the tournament had thrown flowers, ribbons, and kerchiefs at him today. Not Juliana, though. Aghast, Gray realized that the thought rankled. No, it infuriated him.

Why couldn't she play her part in *l'amour courtois*? No doubt she was ignorant of its finer aspects since she wasn't married. If he weren't so irritated, he might teach her what he'd learned from the traditions begun by Queen Eleanor and her daughters, even though it was the married woman who was supposed to be the prize in that dangerous game.

He was still nursing a foul mood when a page announced the maid called Alice. The woman rushed into the tent without leave and began babbling at him.

"Oh, my lord, you must come quickly. I think she be going to kill him, and if His Lordship finds out, oh, I can't imagine—"

"What are you gabbling about?"

"Master Strange, my lord. He be calling for you. You must come to his chamber in the castle. They're quarreling, the mistress and him. I shut the door so no one could hear, but I'm afeared they'll come to blows."

"God's pity," he said as he pulled on a robe over his mail and boots. "You left them alone. Hurry, woman."

Alice led him to a room in one of the guard towers set in the curtain wall. They passed through a room that served as barracks and went up the stairs. As he followed the maid, he could hear muffled voices. They grew louder as he gained the second floor. Alice stopped outside a closed door. As she put her hand on the latch, something crashed against the door and broke. Alice cried out and removed her hand.

Gray shoved her aside and pushed through the door. His cousin lay on a narrow bed, his bandaged foot propped up on pillows. Juliana stood near the bed, her arms folded across her chest, her foot tapping on the floor. Gray stepped over the fragments of a ceramic cup and avoided the splatters of its contents that graced the floor. When they saw him, they spoke at once.

"Cousin, help me. She's trying to poison me."

"Go away," Juliana said. "I can only endure one vain rooster at a time."

He ignored her. "What's your lament, cousin?"

"She's trying to make me drink some foul brew. I vow she hates me and is trying to poison me."

"I think not, cousin. Feeble-witted as she is, she knows she's the first one we'd suspect if you were to die."

"Oh!"

Juliana picked up a clay bottle from the table beside the bed. He thought she was going to throw it at him, but instead she marched up to him and thrust it into his hands.

"He thinks I poisoned this. Why don't you serve as his taster since you're so sure I haven't?"

He tried to concentrate on what she was saying, but her anger had caused her to breathe quickly. The rapid heaving of her breasts interfered with his wits. He remonstrated with himself and dragged his gaze to her face—where he promptly became enthralled with the soft pink of her lips. What had she said?

"Are you going to drink the potion, my lord?"

"What? Oh. There's no need, mistress. I'm certain it's as well made as those you gave Imad."

Edmund scrambled around in the bed until he was sitting straight. "I'll not touch it."

"Excellent," Juliana replied with an evil smile. "Then you'll be in pain the whole night."

"You malformed bitch!"

Gray was at the bed before the sound of the words faded. He grabbed Edmund by the neck of his shirt and twisted the material until his cousin began to gasp for breath. As Edmund clawed at his hand, he spoke quietly.

"If you ever speak so to her again, I'll make you swallow my war axe."

Smiling and calm, he watched Edmund turn purple before releasing his grip. His cousin fell back on the pillows and lay there gasping. He turned to Juliana. She sheltered behind the door, her eyes wide. When he looked at her, she was regarding him with a look of startled surmise, as if no one had ever defended her before. Perhaps no one had. Her eyes were bright, glassy. Was she going to cry? God, his sodding cousin had hurt her, and he wanted to take the pain away.

He spoke softly, "Juliana, my joyance . . ."

She gave a whispery little cry and was gone. He heard her light steps running down the stairs. When they faded, he was left with the scent of violets in the chamber and a chastened Edmund.

Hemlock

 This herb, if often drunk, destroyed the great appetite of lechery.

• *Chapter 9* •

AT DAWN ON THE MORNING OF THE SIEGE OF
the Castle of Love and Beauty, Juliana said her prayers at
the small altar in her chamber, picked up the clay bottle
she'd taken from Edmund's chamber, and climbed to the
top of the Maiden's Tower. She had kept the vessel in her
room as a precaution.

Using a key suspended from her girdle, she unlocked
the door to the room she used as her herb chamber. Dry,
breezy, and equipped with shutters of exacting fit, the
room contained dozens of shelves for her pots and jars.
There were two worktables, mortars and pestles, braziers,
and drying racks. The Wellesbrooke carpenter had fashioned more racks suspended from the ceiling and even a
stepping stool so that she could reach them. Herbs and
flowers hung in bunches overhead.

When the castle wasn't infested with tournament-
goers, she spent much of her time making infusions, de-
coctions, and ointments. Juliana loved her herb chamber.
Special shelves were fitted with heavy curtains to protect
the more fragile herbs from the diffuse sunlight that
showered through the windows. The carpenter had fashioned dozens of small wooden tags engraved with the
names of herbs and various medicinal preparations.
These she attached to her pots and jars with twine so
that the contents were easily recognizable.

Juliana walked to a great chest set against one wall,
deposited the bottle inside, and locked it. Gray de Va-

lence was unpredictable; she wouldn't be surprised if he appeared in the herb chamber, and she didn't want him finding the bottle. Fists planted on her hips, she frowned at the chest. She'd put only a little of the herb spurge in the concoction. Not enough to harm Edmund, just enough to keep him hovering over his chamber pot for a few hours. The man had the honor and chivalry of a newt. He deserved far worse at her hands.

If only de Valence hadn't interfered. She had been furious with Alice for bringing him until he'd defended her against Edmund so honorably. Since his intolerable treatment of her at Vyne Hill, she'd been ready to dose him with every evil potion in her healing box. And then he'd taken such violent offense against Edmund on her behalf that she'd been dazed.

"I don't understand him," she muttered to herself. "Throwing me across his saddle like a—like a—. He's a man of foul, brazen, unchivalrous conduct."

She flushed at the memory of her body resting on his thighs. She went to a worktable and touched an infuser pot. Her fingers drifted over several ceramic filters used to strain plant substance from infusions.

"But he defended me," she whispered. Edmund's epithet still scalded her soul—*malformed bitch.*

Most of the time she forgot about her leg, deliberately. When Edmund had snarled those evil words at her, she'd nearly bolted from the room with shame. She'd been certain that his cousin's contempt would taint Gray's view of her. Instead, de Valence had blamed Edmund and threatened his life. Over an insult against her. When shortly before he'd treated her like an insolent harlot. In that short moment he'd placed himself among a rare minority—those who didn't believe her deformity was God's curse.

She didn't understand. It was clear he was seeking the

favor of Yolande, and yet he couldn't seem to keep clear of plain old Juliana. Now he'd succeeded in appeasing her fury, something she never would have thought possible. Memories of that ignoble ride home faded more each time she recalled the way his voice lowered and grew rough when he said, "Juliana, my joyance."

Juliana picked up her herb knife, held it with the point on the table, and spun it. "My joyance," she murmured with a slight smile. A knock at the door brought a sigh as Yolande entered the chamber. Osbert, her personal guard assigned to her by the Earl of Uvedale, stationed himself outside the door. Osbert accompanied her almost everywhere to guard against abduction.

"I knew you'd be here." Yolande closed the door and rushed over to wave something in Juliana's face. "Look! See what the Sieur de Valence sent to me."

"De Valence?" Juliana asked faintly.

Yolande nodded rapidly and waved her prize again. Juliana snatched her wrist and held it still. Yolande held a pair of kid hawking gloves embroidered in shining green and gold. On the back of each was a winged dragon. Dropping the girl's wrist, Juliana dug her nails into her palms until they pierced the skin.

"A fine gift."

"Oh, yes," Yolande said as she began to dance around the herb chamber waving the gloves. "I always wanted a suitor pleasing of countenance and manner. By Our Lady of Mercy, he's the most chivalrous and comely knight in Christendom."

"And the most inconstant."

"What?"

"Oh, naught." She was going to feed him hemlock, which destroyed the appetite for lechery.

"I can't wait for the siege," Yolande said, lifting her skirts and dancing past Juliana. "I'm the Queen of Love and Beauty because of him, and I'm sure he'll lay siege to me alone."

Yolande curtsied and capered. "And I'll be sure to let him catch me."

She had to control her rage. Her nails were drawing blood. Unclenching her fists, Juliana took several deep breaths. To think she'd believed him capable of honor. His marrow was infused with deceit, and he was hunting poor Yolande.

"Yolande, de Valence has an evil reputation."

"Now don't you be taking against him. I know you detest rooster knights, but my lord isn't one of those. There's no falsity or villainy in him."

"But—"

"I know how hard it is to mend the wound Edmund caused." Yolande's little face grew solemn and cheerless for a moment. "I—I too was hurt."

Juliana felt a rush of pity and regretted her outburst. It was true. Edmund had abandoned Yolande in pursuit of yet another heiress and almost destroyed the girl's heart. Juliana had never resented her friend for Edmund's behavior. Yolande hadn't intended evil, and she'd had a difficult life.

Because of her value, she'd been kept well guarded in various towers and fortresses during her childhood. Her lot had been privileged loneliness and isolation until she'd come to Wellesbrooke. Her every word had been a command to those serving her, but she had few companions her own age.

Because of her upbringing, she'd assumed that everyone's lot was to please her. But battles with three other girls and Havisia had eventually taught her lessons in humility, generosity, and tolerance. No longer did she demand the best cut of meat at table or beat her maid for honest mistakes. Having grown into sweetness and charity, Yolande had won Juliana's enduring affection. And Juliana wasn't going to let Gray de Valence hurt her friend.

"Oh, I forgot the reason I'm here. Your mother says it's time to begin dressing for the siege."

"Thunder of heaven. There's plenty of time. I want to talk to you about—"

"I think your mother has allowed for the time it will take to convince you to dress. If she begins to warn you now, in an hour you'll come down to your chamber and put on that beautiful gown. Come, Jule. I always knew I would have a great man, and now God has provided him. I want to share this day of happiness with you. Please, please, please."

Juliana sighed at the wheedling tone that crept into Yolande's voice. Throwing up her hands in surrender, she said, "Then I might as well come now, for I'll get no peace. After you, she'll send Laudine, then Bertrade and so on."

Seeing Yolande's bright eyes and jubilant expression, she closed her mouth on the truths she'd been ready to reveal concerning de Valence. His attentions seemed to have revived Yolande's old belief in her own paramount importance. Juliana's story wouldn't be welcomed, indeed, would probably be blamed on jealousy. She would try to ruin his evil plan without involving her friend.

Locking the herb chamber, Juliana descended to her room, snorting and muttering contemptuous imprecations against rooster knights. After dressing in the white and gold raiment of Virtue, she stalked into Laudine's and Bertrade's chamber to help her sisters dress. Laudine was a bit disgruntled at having lost the title of Queen of Love and Beauty to Yolande, but she brightened when she donned her gown that was the color of rubies. As Chastity, Bertrade was satisfied with her azure and white costume. Juliana was disgusted when Laudine insisted on taking down her hair, which she'd bound in braids.

"We're maidens, Jule. Men like to see women's long, unbound hair. It sets them afire, and I intend to set plenty of them in flames. Here, this circlet is yours."

Juliana grumbled as Bertrade combed her hair and Laudine set a headdress of gold and pearls on the back of her head. She didn't stop grumbling until she had followed her sisters out of the castle to join the chattering group of maidens on the tournament grounds. All around them, in the lodges and behind the palisades, had gathered merrymakers of high and low birth.

It was the mock castle that silenced her grumbling. The Wellesbrooke carpenters had constructed a replica of the castle and painted it white and gold. Behind the façade was scaffolding upon which the ladies would stand as if atop battlements. From there they would pelt the invading knights with flowers and cakes.

A maid handed Juliana a basket filled with these missiles. Insubstantial weapons, Juliana thought. She chewed her lip while she studied the basket, then hooked her arm through the handle and turned back to the castle while tossing a comment over her shoulder to Laudine.

"I'll be back in a moment. I forgot my kerchief."

"Juliana!"

"I said I'd return."

"If you run away, I'll make you sorry," Laudine called after her.

True to her word, she returned in time to enter the mock castle and climb a ladder to the scaffolding. Once atop the structure, she squeezed by several young guests and nudged her way between Yolande and Laudine. She had no sooner taken her place than a trumpet call announced the approach of the knights.

Cheers went up from the lodges and the palisades.

Juliana's eyes grew round as she heard a roll of thunder. Only it wasn't thunder; it was the pounding of hooves from giant destriers. A long line of knights rode toward them, banners high, swords waving in the air in time to battle cries. Around her shrieks went up from the ladies, and Yolande urged everyone to wait until the men were within throwing distance.

As the first knights reached them, Yolande cried, "Now! Defend yourselves, ladies."

A hail of flowers and cakes pelted the men as squires ran onto the field bearing ladders. Sir Lucien managed to plant his ladder below Laudine, but she gripped it and pushed it away to the cheers of her friends. Juliana remained motionless, watching. She searched the crowd of knights until she found Gray de Valence at the head of a group carrying a ladder to the wall below Yolande's position.

"I thought so," she said to herself.

Grabbing a flower, she tossed it halfheartedly at a knight who was tottering on one of the lower battlements. Not far away, Bertrade shoved a man by his helmet, and he fell amidst the guffaws of his fellows. The crowd cheered the maidens loudly when yet another ladder was repelled from the walls.

Juliana never took her gaze from de Valence. Gray had his own men hold the base of his ladder, so when Yolande tried to push it, she couldn't move it. Laudine's plump curves suddenly appeared, bouncing Yolande away from the ladder. Yolande gave the intruder another of those flat-headed cat looks and darted, arrowlike, between Laudine and the ladder. To prevent a wrestling contest Juliana slipped between the two. Then she and Yolande began to hurl their missiles in earnest as Gray removed his helmet.

Shoving back his mail hood and padding to reveal

moonlight hair, he began to climb. He dodged the cakes that sailed at him. Flowers were ignored, though they hit him in the face. He looked up at them, then signaled for his knights to follow.

"To the fair Queen of Love and Beauty!" he cried.

His men echoed the call, and soon there were knights scrambling all over the edifice. The defenders shrieked and redoubled their efforts, raining flowers and cakes without end. Gray had almost reached them when Juliana set down her half-empty basket. Yolande gave a delighted cry as his head appeared over the top of the wooden wall.

Juliana stooped to gather something in each hand from her basket. By the time she returned to Yolande, Gray was lunging up, arms extended to capture his prize. A cheer rose up from the knights, along with laughter. Gray's hands opened wide to grasp Yolande, who was pelting him with lilies. He bent over the wall, grinning, but Juliana thrust herself between him and Yolande.

"Begone, fiend of Satan," she said as she thrust a pan of butter into his face.

He gasped, sputtered, and choked, bending toward her over the edge of the wall. He righted himself, tottering, and wiped butter from his eyes. As he spotted her, Juliana calmly swiped him on the head with a joint of beef gripped by the bone. Butter splattered everywhere, and Gray roared at her.

"Juliana, what are you doing?" cried Yolande.

Gray dodged another swing of the beef joint. "Fires of hell!" He wiped butter from his armor and glared at Juliana. "By God, it's the evil-tempered witch!"

"Better a witch than a man without honor," Juliana said, and she swiped him on the head again.

Gray swore, then ducked as the joint came down at him again. Thrusting himself upright, he snarled and hopped over the wall to the scaffolding. Juliana hadn't expected him to recover before she could toss him off the wall. Aghast, she backed away, hurled the joint at him and scurried along the scaffolding.

Gray batted the missile aside, his clothing slick with butter and his face red from anger. He lunged at her, and for the second time, Juliana was plucked off her feet. She sailed in the air and landed across his shoulder with her bottom uppermost. She let out a wild cry of rage, but it was smothered by the laughs and cries of the men and women around them.

Her vision blurred as Gray jounced her across the scaffold, over the wall, and down the ladder. Her hair prevented her from seeing much, so she was horrified when her enemy lowered her so that she rested on his hip. More laughter from the onlookers told her just how ridiculous she appeared as Gray mounted his horse with her under his arm like a sack of meal.

Suddenly the world spun, and Gray hefted her across his lap. Without a word in answer to the thunder rolls of knightly laughter and feminine jests, he kicked his mount into a gallop. Juliana gasped as she was bumped and jostled across the lists. All she could see was dirt and grass flying by.

The sounds of the tournament faded as the horse slowed, and they clattered across the drawbridge into the bailey. When the animal stopped she saw packed earth and heard gasps and excited cries. Suddenly she sailed upright and was thrown over Gray's shoulder again.

"You cankerous sodomite, put me down!"

"Thy will is mine, noble lady."

He righted her so that she rested in his arms. She glared up at him; he gave her a buttery, wicked smile. She drew back her fist, ready to pummel that smile off his lips. He dropped her. She fell into a great washtub filled with soapy water and sank like a foundation stone.

Gray water invaded her nose and mouth. Juliana gagged and thrust herself to the surface, sputtering and choking. Gray was standing there, arms folded over his chest, grinning, while around him washing women, stable boys, and servants stared in astonishment. Several noble guests came out of the new hall, and Juliana heard two women whisper and giggle.

When she caught her breath, she began to shout. "You unchivalrous heathen, rabid cur, lascivious knave!"

"Certes, good folk," Gray said to the onlookers. "Mistress Juliana is a right ill-tempered and discourteous maid in need of correction."

"Aaaahhhrgh!" Juliana swept her hands up and sent a wave of dirty water into his face.

It was Gray's turn to choke and sputter. He dashed water from his eyes, and when Juliana beheld his expression, she turned and waded toward the opposite side of the washtub. She wasn't quick enough.

Hands fastened around her waist. Desperate, she twisted around and shoved him. He didn't budge, and she was lifted out of the water. As she went, she planted her feet against the side of the tub and pushed. The force of her movement pulled Gray off balance. Juliana cried out as his feet lost their purchase and he fell on top of her into the tub.

Her head hit the side of the tub as she fell. Underwater, she hit bottom with a bounce, and Gray's body followed, touching hers. Juliana thrashed about only to feel Gray's hands slide over her breasts as he searched blindly. He slid them down to her waist, gripped her, and lifted.

Her body hurtled upward, and she was set on her feet. She stumbled and fell against him. His arms surrounded her and held her steady. With her cheek pressed against his chest, she gulped in deep breaths of air. She couldn't be sure, but she thought his fingers touched her cheek and lips with the lightness of an angel's breath. Then she heard him chuckle.

"You're a most inconstant, mad creature."

"Inconstant!"

Juliana thrust herself out of his grip. Her gown clung to her legs and nearly tripped her. She slicked her hair back so that she could see him clearly.

"You're the inconstant, you foul corrupter of other men's wives. You're plying poor Yolande with courtly wiles when not a few hours ago you spewed honied words at me."

There was a sudden silence. The area around them emptied of washer maids and servants. Gray had been looking down at her with amused mockery. Her words drew a veil across his features. His eyes reflected the still iciness of a snow-bound winter night.

"I promised myself never to answer such slander again. I've heard talk about you too, Juliana, and now I understand why you're to take vows of chastity and leave your father's house. Were I he, I would have clapped you in a nunnery long ago, but I'm sure no worthy order would take you."

Turning his back on her, Gray leaped out of the tub, mounted his horse, and galloped out of the bailey. Juliana watched him while she shivered in the middle of the washtub. She hated him for looking so magnificent, all those wet muscles moving beneath clinging fabric and mail. He'd deceived her for the last time. She promised herself and God that she'd make him a greater spectacle than he made her. By this evening, she'd have every tournament-goer, from the haywards to the noblest baron, laughing at Gray de Valence.

Cuckoopint

If you would make your face white and clear, take powder of the roots and lay it in rose water and set it in the sun till it be consumed, twice or thrice. Rub your face with the powder.

• Chapter 10 •

SHE WAS SUPPOSED TO BE IN HER CHAMBER,
overcome with the mortification of the scene with de
Valence. Juliana hugged a patched and tattered cloak
around her body and poked her head around the central
stone newel of the stair in the Maiden's Tower. She was
listening for her sisters' chatter.

Earlier Yolande had come to her chamber while she
was bathing away the grime of the washtub and accused
her of trying to steal her suitor.

Once again Osbert had stood guard outside the closed
door, but Juliana was sure he could hear Yolande's bellowing.

"How could you disgrace me so!" From her bow-
shaped mouth to her tiny slippers, Yolande was quivering.
"By the wrath of God, you've committed a great sin
against me. Everyone saw how you tricked him. Everyone! You shamed me, made me a laughingstock."

"But I was trying to save you from him."

"Save him for yourself, you mean. Everyone laughed at
me. At me, me, me, *me*."

Yolande's voice rose to a screech. Juliana had forgotten
how shrill Yolande could be when aroused. But this was
more than anger; this was rage. All reason left her eyes,
and she came after Juliana with her fingers curled into
claws. Juliana backed away until she hit a wall, then
slapped Yolande as she struck with those talonlike nails.

Havisia had appeared to take Yolande away and calm

her. Juliana had been left alone to suffer remorse and grow even more furious at Gray de Valence. He had a great sin upon his soul.

Juliana decided that the Maiden's Tower was deserted. Everyone was at the dance being held before the mock castle. Now all she had to do was get out of Wellesbrooke unnoticed. Turning away from the stair, she went through the narrow door of the garderobe, edged around the stone convenience, and began to shove at a portion of the wall behind it.

With much exertion, the concealed door swung open. She lit a torch sitting just inside, closed the door, and was soon on her way down a passage. The corridor led beneath the bedrock upon which the castle sat to a sally port in the curtain wall. No one camped near it because the garderobe drain was nearby.

She and her sisters had found the passage years ago while playing hide and seek. Their parents assumed they knew nothing of it, and they hadn't revealed their knowledge. Why ruin an excellent hiding place when it was so convenient for escaping lessons? Neither Bertrade nor Laudine used the passage anymore, but Juliana did.

She reached the end of the corridor quickly. Dousing the torch in a pot of sand, she opened the door. The sword at her side scraped the portal. Cursing herself for her carelessness, she clamped the weapon against her leg and peered outside. The small expanse of land between the sally port and the riverbank was deserted.

Before going into the open, she checked to make sure her hair was stuffed beneath the pointed hood of brown wool. It covered her head, neck, and shoulders. Tightening the squire's sword belt that bound her tunic at the waist, she stuffed her leggings into a pair of Tybalt's old boots. They were too big and wrinkled at the ankles, but she'd had the cobbler fix the soles like her other footwear.

Using ashes from the torch, she dirtied her face, then slipped outside. The door swung closed to blend perfectly with the rest of the stones around it. During a siege, the passageway would be blocked from inside with boulders, but Wellesbrooke was at peace at the moment. Juliana hurried away from the sally port. She had to breathe through her nose to keep from gagging at the stench of the drain as she hurried around the base of the wall to mix with the traffic crossing the east bridge.

Soon she was walking through pastures and fields into the Hawksmere Forest, leaving behind the crowds of merrymakers and the scores of vendors and entertainers who had descended upon Wellesbrooke hoping to turn a penny. She left the well-traveled path that led north through her father's domain to the lands of Chessmore and chose her way carefully through thick stands of oak and dense brush until she came upon a small ravine.

There she found Eadmer, Warin, Bogo, and Lambert, all dressed as she was and keeping watch over five horses. She emerged from the trees with a whistle. The four waved at her, and Bogo hurried over to her. He was the smallest of the four, but also the widest, and when he smiled he revealed a gap between his two front teeth.

"God save you, mistress. We been waiting a perilous long time."

"I was delayed by a—an accident. Did you bring your bows?"

"Oh, aye, mistress. Now will you tell us what ill-willer has offended you?"

"Not yet. We must ride to Hawkesbrooke quickly. Once we're there, I'll tell you."

"Yes, mistress," Eadmer said as he pulled his horse alongside hers. "And on the way, will you tell us another story of chivalry? I liked the one about Roland and Charles the Mange."

Juliana winced. "Charlemagne, Eadmer, not Charles the Mange, Charlemagne."

Eadmer repeated the name several times. His watery eyes were bright above a nose that seemed permanently red and crisscrossed with tiny crimson veins.

"I liked them laws of love," Warin said as they all mounted. "Avoid avarice and falsehood, obey your lady love, and speak no evil. Never reveal a love affair, and ever be polite and courteous. Do you think I could win Jumping Jean if I was to be chivalrous to her?"

The taciturn Lambert, who was skilled with the long-bow, merely grunted, but Eadmer laughed.

"Blessed be God, Warin. You'd do better to give her gold. They say she jumps from one man to the next by the weight of his purse."

"You're a liar!" Warin hauled his mount around and would have cuffed Eadmer if Juliana hadn't interfered.

"For God's pity, keep silent," she growled. "You two have this same quarrel at least once a month."

They arrived at Hawkesbrooke, a small stream that cut through the forest to join the Clare. In a short time Juliana had positioned her men and settled down with Bogo to wait. She and her companion were perched on the thick branch of an ancient oak. It arched over the brook, and its leaves concealed them as it shaded the water. Warin lurked on the opposite bank, his body stretched out along another branch of a tree. Eadmer had taken up a watch high in the top of another oak.

Juliana signaled to each of them, and they pulled lengths of dark cloth over their faces. Through slits in their masks, she and Bogo watched the track that emerged from the direction of the castle. They would rely on Eadmer's signal, for the dancing water in the brook would drown out the sound of someone approaching.

Bogo was hugging the branch with one arm while he carefully laid down his bow. A quiver was slung across his shoulder. "Mistress, who's the unfortunate we're after this time?"

"Um, it's better you don't know."

Bogo pulled an arrow from his quiver and glanced at her with widening eyes. "Better? How better, mistress? You said we'd never have to worry about getting caught. You promised—"

"Fear not. Alice sent him here, and there'll only be one or two men with them since everyone else is dancing."

"But mistress."

"Very well, it's Master Edmund Strange."

"Ohhh, mistress. What are you going to do to him? I thought he'd hurt his leg."

"He has. Alice has told him he must soak his ankle in this pure, cold water to take away the swelling."

Eadmer uttered a robin's call. Juliana drew a knife and held it by the blade, ready to throw. Bogo nocked an arrow.

"Um, Bogo," Juliana said as she crouched on the branch and prepared for the attack.

"Yes, mistress."

"There is someone else with Master Strange."

"Who be that, mistress?"

"The Sieur de Valence."

Bogo made a strangling sound. Juliana clamped her hand over his mouth.

"Shhh!"

"De-De Valence," Bogo hissed. "May God assoil my soul. De Valence. What—what— We can't. No one goes against—"

"Shhh, Bogo. They're here."

Bogo groaned. "He'll draw and quarter us. If we're fortunate."

"One more word, and I'll help him. Now you get ready to release that arrow."

Silence fell as a party of four emerged from the trees along the bank of the stream. Juliana watched Gray de Valence dismount and help his cousin from his horse and convey him to the bank. Two youths, servants, assisted. One of them was Imad.

When the boys had led the horses away, Juliana whispered to Bogo, "Now."

Bogo drew back on his longbow and released an arrow. Juliana heard a familiar angry buzz, and the arrow shot into the ground at the feet of Gray de Valence. At the same time she and her men let out raucous hooting cries. More arrows rained down on the men below, spearing the ground around them until they were surrounded by a feathered half-circle of missiles.

After the first shot, de Valence had slipped behind a tree and drawn his sword. Edmund was scrambling in the leaves and dirt to hide behind a boulder at the edge of the water. The two servants dodged behind a stand of bushes, kept there by the threat of Warin's bow.

The first volley over, Juliana thrust her legs through the dense leaf cover and swung to a lower branch. Balancing there in sight of her victims, she bowed.

"Well met, my lords." She'd had practice at lowering her voice. She sounded more like a youth than a man, but at least she didn't sound like a maid. "I greet you well."

Gray's bright head appeared from behind the tree. "You've chosen the wrong men. We brought no gold with us."

"That's a great heaviness to me, noble sir. What's a

poor thief to do when great barons become sparrow hawks?"

Her men laughed and called down jeers and insults. Edmund cowered behind his rock and whimpered at de Valence, who ignored him.

"Well, lads," Juliana said. "We've chosen to rob men of such poor condition that they've no coin at all. What shall we do with them?"

"Hang them!" cried Warin.

Edmund tried to burrow under his rock, but de Valence laughed.

"You're only safe at a distance, fool. If you get within sword's reach, you're dead."

His unconcern annoyed Juliana. She let her men taunt the victims a bit longer, then said, "Right well said, my lord. Then I suppose the only thing left to do is run away."

"I would suggest it," de Valence replied.

"But first," Juliana purred, "I'll have your clothes."

"What?" Edmund shrieked. "Oh, God, I've heard of this churl. He's called the stripping bandit."

"Quickly, noble sirs."

De Valence scowled at her, and she was pleased to see that he had no ready reply this time.

Edmund shook his head. "No, I'll not give you one scrap!"

Juliana sighed, put two fingers in her mouth, and whistled loudly. At the signal, arrows shot out to impale the ground a finger's width from Edmund's cowering figure. The man yelped and began removing his cloak.

"Tie them in a bundle and throw them into the forest across the brook," Juliana said.

Gray hadn't moved.

"Your clothes as well, my lord."

"I think not, master thief."

Juliana grinned and glanced at Eadmer high above her. "Convince his lordship."

There was a click and a furious whir as a crossbow fired. De Valence jumped at the impact of a bolt in the trunk of the tree. It had pierced the wood beside his head.

"You should learn humility, noble sir. God has sent me to be the instrument to teach you. Your clothes, my lord. The next shot won't be so wide of the mark."

Even from a distance she could see the muscle in Gray's jaw quiver as he tried to master his temper. Juliana was grinning wider by the moment. De Valence shoved away from the tree and removed his cloak. It spread out on the ground, to be followed by his tunic and belt. More clothing sailed through the air to land on top of these, and Juliana's smile vanished.

His gaze never left hers. She knew he was trying to wish away the cloth that covered her face. Defiance in every movement and in the grim set of his mouth, de Valence unlaced his hose. Juliana had grown silent as the disrobing revealed a lean, tapering torso sculpted with subtle hills and knolls of muscle.

He removed his boots, and his hands went to the top of his hose and undergarment. Juliana usually turned away at this point. She always had before, but he was staring at her in such defiance. Curse him, he wasn't shamed at all. He didn't try to cover himself with his hands; he stood there, open and oblivious to his own body.

Her legs wouldn't move, and she was growing hot. The finely knit cloth slipped down over his hips. She glimpsed hair a shade darker than that on his head. Her mouth was so dry she couldn't swallow; her mask was going to smother her. He bent and removed the last of his clothing, dropped it on the pile and straightened.

She had seen men before. As a healer, she'd seen many men, and come to the conclusion that they were all alike and uninteresting. Then why couldn't she remove her gaze from him? The sight of his body disturbed her. She'd seen muscles before, long legs before, everything before, but not covered with smooth skin that seemed touched with gold. And the only curved part on him drew her gaze as he turned to the side to speak to Imad. *Juliana Welles, you're staring at a man's backside.*

She recalled the feel of him against her when he'd thrown her across his saddle. There had been hardness, an unexpected hardness and firmness. She understood the cause of that hardness, but had refused to connect it with herself until now. Juliana forced her gaze to his thighs, remembering their strength, and then started as Bogo cleared his throat.

"Be it time to go?"

She nodded, unable to speak. She was shaking on the inside and desperate not to shake on the outside where he could see it. Dear God, why wouldn't he look away from her? While the rest of them held their victims at bay, Lambert had dropped to the ground and gathered clothing from the men and their servants. He was leaving when Juliana came out of her trance and dragged her gaze away from de Valence.

"Wait," she called. "Leave a cloak for the heathen lad. He's been ailing."

Lambert tossed a cloak to Imad while Eadmer led their victim's horses beneath Juliana's tree. She and Bogo climbed down and dropped into the saddles. Gathering the reins, Juliana took the clothes while Eadmer and Bogo aimed bows at their quarry. By the time she looked at de Valence again, she'd regained her composure. But she kept her gaze above his shoulders.

"A most profitable encounter, noble sirs. I urge you to

hurry back to the castle, for evening approaches, and the night mist makes for a chilly evening stroll. God give you peace, my lords, as he's given me your clothes."

Loud guffaws from her men caused Edmund to hurl curses at her, but de Valence remained where he'd been all along. His arms rested loosely at his sides. He still made no attempt to conceal his body. No flush of shame reddened his cheeks, and he continued to stare at her. He was frowning, as if puzzled. Suddenly he moved, walking with the grace of a wolf at home in the forest, alert, stalking, menacing. She backed her mount away, and he paused, resting his hands on his hips and gazing at her with that perplexed expression.

"Good e'en to you, my lord," Juliana said. "There are no hamlets or villages between the brook and the castle. And the walk leaving the forest is exposed all the way to the east bridge. You should give the castle folk a right heady sight parading home. I wish I could see it."

Gray flushed. "You meant this all along, you impudent catamite. You weren't after gold."

More jeers from her men filled the air.

Juliana hooted. "Blessed be God, men. He thinks we came all the way through the forest to look at his pretty arse!"

At last she got a curse from Gray de Valence. He stalked toward her only to halt as a crossbow bolt shot into the ground at his feet. Laughing, Juliana turned her horse and kicked it into a gallop, leaving Gray de Valence staring after her in splendid, furious nudity.

Anise

This herb unbound the stopping of the liver and of wicked winds and of great humors.

• *Chapter 11* •

GRAY COULD SEE THE TURRETS OF WELLES-
brooke growing larger and larger. He took another step in
his journey across the fallow field and hit a sharp stone.
Yelping, he hopped on one foot while grabbing the other
in both hands.

The soles of his feet were covered with nicks and
bruises where he'd stepped on thorns, pebbles, and sharp
twigs on his way through the forest. Once they'd been
tough from going barefoot as a slave. Every step reminded him of old shame, old degradations. Releasing
his foot, he limped over an old furrow and vowed to
catch the bastard leader of those thieves if he had to stay
at Wellesbrooke through winter. He'd left the others to
await the rescue party he would send once he reached the
castle. Gloom settled over him.

He'd already had a miserable day. First that mad-tem-
pered harridan Juliana had attacked him, and then Yolande had sent back the gloves he'd given her. She had
sent word through the Earl of Uvedale that she wanted
no more gifts from him, nor did she wish to speak with
him. Until then he hadn't thought about how his carrying off Juliana would appear. Which showed how feeble-
witted the witch had made him. Upon receiving her
message, he'd sought out Yolande and cornered her in
Havisia's well-tended garden. Slipping through a door in
the wall that surrounded the place, he'd crept up on the
girl as she sat alone on a bench reading. His shadow fell

on her as he approached. She didn't look up, but a hiss spewed from her lips. He hesitated, confused by the virulence in her tone.

"Satan's entrails, get out of my light, girl, or I'll sell you to— My lord."

When she saw him, she cut off her words. Her eyes narrowed to slits; for a brief moment he felt as if he were looking into the black-red gaze of an Egyptian crocodile. In an instant the impression was gone, and he was left feeling that he'd imagined it. Gray bowed as she stood and set her book aside.

"I thought you were my maid."

"Sweet mistress, I've come to explain about this morn."

"There is nothing you can say to wipe out the shame of what you did before the whole tournament."

"If you would but listen."

"I heard about the washtub," Yolande said.

It was her voice, that sweet voice. It made her seem more pliable and young than she was.

Yolande ran her fingers through a long lock of gold that hung over her shoulder, twisting and tangling them in the skeins. "I'll not listen to you, because there is nothing that will restore my pride except to spurn you, and I'm determined that it shall be so. Everyone will say I rejected you instead of whispering that you prefer Juliana."

He stared at her, and she stared back at him. Gone was the sweet and guileless maid with whom he'd danced. He faced a young woman, her stance unyielding, her mood implacable.

"Don't be in such haste."

He would have gone on, but she left, slipping through a door concealed by a cascade of vines, and he found himself talking to the bench. He had not done well. Being in the wrong had put him at a disadvantage.

Now there was talk all over the Welles domain that he'd thrown over Yolande for Juliana. Yolande obviously believed it; and once he'd thought about it, he could understand. After all, heirs to great baronies didn't usually squirm around in washtubs with lord's daughters.

No one had believed him when he protested that he'd been furious and wished to pay her back. Arthur had stared at him in wild consternation and muttered something about choosing another, richer heiress rather than Juliana. He still cringed at the recollection of Lucien's knowing smirks.

"By the holy saints, *messire*," Lucien had said. "You must be fair smitten with ardor to wallow with your love in a washtub before everyone."

"I didn't wallow," Gray muttered to himself as he left the fallow field, his feet and legs dusty and sore. Lucien's wit could be nasty at times.

It had been a miserable day. He was furious at Juliana Welles. The woman might have cost him his betrothed, for if he couldn't regain Yolande's favor, he wouldn't force her to accept him. He had more pride than that, and there were other heiresses, by God. What had possessed Juliana to leap on him like that? Was she so foultempered as to wobble on the brink of madness? No, she'd been furious at him for his honorable courting of Yolande.

He was nearing the east bridge. Carts, wagons, and people were crossing in both directions, the last traffic before the gates closed at sunset. He forgot about Juliana as dread engulfed him. He closed his eyes, remembering the docks of Alexandria. It was there that he'd been stripped for the first time, stripped, examined, handled. Those old feelings of shame and degradation settled over him again. Just God, would he never stop feeling defiled?

"Think about what you're going to do to the whoreson

who took your clothes," he muttered to himself. "Where's your courage, fool? Find it again before you have to face everyone."

Feeding his anger with thoughts of hanging the thief naked from the battlements, he left the field and stepped onto the path that led to the bridge. A farmer pulling a hay cart looked his way and stumbled, causing the woman with a basket of bread to run into him. She remonstrated with the farmer, but stopped in mid-sentence to stare at Gray, her gap-toothed mouth ajar. Then she screamed.

More people turned to gape. Several snickered before they recognized him. He stalked over to the hay cart and placed himself against it.

"Don't leer at me, man. Get me a cloak."

"My—my—lord. How—where—"

Gray considered cuffing the man, but was distracted by the sound of giggling. In the shadow of the east gatehouse, Gray beheld a slight, black-haired figure in violet silk. Juliana Welles had covered her mouth with a filmy kerchief, but he would know that rippling laugh if he were struck blind. Uttering a growl, he scoured the battlements to find that he'd attracted the attention of several other maidens. Fortunately, Havisia appeared, glanced over the walls at him, and shooed the girls away.

Peasants, reeves, bailiffs, and dirty children passed around him like flowing water around a rock and gave him looks of incredulity, and derision when they thought he wasn't looking. The children merely sniggered. Blood pounded in his temples. He ground his teeth so hard he thought they'd crack. And Juliana Welles stood at the gatehouse and laughed.

"By the devil's horns!" He pointed at a guard standing beside Juliana. "You, don't stand there and gape at me like some addled court jester, bring me your cloak at once. The rest of you, begone!"

The guard was short, so the cloak only came halfway down his calves. Gray swirled it around his shoulders and marched across the bridge while his abruptly silent audience fled. He growled at the guards standing on either side of the raised portcullis, and they vanished. Then he rounded on Juliana.

"Why are you smirking at me, woman? Get me clothing."

Juliana's smile vanished. "You'll not order me around as if I were a pot boy, Lord Lack-clothes." Her gaze slid down the cloak to his bare legs and sniggered. "Now that you know the discomfort of being the object of amusement, perhaps you'll think twice before tossing ladies into washtubs."

"I'd do it again if I had one handy," Gray rumbled. His legs itched, and he was getting cold. "Now fetch my clothes."

Turning with a sweep of violet silk, Juliana sniffed at him over her shoulder. "Fetch them yourself. I think I'll watch your progress from the top of the gatehouse."

Furious, he lunged at her and spun her around to face him.

"I'm not walking through the entire castle in nothing but this cloak."

"Then spend the night in the gatehouse," Juliana snapped. She yanked her arm free and marched under the portcullis.

As he went after her, something snapped at his ankle. A honk alerted him to danger. He leaped out of the way as one of the castle geese fluttered its wings at him and hissed.

Juliana laughed so hard she had to bend over and clutch her sides. Gray danced out of striking range in a circle around her, chased by the goose. Juliana's laughter attracted the attention of guards, maids, and grooms, who gathered to stare in astonishment.

Enraged all over again, Gray halted his flight, fastened his hands on Juliana's waist and set her between him and the goose. The creature stopped, spread its wings, and honked while Juliana swore at him and tried to pry his hands from her.

"Thunder of heaven! Let me go, you sodding whoreson."

"Juliahhhhnaaah!"

Gray looked over her head to see Hugo charging toward them. As before, onlookers found urgent tasks to occupy them elsewhere. The lord of Wellesbrooke descended upon them, swarthy face umber with wrath.

"What passes here?" he bellowed. "Can you not go half a day without shaming me? No, no indeed. I find you in the castle yard wrestling with—" Hugo noticed Gray's state for the first time. "God save you, my lord. What . . . Oh, no. The stripping bandit has returned."

Gray released Juliana. "The stripping bandit?"

"A God-cursed churl who plays evil jests upon my friends. He hasn't appeared in months. I thought he'd gone, but—by the Trinity! Did you catch him?"

"Would I be standing here naked if I had?"

"Aye, aye." Hugo appeared to remember his daughter. "And why are you brawling with this knight, *again?*"

"He commanded me to fetch him garments as if I were a slave."

"Only after you jeered at me," Gray said through locked teeth.

Hugo's brows drew together in a straight line over his eyes. Then he threw up his hands.

"What's to be done with you?" he shouted at Juliana. "You've made a marvelous spectacle of yourself in front of the whole castle for the third time this day, and I've no more patience. You, eldest daughter, will fetch my lord de Valence's clothing with your own hands and attend him in the Lion Tower as a courteous gentle lady should."

"But Father—"

"I'll have a tub and hot water brought to the chamber on the second floor. Lord Quentin has gone home, and there's no one in that room."

"A tub?"

Gray was smiling now, and his smile grew as Juliana almost turned the color of her gown with outrage.

"You've been sinfully discourteous, my noble demoiselle. I've had enough of your temper, your rashness, and your disregard of noble demeanor. You'll attend the Sieur de Valence for the rest of his stay at Wellesbrooke."

"Father!"

Hugo stabbed his finger at Juliana. "Do it, or I'll lock you in your chamber and sell that manor."

Juliana was silent, more out of consternation than dismay, Gray was certain. He asked Hugo to send a party after Edmund and the others. He'd left them at the brook because Edmund still couldn't walk long distances, and he hadn't wanted Imad to strain himself either. When he'd finished, he looked up to see Juliana stomping across the bailey.

"She'll mend her ways, my lord. I promise you. There'll be no more of this shameful discourtesy."

"I thank you, my lord."

Hugo showed him to his appointed chamber and left to arrange for Edmund's rescue party. Gray sat on the edge of the bed that took up most of the room and examined his bruised feet. He had stretched out on the bed, arms cradling his head, the cloak draped across his hips, when Juliana burst through the door and threw a bundle of clothing in his face. A belt buckle rapped him on the nose. Cursing, Gray lunged up as Juliana fled and caught her from behind in his arms, trapping hers at her sides.

"I've had enough of your maltreatment."

He was ready for her when she tried to stomp on his foot and twisted her around to face him, hugging her close. She grew red-faced trying to wriggle out of his arms. Then he felt her weight shift as she drew back her booted foot. He lifted her off her feet, holding her so that their heads were on the same level. Their eyes met, and he found himself distracted for a moment by damascened brilliance before he remembered his anger.

"What ails you, woman? You've harried me from the moment I arrived, and now you've ruined my betrothal to Yolande."

"I harried you? You're the one who ruined my herb pots. You're the one who—who . . ." She blew a curl out of her face. "And then after that, you play the devil's sweet-tongued serpent with Yolande!"

"Serpent? I but played the courteous knight, you ignorant maid. It's clear you know nothing of the art of love. Maids like to hear such talk from their suitors. Would you have me simply arrange the betrothal and then fetch her for the marriage without ever having set eyes on her? Many men would have done so. Juliana, are you listening to me?"

He watched the progress of her glance, which had switched from his face to his neck, then his shoulders and down the length of their bodies where they pressed together. She gasped and renewed her struggles.

"You're unclad, you knave. Let me go."

He grunted when her knee jabbed his thigh. Wrapping his arms around her more securely, he squeezed her until she cried out.

"Good," he said as she went still and glared at him. He smiled at her sweetly, which caused her to regard him with distrust. "Now, my obstinate wench, how would you suggest I release you without offending your maidenly modesty?"

He wished she hadn't chosen that moment to wriggle, this time using her hips. Gray sucked in his breath, and his face contorted with the pleasure-pain. And she wouldn't stop.

In desperation he staggered a few paces until he could press her against a wall and still her movements. Her head bumped against the white-plastered stone. Fighting an onslaught of desire, Gray pressed his cheek against hers, his body against hers.

"Don't!" he cried when she wriggled again. "By God's mercy, if you value your honor, don't move."

For once she was both quiet and motionless. He bit the inside of his cheek and forced himself to think about his past as a slave to cool his boiling blood. After a few moments, he could breathe evenly.

He lifted his head. "For God's pity, I never thought doing my duty would be so difficult."

"Now will you let me go?"

"Not until you tell me why you've tried to ruin my plans to marry Yolande."

Those silver eyes were cutting through him again.

"You care naught for Yolande. You only want her lands and riches, like every other rooster knight in Christendom.

"Now I know you're feeble-witted. What is marriage but an alliance? Haven't I just said I was trying to make friends with the girl so that we'd make an amiable match? Marriage among such as we is a duty, an obligation, an alliance for security and power. Unlike most, at least I had a care for her feelings. But you interfered. Why?"

"Thunder of God! Because you don't care for her. I've watched you. You're not even interested in her. When you mouth those pretty words to her, your eyes are like ice."

"You think love and marriage belong together? You know such a thing isn't possible for a baron's heir. I must marry for the sake of my family. But after all, you must realize Yolande is very young. She doesn't excite me, not like—"

Gray stopped and let his gaze drift over Juliana's features. Eyes with the gleam of steel and the sparkle of shooting stars, rose-tinted lips, and a determined little nose. The longest neck he'd ever seen, one whose line descended to those breasts he dreamed of. He was growing warm again. Long moments passed while he chased new and unlooked-for thoughts.

Juliana had appeared out of nowhere to devastate his peace. After his years of enslavement, he rarely lost sleep because of sensual cravings, not until he'd met her. Yet after only a few days spent near her, he'd given up trying to banish her from his nightly imaginings.

The longer he knew her, the more she plagued his existence. When he ate, he thought of Juliana. When he rode his horse, he thought of Juliana. When he jousted, he thought of Juliana. Worst of all, when he had been wooing Yolande, he'd been thinking about Juliana. The one was plain porridge, while the other was pure pepper and cinnamon.

All at once he realized he didn't want to spend his life eating plain porridge. He'd been a fool to think he could. His senses were filled with Juliana, and now he knew they always would be. Even now he ached for her.

"You know," he said lazily and softly. "In spite of her

riches, Yolande is quite ordinary. While you, my joyance, are above all that's mundane. Do you taste as spicy as you behave?"

She began to struggle again. "Foul lecher! That's just why you should leave poor Yolande alone. Why should she be cursed with a husband who thinks she's ordinary?"

"Aye, and why should I be saddled with a wife so ordinary, when I could have you?"

She stopped struggling again and stared at him open-mouthed. "What?"

"Yes," he said, more to himself than to her. "You've infected my blood, it seems, so why not?" He looked down at her half in speculation, half in anticipation. "After all, my sweet joyance, lust and power often intertwine with each other. Do they not?"

He emphasized his point by moving his hips against hers. She blinked at him, and he could see that she didn't understand. But he also saw the throbbing of the pulse in her neck and the slow flood of color from her cheeks to her neck. He looked at her open mouth, and placed his lips over hers. She tried to close them, but his tongue slipped inside her mouth. She went still, as a deer does when startled. He teased her with his tongue, then kissed his way to her ear.

"My sweet joyance," he whispered. "Would you have me beg? You're famed for your sweet care of others. You suffer when they suffer. Don't make me suffer."

Abruptly she seemed to dissolve against him. All resistance left her body, and he loosened his hold on her. Her arms came up to his neck. He delved into her mouth, then nuzzled his way from her cheek to her throat.

His hands slipped inside her dress, sliding over her breasts. The overgown impeded him. His head and sex throbbed together in time with the pulse at her throat, which he covered with his mouth. When her hips surged against him, he lost all control and tore the overgown. His palm cupped her breast while he returned to her mouth. He was about to tear the undertunic when something behind him banged.

Gray lifted his head, turned, and found Hugo Welles glaring at him like a chained bear. Behind him stood four boys carrying a tub. Juliana cried out, then quickly slipped around him to stand so that she concealed him from her father. Gray raised his eyes to the ceiling.

"This is truly a cursed unlucky day."

He expected roars, bellows, and howls. However, Hugo behaved most unlike himself. He put his fists on his hips, studied them in silence, and then began tapping his foot.

"Er, Father," Juliana said. "Nothing has happened."

Hugo shoved the boys back out to the corridor and slammed the door. Rounding on them, he said, "Which is it to be, de Valence, marriage or death?"

Gray threw back his head and laughed so hard Juliana turned to gape at him. Her frown deepened into a scowl the longer he laughed, but he couldn't seem to stop.

"Why, marriage of course, my lord."

"Marriage!" She backed away from him, noticed his bare body, and turned her back. "Thunder of God, I'll not be handed over to a debauched villain with an evil past and, and—"

"Daughter, you're going to marry this man, and that's my final word."

"He's a rooster knight! And at the tournament he didn't ask for my—"

"Now Juliana, you liked me a moment ago." He should have explained himself to her, but she was too angry, and Hugo and she together produced sparks and flames that made calm reasoning useless. She was glaring at him over her shoulder. Her dark hair reflected the deep violet of the silk she wore and made her silver eyes gleam in contrast.

He couldn't help giving her a lurid smile. "Not a moment past you found me right pleasing."

"You wove some spell against me. You lost Yolande, and now you're only taking me because you're trapped."

Gray came up behind her and put his hands on her shoulders. "I want to be caught."

"I don't," she retorted, shaking off his hands. "It's too late, for I've discovered your true nature. You're as bad as any of them, worse, for you use your appearance and your —your lewd skills to get what you want. Any woman who marries you will have to watch you rut and plow among her serving women and any hapless village wench or farmer's wife who steps into your path. I've seen Edmund Strange behave so, and you're no different. I'll not have you, my lord. Not if you were dipped in marchpane and served with feathers on."

Juliana cast an evil glance at him that went no lower than his chin, then marched out of the chamber, banging the door behind her. Hugo watched her go before addressing Gray.

"Pay no heed to her mad rantings. She'll marry you. I'll see to it."

"I've no doubt, my lord."

"I'll send your servants to you. We'll speak about the settlement upon the morrow, de Valence, the first business of the morning."

Gray nodded to the older man. Welles left him and sent in the boys with the tub. Gray went to sit on the bed while the tub was filled with hot water.

He'd done a mad thing: he'd tossed aside the king's gift of a rich heiress for a woman who thought him Satan's minion. He'd allowed his cock to govern his head. Juliana Welles was no great heiress. Her family was prosperous, but not the rich match the heir to Stratfield should aspire to. He'd have to fight his ailing father, the whole of his family, to keep her. Not that he would let that prospect interfere. He was going to have the tumultuous Juliana and no other.

It was unexpected, and yet utterly pleasing, this new idea of marrying Juliana Welles. Now that he thought about it, he realized that when he was with her, he forgot the corruption in his soul. Just now, when he saw her at the gatehouse, he'd forgotten the ugly memories of Saladin and slavery and nakedness. Who had time to grieve about the past when dueling with a lady whose wit was as sharp as his battle sword? And she made him burn as no woman had ever done, not even the skilled artisans to whom Saladin had introduced him.

He shied away from the memory. Saladin had been a twisted man who enjoyed watching Gray perform with his other slaves. He'd complied to save his life—and hated himself. But Juliana banished the shame and the hatred. All the ugliness seemed to burn away in his passion for her, in his desire to entice and conquer her. He'd been so intent upon his duty to marry and his schemes of revenge that he hadn't seen it earlier. Now his vision was clear.

He would marry Juliana Welles. Of course, he would have to woo her, and much differently than he had the sweet-natured Yolande. Juliana would be a far greater challenge. And while he was courting the lady of the damascened eyes, he would find and hang the thief who had stripped him and humiliated him before her.

Vervain

Vervain was thought to be good for the stomach, liver, and lungs, or externally for the bite of venomous beasts. It was used against fevers, and all poisons. If a man kept vervain in his clothes in battle, he would escape from his enemies.

• *Chapter 12* •

JULIANA RACED ACROSS THE BAILEY. SHE turned a corner of the new hall and ran inside past dozens of servants setting out the trestles and benches in preparation for dinner.

Marry Gray de Valence, by God. Once she would have welcomed it to the depths of her soul. If only he'd been so attentive and seductive the night she'd treated Imad, or the next morning when she'd been as full of timid excitement and infatuation as a lady in a troubadour's song, ready to give her favor and her heart. But she knew better now. She wouldn't be fooled again. She wouldn't be hurt again.

Clutching her ripped overgown, she blew strands of hair out of her face and stopped to ask the butler overseeing the work in the hall where her mother was. Then she charged out of the hall, down an inner stair, and into one of the large storerooms beneath the structure.

Hardly pausing to allow her eyes to adjust to the dim candlelight, she hurried over to her mother, who was inspecting food supplies. Laudine was counting bags of flour while Bertrade sat on a barrel with quill, ink, and the inventory list.

"Mother, you must do something!" Juliana paused beside a barrel of vinegar, leaned on it, and panted.

Havisia stopped counting jars of oil. "What have you done now?"

"Naught," Juliana said as she gulped in air and patted

her brow with the torn edge of her overgown. "Father says I have to marry that corrupt spawn of the devil, and you must prevent it. Yolande won't have him, so he's trying to—"

"By the Holy Mother," Havisia said. "Are you saying Gray de Valence has asked for you instead of Yolande?"

Laudine clapped her hands and laughed while Bertrade let out a sigh and gave Juliana one of her beatific smiles. Juliana nearly growled at them, but persevered with her mother.

"He's worse than Edmund Strange. He's not been here a week and he's cast aside the lady he was wooing before everyone."

"But you're the one who didn't want him to have Yolande," Laudine said. "And now we know why."

"You be quiet. Go count dried fish. Mother, I'll not be enslaved to the prince of rooster knights. Since we met he's run me into a mud hole, thrown me over his saddle, and tossed me into a washtub."

Havisia sighed and rubbed her temples. "I fail to understand you, daughter. Are you saying Gray de Valence has asked your father for your hand?"

Not wishing to reveal the lurid circumstances that precipitated the tangle, Juliana only nodded vigorously.

"Even though you've behaved in a most discourteous and insolent way toward him? And don't deny it, Juliana. I saw you throw butter in his face and beat him with a joint of beef. And I was witness to your disrespect at the east gate. You've treated him worse than the meanest pot boy, and yet he has asked for you."

Feeling misunderstood and ill-used, Juliana stamped her foot. "He only agreed because Father caught us—"

Too late she realized her lack of wisdom. Havisia swept over to her and fixed her with a sharp gaze.

"Out with it, daughter."

Juliana worked the edge of her boot between two floor-boards and mumbled, "Together."

When she risked a glance at her mother, Havisia was staring at the rip in her overgown.

"I shall speak to my lord about this."

Juliana let out a long breath. "Oh, thank you, Mother."

"A betrothal must be announced quickly to stop evil tongues from ruining your honor."

"Mother!"

Laudine laughed again. Bertrade tried to pat her shoulder, but Juliana shook off her hand and followed Havisia as she resumed her inspection of ale barrels.

"Mother, you can't mean you want me to marry this—this Viking. I won't. I'm going to take vows of chastity . . ." She faltered at this, for she recalled how Gray de Valence made her body tingle and burn. "I—I'm going to live at Vyne Hill."

Her mother was watching her, and Juliana found herself avoiding that penetrating gaze.

"I'll admit your wooing has been unusual," Havisia said. "But you're not an ordinary maid."

"Wooing!"

"Yes, daughter, wooing. What else have you two been doing?"

"Fighting. That's what we've been doing."

"Perhaps. But few knights would endure from you what de Valence has and thrive at the prospect of more battles. No, don't belabor me with more protests. De Valence is a brilliant match, one I never hoped for, especially for you, my willful, hot-tempered little fury. The only reason I agreed to this plan to cloister yourself was because I never thought to see you matched with anyone after Edmund Strange. Now run along and change your gown. You don't want to dine with Gray de Valence looking like that."

"Mmm, mmm, mmm, sister. What will Yolande say now that you've stolen her lover for certain?"

"Oh, Laudine," Bertrade said. "Juliana wouldn't steal. Yolande has already refused him."

Juliana's eyes widened as she stared at her mother and sisters. "You—I didn't— Thunder of God, you're all mad!"

A noise made her whirl around to face a figure gliding down the stairs. For once Juliana was speechless as Yolande floated toward her, her pace slow, her complexion pale. Clutching an account book to her breast, the girl came to rest before Juliana.

Twisting her fingers together, Juliana began to stutter apologies, but her earlier fit of rage seemed to have drained Yolande of her anger over de Valence. Her head drooped as she lifted a hand to stave off more of Juliana's explanations.

"None of this is your fault, Jule. I know that now. There's something in your temperament that calls to the Sieur de Valence." She sighed and managed a smile. "Besides, my lord de Valence was becoming wearisome. He never wanted to play games, nor did he want to dance long enough to suit me. I have rejected his suit. You take him. He's more amusing when he's quarreling with you."

Aghast, Juliana backed away from Yolande. "Amusing! Thunder of heaven, you're as mad as all the others."

She stormed out of the storeroom, running up the stairs and out of the new hall. She nearly ran into Alice as she crossed the yard between the hall and the old keep.

"Mistress, I been looking for you everywhere." The maid fell in step beside her, brandishing a kerchief. "Oh, I be terrible spent. Ah-choo!"

"What is it?" Juliana snapped.

"Long Tom has drunk too much ale again. He hasn't stopped since the tourney began, and now his wife says he has a fever and a terrible ache in the head."

"It's God's judgment, no doubt. Come along. I must change my gown and fetch my healing box, and we'll need to fetch more vervain from the herb chamber."

Long Tom was a drunkard, but Juliana blessed him all the same. His misfortune was her good luck this evening, for Long Tom lived in Wellesbrooke village near the mill. She would be able to extend her duties there until everyone had gone to bed, thus avoiding another encounter with de Valence. She needed time to think and time to devise a way to save herself from his mad fancy.

Late that night Juliana returned to her chamber and sent Alice to bed. Long Tom hadn't been the only villager suffering from the effects of tournament celebrations. She'd ministered to three other men, the miller's wife, and the hayward's daughter. Her activities had distracted her from her predicament.

She was weary, but couldn't sleep once abed, and she was still as confused and apprehensive as she had been when Gray de Valence first said he wished to marry her. Knowing she would toss and turn if she tried to sleep, Juliana pulled on a cloak and went to the herb chamber. There she busied herself with notes she was collecting for an herbal. She had learned her craft from her mother and also from Friar Clement and Mother Joan in the village. No one had bothered to write down all the herbs, their preparations and uses, and Juliana was determined that the lack be remedied.

She began to read over her notes by the light of a single candle. Gillyflowers were good for hard labor in childbirth and for dropsy. Wormwood taken with spikenard abated wicked wind of the stomach and comforted the heart. Pennyroyal had many uses: for cold humors of the head, for phlegm, for ailments of the belly, and itching boils.

"That's what he is, an itching boil," she muttered to herself. "The vile wretch set me in Yolande's place, as if we're interchangeable pawns on a chessboard."

Juliana set aside her notes. She was perched on a stool before her worktable. Resting her elbows on its surface, she put her face in her hands.

"Why? Why has he done this mad thing?"

Never had she been so bewildered. Gray de Valence could marry any of the most beautiful and noble of women. She had seen the way maidens and dames alike quivered and sighed when he looked at them. He had but to enter a room and Laudine began to arch her back and purr. Once he'd been talking with Richard and happened to glance at Alice and smile. Juliana had heard a colorful description of how that glance had affected her maid.

"Oooo, mistress. He looked at me, and me knees turned to potage, they did. I almost fell on me face. I thought my insides had turned to hot butter."

What would a man of such sensual power want with her? Nothing but one of those passing tumbles for which he'd gained fame in the courts of France, Aquitaine, Burgundy, and England. Yes, that was it. He'd been about to seduce her when Hugo interrupted. He was a skilled deceiver, and he was trying to dupe her and Hugo too. No doubt he found it easier to agree with Hugo's demands for the moment. That way he could trick her into satisfying his lust, and then find some excuse to rid himself of her later.

Juliana raised her head and gasped. She stared at the candle flame. Perhaps he would use the same excuse Edmund had to escape marrying her. If Gray de Valence spurned her openly . . . Lowering her face to her hands again, Juliana moaned. She couldn't endure that again. She had tried to forget that scene in the new hall bed-chamber, forget his glance like that of a leech inspecting a leper. The evil feelings came back to her. Her body felt suddenly hot and cold at the same time. *No*. Better to die than to be shamed before the world a second time.

The prospect chilled her heart and brought tears to her eyes. She nearly sobbed with the pain and fear. She wanted to run away, into the hills, where she could dig a deep tunnel in which to hide like a sick rat.

Juliana scooted off her stool and began to pace around the herb chamber. Her eyes burned from weariness and unshed tears, and she felt a vague queasiness in her stomach, the result of fear. She wouldn't be fooled by false hope and that pretty face again. In spite of her determination, images of Gray de Valence, all moonlight hair and male sensuality, formed in her head. He stood in the Wellesbrooke chapel along with her family and a great crowd, raised his arm and pointed at her, called her malformed. Everyone stared at her in horror, and she ran.

But she couldn't run away, not really, not forever. Father wouldn't let her. Hugo was as delighted to ally himself with de Valence as Mother was. No one would listen to her.

"What am I going to do?" she asked aloud.

No answer came, and she continued to pace. After a while, she returned to the stool. Resting her elbows on the table, she propped her chin on her laced hands.

"Friar Clement!" she whispered.

He would help. If she said vows before him, even Father wouldn't interfere. Friar Clement wouldn't want her to be given to a man who so easily abandoned one woman for another. Dedication to God and charity ranked above marriage, even for women. Relief flooded through her, and with it returned her fatigue. She rested her head on her arms and closed her eyes. A tear formed and slid down her cheek.

Troubadours sang songs about the love of knights and ladies. If her life were like those songs, Gray would have been enthralled with her at first sight. He would have wooed her gently with poetry and pleading. He would have sought her favor at the tourney, chosen her Queen of Love and Beauty, scaled the walls of a mock castle to claim her. But he did none of those things. He cornered her in mud holes and washtubs to ply her with lurid, sinful touches and the temptation of his body. He tossed her over his shoulder and threw her across his saddle like some Viking raider.

Gray de Valence didn't court her, he marauded and plundered. But she wasn't going to be one of his victims. She wouldn't allow him the opportunity of hurting her like his cousin had. Thunder of God, what was she saying? If she wasn't careful, this silver-haired invader would do her more harm than a thousand Edmunds.

She would refuse this marriage, despite Father's commands. If she refused to give way and returned Hugo's bellows with shouts of her own, she would at least gain a reprieve. She would use the time to make Gray de Valence rue the day he attempted to use her for his amusement. Soon he would beg to be released from his commitment. Juliana smiled as she imagined divers fascinating ways to make de Valence eschew their betrothal. But as she began to fall asleep, visions of evil tricks gave way to those of him standing tranquilly and beautifully naked in the midst of her bandits.

"Mistress, wake up, wake up."

Juliana's eyes fluttered open. She raised her head from the worktable and winced at the pain that shot through her neck. Looking up, she saw Alice hovering beside her.

"Oh, my neck. God's mercy, I slept on this table all night."

Alice was grinning at her, which sat ill with Juliana as she recalled the misery of her situation. "What are you so mirthful about? Don't you have a backache or a sneeze coming on?"

"No, mistress. Oh, it's a happy day. They be in the new library at this very moment." Alice clasped her hands together and almost danced with merriment.

Juliana stood and winced again as a muscle in her side protested. She rubbed her numb bottom. "Who is in the library?"

"Your lord father, of course, and *him*."

Placing her hands on the small of her back, Juliana stretched backward, then forward to work out the kinks in her muscles. "Him who?"

"Why, the Sieur de Valence."

Juliana whipped herself upright, spun around, and grabbed Alice's arm. "What do you mean? Why are they in the library?"

"Ouch! You're pinching me, mistress."

Juliana dropped Alice's arm and raised her voice. "What are they doing in the library, damn you?"

"Why, composing the betrothal documents, discussing your dowry and jointure—"

"Spawn of Satan!"

Alice covered her mouth with her hands. "Oh, mistress."

Juliana rushed to her chamber with Alice trailing behind. "It's late in the morn. How long have they been talking?"

"Almost an hour," Alice said as she stared at her mistress.

Juliana pulled off her clothes, washed quickly in a basin, and donned one of her work gowns. Alice tried to comb her hair, but Juliana thrust her aside and ran her fingers through the long locks. She rushed to a casket and riffled through it.

"Where are my knives, my knives? Ah, there they are."

Alice was watching her with a startled-cow expression. "What do you need with a knife, mistress?"

She selected one with a long blade and slipped it into a sheath and threaded her leather girdle through the sheath.

"Mistress, what are you going to do?"

She tied a leather thong around her head to keep her hair out of her face. Grabbing another knife, she rushed out of her chamber. Alice babbled protests and came after her. Juliana stopped before she reached the stairs and turned on the woman.

"Stay here."

"But mistress—"

Snatching Alice's arm, Juliana propelled her back into the chamber and slammed the door. She ran until she reached the landing outside the library above the new hall.

At that moment a clerk opened the library door, started, and gawked at her.

Flustered, the clerk bolted back inside the library and shut the door. Juliana thrust it open again, sending it crashing against the wall, and startled a room full of men. At a long table Hugo's steward and clerk had been scribbling notes, flanked by her father and Gray de Valence. Arthur Strange and Lucien had been consulting parchment documents while Barnaby engaged in a serious discussion with Hugo and Gray. Everyone had looked up when the door banged.

She raised her arm and pointed at Gray. "I'll not betroth myself to that man."

"Now, daughter," Hugo said. "You're fevered."

Juliana nearly roared. "Thunder of God! I'm not fevered. I'm not ill at all. I won't have him."

She fingered the knife she was holding when Gray threw back his head and laughed. Turning crimson, Hugo jumped from his chair and bellowed back at her.

"I'll not be ranted at by my own daughter. Get yourself from here at once. I'll make my arrangements known to you when we're finished." Hugo turned his back on her. "Now, about Vyne Hill."

Juliana uttered a furious growl and took a step into the library. "You're not giving him Vyne Hill!"

"The use of your possessions will pass from me to your husband," Hugo shouted. "Now begone."

This new peril robbed her of speech. Juliana wavered, squeezing the knife blade between her fingers, and looked from Hugo to Gray. Gray was regarding her with amused appreciation, as if she were a prize colt. He had propped his legs on the table, and his hand rested on the draft of the marriage agreement. She saw a list of her possessions, and her brows drew together.

Gray chuckled when he saw the direction of her gaze. "Are you going to fight me for every pin and bag of grain?"

She felt a muscle in her jaw twitch. In a blur of movement, she cocked back her arm and threw the knife. The blade sliced through the air. There was a snap, and the point stabbed into the parchment between Gray's second and third fingers. The clerk and the steward gasped.

Gray's smile vanished, but that was the only reaction he displayed. His hand didn't move. He didn't look at the knife; he looked at Juliana, his eyes narrowing. Even Hugo was silent.

With their eyes locked, Juliana gave him a cold smile. "Unless you want to end up like that parchment, you'll withdraw your offer."

"Unless you want to end up in another washtub," Gray said with a look that spoke of battlefields and ruthless slaughter, "you'll cease interfering."

Juliana put her hand to the hilt of the knife on her girdle. As she did so, Gray swept his legs from the table and stood in one swift movement. Juliana faltered, remembering his speed and strength; Gray vaulted over the table. Crying out, she ran from the room. She heard Hugo as she fled.

"By the Trinity, my lord, you're the only man I've ever met who could make Juliana turn and run. You're the husband for her."

Gray's laughter floated after her; he hadn't bothered to chase after her. Red with fury and humiliation, Juliana ran to the stables. Her glowers and bullying forced a groom to saddle her mare. She jumped into the saddle, kicked her horse into motion, and fled before Gray de Valence decided to come looking for her.

Wormwood

When drunk with spikenard, wormwood assuaged the wicked winds of the stomach. Mixed with the gall of a bull and put in a man's eyes, it put away all manner of impediments of sight.

• *Chapter 13* •

GRAY TRIED TO KEEP HIS MIRTH CURBED AS HE resumed his perusal of the marriage-agreement draft. Juliana had burst in upon the meeting and set his senses aflame with her wildfire presence. She'd been so furious he thought lightning would shoot from the tips of her fingers, and she'd had that polished-steel glint in her eyes. He thanked God that he was sitting, or Hugo would have notice the effect on his body.

Late into the night he'd wrestled with his conscience. He would create a furor among the English barons with this marriage that brought little gain. But after hours and hours of thought, he still wanted Juliana.

Before she had interrupted the discussion, his head had felt leaden and he couldn't shake weariness brought on by a disturbed and restless sleep. Thrice he awakened in a fit of swollen lust, roused by the ferocity of his desire for her. Thrice he'd emptied cold water over his head to quell his appetite. With no such remedy open to him at the moment, he was reciting Psalms. *The Lord is my shepherd; I shall not want. He maketh me to lie down in green pastures; he leadeth me beside the still waters.*

"Still waters," Gray muttered under his breath as he tried to master his body. "Right still, placid, calm waters. *Still.*"

"Are you well, my lord?" Hugo stood over him holding out the list of Juliana's dowry.

Gray swallowed. "Right well, my lord, now that I am to take your daughter to wife."

"Ah, about Juliana. She's a most obdurate child, always has been. But you must understand that for all her raucous ways and willfulness, her heart is full of compassion. She never spares herself when there's sickness abroad, and she looks after those folk at Vyne Hill as if they were her kin. And she's a sensible girl, not like my other two. She'll keep your households in good order."

"My lord," Gray said before Hugo could continue.

"Yes?"

"You've no need to convince me of your daughter's virtues or to warn me of her faults."

Hugo stuck his thumbs in his belt and bounced on the balls of his feet. "I want no repetition of the disaster with your cousin. Thus I'm plain with you now. I'll have you know Juliana's faults and imperfections. Have you heard the tale of their betrothal?"

"Yes."

"I'll have you know the truth of it, though. My Juliana has a small imperfection of the body."

"I know," Gray said. "Is there anyone born of woman who doesn't have at least one? This is a matter of no consequence to me."

Hugo glanced around the room at the men listening. "It's good you say so before these witnesses, for I'll not have my Juliana shamed again. Be warned, my lord. Though you be a powerful knight and beloved of the justiciar and the king, I'll have your teeth for a necklace if you hurt her."

"Have no fear," Gray said with a smile. "For I'd rather burn at the stake than hurt her."

Lord Welles fixed Gray with a severe stare, then nodded his satisfaction. "I also feel obliged to warn you that my daughter will no doubt contrive some plot to try to force you to give her up."

"I'm looking forward to the contest."

"You are? By God's grace, I do think you're a fine match for my Juliana if you can contemplate such a battle with pleasure."

"Have no fear. I can deal with Mistress Juliana," Gray said. "Shall we leave these good gentlemen to their scrivening?"

"Then you agree to the settlement?" Hugo asked in surprise.

Arthur interrupted, placing his hand on Gray's arm and drawing him aside. "Cousin, I must ask you to reconsider. You can still have the de Saye girl. What does it matter if she's annoyed with you? The Welles woman is worth less than half—"

"No. Mistress Juliana is worth more to me than the treasures of Midas. Come, don't take the same side as your brother, not after all these years."

Arthur gave him a bitter smile. "I did so love the way you can send him running from the room. How you do it with but a whisper in his ear?"

"There's no secret to frightening men, cousin. You only have to be willing to kill. I've seen you do the same. It's only with your brother that you hesitate. Now leave this talk against my marriage."

"But your father will never agree. Every man who is an heir is expected—"

"I'm not like most heirs," Gray said quietly. Their eyes met, and Arthur looked away.

After an uncomfortable silence, Arthur said, "Indeed, cousin, but your duty lies in furthering the position of your family."

"I know my change of course seems precipitous to you, but I've thought about this all night. My family loosed me upon the world to make my own way when I was eight, and when I was falsely accused of dishonor and begged for aid, not one of them bothered to stand at my side. Why should I sacrifice myself on the altar of English barony when it near destroyed me? I'll govern Stratfield well, but if I'm to devote my life to others, I'll have Juliana for myself."

"But your father won't agree."

"My father will abide by my decision if he wants me as heir to Stratfield. Otherwise I'll return to Valence, which more than equals my English inheritance. I don't need Stratfield or its riches. The French king would be happy to welcome me back. After all, he gave me my lands there for my service to him." Gray watched Arthur's mouth work, then laughed. "Take cheer, cousin. You should be happy I'm risking my father's banishment. If I leave, Edmund will inherit, and you're his heir."

"Edmund! That's too horrible a cost." Arthur lowered his voice. "You know he's more concerned with the hunt and burying his cock in every woman in sight than with caring for his manors. He'll ruin Stratfield as he's ruining our own demesne. Gray, you're driving me to a frenzy with this mad course of yours."

Gray clapped his cousin on the back. "I'm full sorry, Arthur, but I've no choice unless I want to end up demented from unrequited—er—I've no choice."

He returned to Hugo to give his formal consent to their arrangements. Taking leave of his future father-in-law, Gray hurried from the castle to his pavilion, calling for his palfrey.

"Imad!"

"Yes, master."

"Did you see where she went?"

"She rode west, master, into the hills. I sent your

squire to follow her, but he returned saying he lost her when she left the track."

"Christ's curse," Gray said as he mounted. "Simon, Simon, you young fool, where are you? Oh. Well, don't gawk at me. Get your horse and show me where you lost her. Imad, what of the search for that cursed bandit?"

Imad stuck his hands in the sleeves of his robe and bowed. "No luck yet, master. He and all his minions seem to have vanished like a whirlwind in the desert. May Allah bless our search."

"If I'm back in time, I'll take a party out to search. And Imad . . ."

"Yes, great master."

"Don't tell Hugo Welles where I've gone."

"My silence is the silence of the dead, o wondrous lord."

"Verily, I trust it is so," Gray said. "For I've a great deal to say to Mistress Juliana, and I'll never be able to talk to her if my lord Welles keeps intruding upon us."

Friar Clement was a Franciscan and thus lived by what God provided. He wandered the Wellesbrooke domain ceaselessly, and refused all offers of permanent shelter. Juliana wasn't sure he would be at the cave, but it was the only place he stayed with any regularity. Juliana rode into the tree-shrouded hills west of the castle. At the summit of the first slope, she had to dismount and lead the horse through thick underbrush and over fallen rocks.

The going was hard what with the lack of a trail and the preponderance of loose rock and soil, but she finally made her way deep into the hills. She rode across a ridge and around to the west side of a high knoll before dismounting again. Now she could no longer see Wellesbrooke, its surrounding farmlands, pastures, villages, or gardens. So isolated was her destination, she seldom met anyone except a lone shepherd and his flock. Today she encountered no one.

Pulling her mare behind her, Juliana found a concealed, narrow tract that skirted precariously along a slope until it suddenly twisted and darted behind thick shrubbery and stunted trees to end in a small clearing. Not far off, she could hear the cascading of water. Leading her horse toward the sound, she came to a place where water splashed from rocks in the hillside and danced its way down to a basin worn into the stone. Juliana tethered the mare where she could drink and graze and stepped into the shadows formed by a stand of ancient gnarled and twisted oaks that hugged the hillside.

In the midst of the darkest shadows lay the entrance to the cave. She walked into cool darkness and paused to allow her eyes time to adjust. The cave was a little larger than her herb chamber, but narrow and deep rather than square.

In the darkness just before the point where daylight from the cave entrance faded completely, a young man in a gray robe and worn sandals lay asleep on the bare, packed earth. Around him were strewn flowers—red campion, wild hyacinth, and sprigs of blossoming holly. A tiny robin was pecking at seeds that had been scattered on the cave floor, but flew away when she appeared.

Juliana knelt beside Clement. He was young, a few years older than her. His face was lean, with a hollowness of jaw gained from scant meals and nights spent in the open. If Juliana hadn't known how many women shoved bread, cheese, and other food into his hands, she would have worried. But Clement's haggard appearance had more to do with his lack of interest in food than its supply. Not even Mother Joan's puddings could put flesh on Clement's prominent bones. His hair was an indeterminate shade between blond and brown, long and cut unevenly. The skin on his hands and feet was dry and cracked from exposure to wind, sun, and cold.

Touching the sleeve of his robe, Juliana spoke to him quietly. "Friar, Friar Clement, please."

He mumbled something, then opened his eyes.

"Mistress Juliana." He sat up and rubbed his face. "Peace and good to you."

"Peace and good to you, friar, I'm in great peril."

Clement yawned. "Have you harried another poor knight and sent him wandering about the countryside without his clothes?"

"Yes, but that's not why I'm in peril. Please, come into the light where we can talk. I don't know why you eschew candles. Even a torch would be welcome. And I wish you'd store some food here. I haven't eaten since yesterday."

"Now Juliana, you know Francis of Assisi follows the promise of Christ. We must have faith in the providence of God, who will provide." Clement rose and dusted off his robe. Sprigs of hawthorn and saxifrage tumbled from his sleeve. "Remember the sacred words: 'Take no thought for your life, what ye shall eat, or what ye shall drink; nor yet for your body, what ye shall put on. Is not the life more than meat, and the body than raiment?'"

Juliana returned with Clement to the mouth of the cave where she sank to the ground. "Our lord also said not to take thought of the morrow because the morrow will take thought for itself, but if I do that, I'll be enslaved to a barbarian Viking with no chivalry or honor."

"What do you mean, enslaved to a Viking?"

"He's an evil man!" Springing to her feet, Juliana strode back and forth across the cave entrance waving her arms. "He tried to woo Yolande, and when he failed, he tried to seduce me."

"For God's love, mistress, start anew and tell the tale from the beginning."

With wide gestures and many exclamations regarding Gray's boundless faults, Juliana complied. When she finished, her steps faltered, then ceased, and she touched the sleeve of Clement's robe.

"Remember those vows we discussed a few months ago? Now I must take those vows quickly to foil this marriage arrangement."

Clement was staring at her with a dazed expression. "You say you've quarreled with him from the moment he set foot in your father's demesne?"

"Yes. He's Satan's curse upon the world."

"He came upon you in the wood and you fought with him? Wrestled with him in the mud, exchanged threats while dancing, then fought again at Vyne Hill and the Wellesbrooke mock siege, all within the space of a few days?"

"And he's a dissolute man."

"Wherefore do you know this?"

Juliana turned pink and looked away from Clement's startled gaze. "From the first he has behaved most unchivalrously to me."

"How so?"

"He's given me much tribulation with his unruly hands and heathen wiles!" Juliana turned back to the friar and plucked at his sleeve again. "Don't you see, he's bent on seducing me to satisfy some mad lust of his, and then he'll find a reason to annul the marriage agreement. Why, the only reason he offered the alliance was because Father caught us in the Lion Tower."

"Caught you," Clement said gravely. "Caught you doing what? Come now, Juliana, you must tell the whole of it."

She had never been able to lie to Clement. "Well, he was naked, and—"

"Naked!"

Juliana studied her fingernails. "I told you I'd played another of my small jests."

"Oh, no. Not with the heir to Stratfield."

"Thunder of God, he deserved it!" Juliana caught Clement's somber gaze and muttered, "Forgive me. But it was a most cheerful thing, watching him, the prince of rooster knights, stumble across fields without his clothes." She smiled at the memory, but Friar Clement didn't.

"Go on."

Clearing her throat, she managed to tell the tale of her encounter with Gray in the Lion Tower and its disastrous result.

"And so I must take the vows of chastity and dedication to a life of service, like the lay brothers and sisters of the Franciscans and other orders. Even Father won't make me marry once I've taken such a vow. Please, Clement, I must do it now."

Clement turned away from her, and Juliana tried to contain her impatience. The afternoon was waning, and she wanted to return to Wellesbrooke as soon as possible and stop any further arrangements for her marriage. She would ask Clement to come with her as witness of the vows.

"I can't do this," Clement said as he came back to her.

Juliana shook her head. "You must. I'll be lost if you don't."

"Such vows can't be taken in haste and secret."

"But—"

"No, Juliana. Even if I was certain of your intentions and dedication to God, I couldn't allow you to deny what you so obviously feel for this man."

Her jaw dropped. "What?"

"I, like Francis of Assisi, was a knight before I became a friar, mistress, and I know what passion and love are."

"Then you should know I feel neither for this—this—this—this churl."

Clement gave her a calm smile. "You see? Even speaking of him thrusts you into a fit of passion."

He began picking up the flowers strewn on the ground. Juliana followed him as he progressed into the darkness of the cave.

"By my troth, Clement, I hate him. I do! Why, I've much greater affection for you. You're a wondrous honorable man. Not like him." She lowered her voice in silken entreaty. "Dear, sweet, gentle Clement, please, I beg of you."

A shadow fell across the mouth of the cave. At the same time Juliana heard the hissing sound made by a sword being drawn.

"What good fortune that I found you," said Gray de Valence. "Have you a lover, my joyance? Come out dear, sweet, gentle Clement, so I can kill you."

Pennyroyal

This herb was good for cold humor in the head, phlegm in the breast, disease in the belly, and cramp.

• *Chapter 14* •

WHEN SHE HEARD GRAY'S VOICE, JULIANA cried out and whirled around to face him. She glimpsed wide shoulders that blocked her view of the outside world, a body clad in black leather and doeskin. His anger made him seem taller and more menacing than ever. She wouldn't let him unsettle her.

"You followed me. Go away."

Ignoring her, Gray raised his voice and his sword and stared into the darkness of the cave.

"Come out, you rutting bastard, or I'll come for you with my sword."

"Don't you speak so to Clement," Juliana snapped as she marched up to him. She had to get rid of him, or he was going to ruin her scheme to rescue herself.

Clement chose this moment to emerge from the shadows. Gray thrust her aside and pointed his sword as Clement came into the light. Juliana watched confusion pass over his face and smiled.

Then Gray gave a wordless snarl. "What foul blasphemy is this?"

The point of his sword came up to prick Clement's robe over his heart. The friar cried out in alarm, and Juliana lost her temper. Darting at Gray, she shoved him off balance. As he stumbled, she put herself between him and Clement.

"There's no sin or blasphemy here, except in your evil thoughts. Friar Clement is a most holy man. But I shouldn't wonder that you fail to recognize it, for you're deep in the mire of sin and deceit and no doubt blinded to all good." She backed up as Gray stalked toward her with an angry-wolf glare.

"Then what are you doing here addressing a friar in such a wheedling tone?"

Clement sighed and shook his head as he held up both hands and stepped between them. Juliana was relieved when Gray stopped coming at her to scowl at the friar.

Undisturbed, Clement said, "Peace and good be with you both."

"You're a Franciscan," Gray said.

"Yes, my lord."

"Forgive me, Friar, but Juliana has tried my patience past bearing with her ungovernable ways, and when I heard her, I thought—"

Now Clement was flustered. "Yes, yes, well, no ill was done."

"Now you know who he is," Juliana said, "so go away."

Gray shook his head. "You and I have much to talk about. But first I want to know why you're here. What cause have you to plead so with this friar?"

"You have no right to question me."

"She wished to take vows," Clement said calmly. "So that she couldn't be forced to marry you."

"Clement, no!" she exclaimed.

To Juliana's annoyance, Gray let out a bark of laughter.

"Vows," he chortled. "Juliana Welles, you know you're not meant for holy vows. Didn't we prove it so in the Lion's Tower? Vows. God save me."

Turning red, Juliana appealed to Clement. "You see? He has no reverence or honor."

Gray's laughter broke off, and he gave her a stern look.

"I grow weary of your sharp tongue. You and I are going to settle things between us this day. I'll not have a contentious and unruly wife, for all that she rouses me to unbounded lust with her hot and heady manner."

"Arrogant liar." Juliana's hand went to the knife in her belt.

Gray lunged at her, and he snatched the knife as she drew it. Juliana tried to get it back, but he held it high above her head.

"I'm in no mood to let you impale me just because you won't admit you want me in your bed, my joyance."

"Ooooo! You piss-ridden, caitiff whoreson."

"Peace, mistress," Clement said. "I beseech you."

Juliana heard the note of chagrin in the friar's voice. Gray had shamed her in front of Clement, just as he'd shamed her at Wellesbrooke. Was there no place she could find refuge from indignity? Juliana made another grab for the knife, causing Gray to hold it higher. As his arm stretched, she suddenly ducked under it and ran. As she dashed from the cave, Clement grabbed Gray's arm.

"Wait, my lord. Remember her temper."

Furious and humiliated, Juliana could only think of escape from her tormentor. Blinking in the sunlight, she rushed toward her mare, but the animal was gone. Gray's doing, no doubt. She heard his voice and Clement's as she ran up the hillside; he would come after her. Her only chance was to hide where he wouldn't find her. There was another, smaller cave almost at the summit of the hill.

Grasping at saplings and tree branches, she pulled herself up the steep slope. The soil was loose, and the footing precarious, but she managed to climb most of the way to the cave before running out of breath. The clearing and Clement's cave were far below now. She stopped, clinging to a stunted shrub and gulped in air. Then she began to pull herself up again.

"Juliana!"

She cried out and whipped around, trying to see how close Gray was, and lost her balance. Her boots slipped on a thick layer of leaves and loose soil. Juliana shrieked as she hurtled down the steep hillside at an uncontrolled run. She couldn't stop herself. Her body seemed to plunge down the slope as if dropped from a cathedral spire. She tried to scream, but her heart was crawling up her throat.

Below her Gray shouted at her and burst into flight. He ran at an angle to catch her, flung one arm around a sapling, and scooped her up as she soared by him. Juliana felt her feet leave the ground. She careened into him, and he pulled her to his chest.

Gripping his tunic, Juliana clung to him, buried her face in his neck, and burst into tears. She tried to say something between pants and gasps, but all that came out was "Oh, oh, oh." Gray braced himself against the sapling and wrapped both arms around her. She felt his lips on the top of her head.

"Are you hurt, my love? Juliana, answer me."

"I—I c-couldn't stop."

Although she hated herself for her cowardice, one look down the sheer slope made her twist her hands in his tunic again and bury her face in his shoulder.

"But you're safe now," he said as he stroked her hair. "Come, we must get you off this hillside before you take flight again."

Sniffing, Juliana wiped her eyes with her sleeve and turned in the circle of his arms. Her gaze met the steep incline. The ground seemed to dip and fall from beneath her feet. She gasped, and her knees buckled as she turned and threw her arms around his neck. He caught her and swore.

"Here, my joyance, put your arm around my waist. See? I've got you. We'll climb down together."

She listened to his calm, soothing voice for a moment. It wasn't the words that allayed her fears and restored her strength; it was that tall, rampartlike body that supported her when the very ground beneath her seemed to give way. She remembered how he'd snatched her from the air with one arm. He wouldn't let her plunge to her death.

Thus assured, Juliana was able to descend the slope with his assistance. Her fear ebbed the farther down the hill they went. By the time they reached the clearing, she'd regained her wits. She loosened her grip on him, intending to step away and leave. Dropping an arm behind her, he bent and swept her up in his arms.

"What are you doing?"

"I told you we were going to talk."

Despite her curses and protests, he carried her back to Clement's cave. The friar was nowhere in sight.

"Clement, Clement, help me!"

"He's gone to the village," Gray said as he set her on her feet.

The moment she was free she tried to rush around him, but he stepped in her path. Juliana almost bumped into him, but stepped back just in time. He was between her and the cave entrance.

"You're over your fright, it seems."

"Let me pass," she said.

He shook his head, but he wasn't looking at her face any longer. His glance had strayed to her chest. Juliana frowned and looked down at herself.

"Thunder of heaven!"

The neck of her gown was laced up the front from a point just below her breasts. Somehow, during her flight down the hill the lacing had come free and her under-tunic had torn. Her breasts were exposed almost to the nipple. Juliana drew the edges of the tunic together and scowled at Gray.

"I'm not going to talk to you. And cease staring at me in that lewd manner."

"Why?"

Nonplussed, all thought seemed to vanish from her mind. Her fingers twisted in the laces and torn fabric at her chest. He was waiting for an answer, his eyes visible to her in the half-light of the cave entrance. She felt so odd under that emerald gaze. Being looked at by this man made her feel hot and disturbed and right lascivious. Each time they'd been alone, he had worked some magic that stirred her senses. Her body spoke in a strange language when she was with him. Holy Trinity, he was smiling at her in that pagan, sensual way that no good Christian ought to. Why, indeed.

"Why, Sir Knave . . ." She stopped for a moment because she sounded like a breathless child. "Because your stare is most unchivalrous."

He took another step toward her and spoke in a compelling, sorcerer's voice. "But Juliana, you hate it when I'm chivalrous."

It was that voice that caused her dread. Not because of its threat, but because it made her want to obey. She stepped back and held out a hand to ward him off.

"I said go away. I'll not speak with you."

"For once you're right," he said roughly as his gaze raked over her. "This isn't the time for discourse."

He came toward her then, and Juliana bolted into the cave. She knew the place, and he didn't. All she had to do was lose him in the blackness and slip around him while he wandered in search of her. She plunged deep into blackness, then stopped so that he couldn't hear her footsteps. She'd heard him running after her, but when she had stopped, he had too.

Quietly and slowly, she drifted over to a wall and began to sidle toward the mouth of the cave. She was still deep in the bowel of the cavern. Although her eyes were open as wide as they would go, she couldn't see a speck of light. She put out her hand, waving it back and forth so that she didn't run into an outcropping of rock. Her palm met cold rock, and she moved her hand in the other direction.

She screamed as Gray snatched her wrist.

"Got you."

Juliana burst into motion. She flailed at him with her free arm and kicked. They wrestled for a moment, and then their legs entangled. Suddenly they both lost their balance. With their feet tripping over each other, they had no purchase. She fell against Gray, who lost what was left of his balance. In the blackness she plummeted toward the ground and landed on top of him.

She recovered from the jolt first. Shoving her palms against his chest so that he gasped, she pushed herself up and slid down his body to land on the cave floor between his legs. As she moved, she heard him suck in his breath. Turning her back to him, she began untangling her legs from her skirt. She got to her knees, but he sat up then and caught her.

Juliana hadn't realized she was still sitting between his legs facing away from him. His arms came around her and pulled her between his thighs and against his chest. One arm snaked beneath her breasts while the other covered her hips. She pounded his legs and arms until he squeezed her hard enough to stop her breathing.

Loosening his grip, he nuzzled through the abundance of her hair until he found her ear and whispered, "I've taken enough of your pounding. No more."

"Then let me go."

"I can't, my joyance."

There was a short silence during which she could hear his breathing grow heavy.

"You should never have wriggled down my body like some wicked incubus," he said harshly.

"But I had to get off you," Juliana said as she began to wriggle in an effort to free herself. "By my troth, you're a troublesome knave."

"Be still!"

She obeyed out of astonishment at the force of his shout. It echoed off the unseen walls and high ceiling of the cavern. They remained as they were, each breathing more and more roughly the longer they touched. Gradually Juliana became aware of her breasts. Her nipples were tingling. The feeling made her want to squirm, and it was all she could do to refrain.

Suddenly she felt him move. The hair that hung down her back was parted, exposing her neck, and he gently raked his teeth along it. Reaction shot through her body as it never had before. Her back arched and a knot of sheer titillation burst into existence between her legs. She heard a gasp, then realized it was her own. His tongue followed the same agonizing path down the back of her neck. This time she groaned.

"Ahhh," he murmured. "So this is the secret."

What secret? His hands rubbed their way to her breasts. His fingers found her nipples. Her eyes opened wide, seeing nothing, and she mouthed a protest. It died in another gasp when he responded by raking his teeth down her neck again. Her back arched, shoving her breasts against his hands.

Never had she experienced such churning, pleasureful torment. Even as she felt his hands slip inside her gown to knead her bare flesh, Juliana realized she might never feel this again. His lips teased the back of her neck. His hands worked down to her breasts, exposed them. Wherever they roamed, they brought heat. The agony between her legs grew, and she began to writhe.

This time she felt something against her buttocks. He was rigid there. Without knowing why, she felt the urge to turn and thrust herself against that hardness. She tried to, but he stopped her by finding her lips and kissing her. One hand roamed over her breasts while the other drifted lightly down to her hip and the inside of her thigh. He urged her legs apart, then stopped.

"Say yes, my joyance," he whispered as she arched against him. "I seek not to pillage and destroy, but to do your good pleasure. "Say yes, I beseech you."

She didn't want to think about the world outside this black cavern, or what might come after. His desire might be fleeting, and she might pay at his hands for her weakness. But his beauty and his artistry gave her such unparalleled pleasure. She wanted it. This she would have for herself, with this man who stirred her past bearing.

"Yes."

He wouldn't let her turn to him. Holding her mouth with his, he slipped his hand beneath her skirts to touch the top of her boot. Fingertips traced a path from her knee to her inner thigh, up and up toward that knot of burgeoning sensation. They lightly touched her. Juliana shrank away then, but his mouth left hers to whisper encouragement and to plead. But her body refused to slacken its rigidity until he nipped at the back of her neck. The teasing bites plunged her into chaos. She nearly doubled over in an attempt to escape, and her hands gripped his thighs.

When her fingers dug into the muscles that ran along the inside of his thighs, his hand returned to her core and began to caress her. At that first touch, Juliana bucked and reached up to tangle her fingers in his hair. Her legs spread wider with each teasing touch. The feeling built and built until they began to rock against each other.

Her body burned and the knot of titillation swelled at his encouragement. Then he pinched her nipple, and she cried out. She thrust up against his hand, and as she moved, he came with her, lifting her and placing her on the ground. His hand returned to bedevil her. Again she arched her back while pulling him toward her without knowing what she sought.

He resisted for a moment, then came down to her. She gave a little start as heated flesh touched her where his hand had been, but she was so aroused that the strangeness soon vanished. His hips thrust against her, and a sudden thought flitted through her mind. Her knowledge of sick men hadn't prepared her for the condition of a man in superb health.

Then the thought was gone, for he was caressing her with himself and with his hand. Her fingers tangled in his hair again, working into its softness as her pleasure built. She felt a turgid, almost painful swelling that climbed, climbed, climbed. She cried out even as he shifted his hips and slipped inside her. He thrust without warning, and she felt pain that vanished beneath the ungovernable urge to push. He moved back and forth inside her, causing the knot of sensation to enlarge so that she thought she would go mad if he stopped.

He moved faster. Pleasure mounted, surged with his penetrations. So intense was the feeling that she finally lifted her hips in an effort to force him deeper. As her body thrust upward, she felt a great, fulminating release. Even as she cried out, his body came down on hers, thrusting her back to the ground. He strained against her, pumping rapidly, and then cried out.

Juliana felt a surge inside her, and a sudden flood. Seed. Life. This man's life and seed. All at once, she felt a rush of amazement and a sense of mastery. Gray de Valence, mighty lord, unruly Viking. *She* could drive him to this desperate passion. His head dropped to her breast. They lay there, linked, breathless, spent, and silent.

Eventually sense began to return to her. With it came fear, for Gray de Valence wasn't the only one driven by lust. She had no honor where this man's body was concerned. Yet hitherto she'd been invulnerable to men's wooing. She should have remembered how small was her experience. It was limited to Edmund Strange's perfunctory gestures rendered because of duty.

Edmund Strange! Remembrance turned her cold; in the concealing darkness, she had forgotten her imperfection. God's mercy, she was still wearing her clothes, her boots. *He'd said nothing.* But he would, and soon. She'd given him what he wanted, and now there was no reason for him to continue this mockery of a betrothal. And she couldn't complain, because he'd asked her, and she'd said yes.

Only now she was more confused than ever. In her new weakness for him, she almost wished his offer were honorable, but her saner self knew just how arrogant and barbaric he could be, more so than any rooster knight she'd ever encountered. And now it wasn't only he who had betrayed Yolande. She had acted out of selfishness.

Juliana sighed, and the movement disturbed that part of him still inside her. He turned his face toward her and kissed her cheek. She touched his hair, and forgot her fears in marveling at its softness. It was heavy, thick, silken, and just feeling it against her skin made her desire quicken. She touched the fragile strands at his temples. He turned to kiss her palm. His lips performed a supple dance on her flesh. Juliana tried to gird herself to tell him she hadn't changed her mind about marriage, but he spoke first.

Propping himself up on his forearms, he found her mouth with his in the darkness and whispered against her lips. "My joyance, once I swore never to allow anyone to enslave me again." He sighed, causing his sweet breath to feather her cheeks. "I think I am forsworn."

Mallow

A plaster of mallow and sheep's tallow was good for gout. Drenched with vinegar and linseed, it abated the wicked gatherings that were engendered in a man's body and kept witches away from the house.

Chapter 15

DID SHE FEEL HIS TREMBLING? GRAY GENTLY withdrew from Juliana, gritting his teeth with the effort, and settled beside her. She would have risen, but he pulled her into his arms and whispered words of comfort. Resting with his back propped against the cave wall, he listened to her breathing as it calmed, slowed, and signaled that she'd drifted into sleep. After nearly falling to her death and then making love for the first time, she should be spent.

He'd never been with a virgin, but his experience as a slave had served him well. He better than most knew what it was to be naked, frightened, and unable to control what was happening to one's body. Was that why he was so disturbed?

No, the reason was darker, uglier. When Saladin had given him his freedom and he'd returned to Christendom, he'd been filled with revulsion. Revulsion for unwanted intimacy, for what had been done to him, for his helplessness to prevent the violations done to him.

Saladin hadn't been physically cruel, although the threat had always been there. No, Saladin had done far worse. He'd allowed Gray a certain amount of freedom, allowed him to serve as a warrior. And then he'd exacted a price for the freedom.

The memory of nights spent performing for his master still haunted him. He'd been so unsuspecting the first time, but then, he'd been young. His experience had been restricted, and thus he'd been unprepared when Saladin required him to couple with slaves while his master watched. Oh, he'd tumbled with maids in barns with friends, but those friends had always been too concerned with their own pleasure to do what Saladin had done. Never had they come close, given orders, placed their hands between bodies.

And so when he'd saved Saladin's life that second time, been freed, and come home, he'd been celibate for over a year. As time passed, he'd gradually recovered, or so he'd thought, until now. Yet he still trembled.

Gray rested his head against cold stone and tried to make sense of jumbled emotions. He felt so unsteady and yet certain of his course. There was no logic in feeling both, but he'd been this way since meeting Juliana. Lowering his head, he nuzzled her hair. She turned on her side and rested her cheek on his chest. Staring out at the cave's blackness, he realized that he'd never had such a moment in his life. Never had he made love in such complete privacy, sharing instead of . . .

That was it. As a slave he hadn't made love, he had performed. For so long it had been no more than a humiliating exhibition, an act of submission in which he had no choice. To escape the memories and the feelings, he'd turned lovemaking into a game of seduction in which he held the power and allowed the favors. And there had been plenty of women at the French and English courts willing to play the game with him. Until Juliana. She didn't play games of courtly love or seduction. She had barged into his life and disrupted his pretense, his façade erected to protect himself against further hurt and shame.

She was stirring. He felt her move against him and heard a tiny snuffle, then a caught breath. She raised her head. He couldn't see her, but he could feel her body tense. Was she in pain? Had he hurt her? She'd been untouched, unlike him. Unlike him. Dear God, she was so sheltered and free of corruption. As she sat up, Gray realized that he couldn't let her know what he'd been. She was so unsullied; if she found out, she would be disgusted.

"You're ignoring me!"

"What?" He jolted out of the past and helped her stand.

"I said—" She stopped and lowered her voice so that it didn't bounce off the cave walls. "I said that now there's no reason to continue this pretense of a betrothal."

"What?" He couldn't seem to leave confusion behind.

"No more lies, Sir Knave. I've succumbed to your licentious trickery—"

"Trickery!" Now he was alert. He searched in the dark until he found her arm and grasped it. "There was no trickery, mistress. I but initiated you into pleasures we'll soon share in marriage."

"I told you there's no need to continue that lie. I'll not play the debauched maid and shriek for remedy in marriage vows."

He would have interrupted, but her fingers found his lips and pressed them into stillness. She went on in a tone that was a little too light, a bit too confident for a young woman so recently seduced.

"I admit I now know why you men feel so, so driven. And I thank you for the—the . . . for what you've done. No doubt you didn't expect this seduction to be so easy, or escape to be so quick. I'll not marry you."

She thought him a vile debaucher of virgins! He shook off her fingers, clenched his fists, and tried to control his fury.

"What ails you?" she asked. "I said I won't marry you."

"Oh. Yes. You. Will." He could hear his own rough breathing.

"No I won't."

He struggled to hold his temper. God, but she was willful. "I've been trying to tell you this since I found you. I understand that a young demoiselle like yourself can be frightened of taking a husband and leaving her family. I'll give you time to accustom yourself to the idea. I still have to catch that whoreson bandit, which may take a while. There are arrangements to be made. You may have a month."

Shrill mockery flew at him. "A month. A month. Thunder of God, he allows me a month!" An abrupt silence fell. Then she whispered, "You mean you insist upon marriage?"

"Have I not said it?"

"Even after—why?"

Now he was in danger. He'd been unguarded before and admitted the truth. He was enslaved by her wildness, her spirit and strength, by her damascened eyes. But he couldn't tell her that. She wouldn't believe him. She already thought him a liar and he'd confirmed to her that he was a seducer of innocents. It wasn't fair, because she'd seduced him before they'd ever entered this cave.

"I asked you why?" she said again.

"Er, I need a wife. I need heirs, and it's a good match."

"No it isn't. Not for you."

"It is. I've thought over my reasons for marriage and come to new conclusions. A great heiress would bring with her a powerful family who would interfere with my life, and I'll not tolerate that. Now come along. I should take you home before your father begins to search for you, and we should repair our clothes. And I have to look for the bandit."

He gripped her arm and began to lead her out of the cave. She dug in her heels.

"I don't believe you. You're not telling me the truth."

"We'll talk again later." What else could he do but delay when he didn't understand himself? "Right now I have men searching the countryside for those bandits, and when I catch them I'll hang the lot of them."

"Hang?"

For some reason her voice was faint. He wouldn't have thought so willful a maid squeamish.

"Aye, hang. They stole from me."

He didn't mention the most powerful reason for his fury. The repetition of what Saladin had done to him— the exposure and humiliation before others—these still gnawed at him as if vultures picked at an open wound. He craved vengeance for that. The bastard had given him renewed nightmares of nakedness and shame, and for that alone he would kill him.

They went to the mouth of the cave and did what they could to repair their clothing. In silence, Juliana cast fulminating looks at him when she thought he wasn't looking and appeared to be engaged in agitated thought. Once she turned her back to him and fumbled with her boots. Upon facing him, she folded her arms over her chest and looked at him through dark lashes, her pliant mouth now stiff.

"I've an idea," she said. "Leave off this hunt for bandits and I'll marry you at once."

His hands froze while buckling his sword belt. He studied her narrowed eyes and rigid body. "Now who is lying? Not a moment past you refused me."

"I've reconsidered, as you have."

"You're a hot and heady maid, Juliana, right obdurate and froward. And you've given me much tribulation of late, so why the sudden change—"

"My lord!"

They turned to look out at the clearing where several of Gray's men rode toward them. One dismounted and gave a salute.

"We met the friar in the village, and he told us where you were. By my troth, what a time we've had finding you."

He muttered under his breath, "God be thanked for it."

He heard Juliana suppress a snicker. Casting a stern glance at her, he nodded at the man.

"We've caught one of the bandits, my lord. We gave up searching the wood and went among the villagers. Right insolent some of them were, but we had Lord Welles's permission. When we came to the blacksmith's cottage, we found a black mask under a pallet belonging to one of his sons, the one with the watery eyes called Eadmer. Keeps howling about Charles the Mange. Must be what the bandits call their leader."

"Hardly a name to inspire fear. I'll come as soon as I've escorted Mistress Juliana home."

"I'll come with you."

He was surprised to find her standing so near. "This is no business for a woman."

"Oh? You mean for a woman who can watch a sick man vomit and risk infecting herself? For a woman who, if she marries you, will command your men when you're away? For a woman who will suffer the agony and spill the blood of childbirth? It's no business for that woman?"

"I'll not have you twisting my words—" He glanced at his men, who were pretending not to listen. Grabbing her arm, he pulled her over to where his squire stood holding their horses and dismissed the boy. "You're not going," he said as he gathered the reins of both mounts. "For once you'll do as I command and return to the castle."

"But there has to be some mistake," she said. "Eadmer wouldn't harm anyone. He's an honest young man, honest and good. What are you going to do to him? Father won't like it if you hurt him. The stripping bandit has outwitted you again by placing this mask where it doesn't belong to delude you."

Startled by this flood of protestations, Gray studied her while smoothing the reins through his hands. She was almost dancing with agitation, and her hands were trembling. She shouldn't be so distressed by the apprehension of a thief—unless she knew him, perhaps had some knowledge of his activities. His fingers wrapped around lengths of leather and squeezed.

"What do you know of this Eadmer?" he snapped.

She'd still been chattering, but the flow ceased with this question while she fluttered her lashes and went pale.

"Well?" he asked. "You were conveniently nearby to watch when I came back after being robbed. Christ's curse, Juliana, have you suspected this man and not spoken?"

"I—er."

She wet her lips and stuttered some more while he stared at her. Then, without warning, she gasped, turned her back to him, and covered her face with her hands. To his consternation, he heard weeping. Dropping the reins, he rushed to her and took hold of her shoulders. They were shaking.

"What ails you? What's wrong? Juliana?"

He held her for a few moments until her weeping subsided. She lifted eyes shimmering with tears and gave him a pleading look.

"Eadmer saved my mare's life once. Her name is Elise,

and I've had her since she was a foal. She hurt her foreleg last year and Father wanted to put her down, but I couldn't. Eadmer saved her. He would never do anything so dishonorable as fall in with bandits."

He could find nothing to say as she dropped her head on his chest and sobbed. He'd known Juliana was soft of heart, but clearly she hid the depths of her compassion and sensitivity from everyone. To be so gentle-hearted in this age of cruelty would mean a life of constant pain. Something in him shuddered, and he was flooded with a fierce desire to protect this woman whose compassion surpassed that of anyone he'd ever known.

"Sweet joyance," he whispered to her. "I can't let this Eadmer go without speaking to him, but I promise to be evenhanded. If he's innocent as you believe, I'll not send him to his death. You have my word."

"I want to come with you."

"No, and don't bother trying to convince me to change my decision."

"Unless you lock me in my chamber—"

"Peace," he said as he stepped away from her. "Don't think I won't if you try my forbearance."

The silver fire returned to her gaze, and he welcomed it.

"Just you attempt it, Viking. Just you try."

He smiled at her, remembering how she'd bucked at his touch in the cave, and saw her flush. "Juliana, do you wish to ride back to the castle tossed over my saddle like a dead doe?"

Her gasp was his answer. She whirled away from him, gathered her mare's reins, and mounted. He tried not to grin as he led the way down from the hills, but battles with her were so hard won it was hard not to gloat.

They crossed the stream near where he'd first

The sun had almost set by the time his plans came to fruition. He had returned Juliana to the castle only to find it in an uproar over the disappearance of cousin Edmund. He hadn't been seen all day. His chamber still held his belongings, and none of his party were missing. Gray suspected he was wallowing in some haystack with a village maid, but he'd been too preoccupied with the need to question the blacksmith's son to worry about Edmund's rutting. He'd gone with his men to the blacksmith's house in Wellesbrooke village where he'd confronted the young man.

An hour's browbeating and rough handling had produced nothing but protestations of ignorance and innocence. Gray knew that harsher methods would bring Juliana's wrath, but he detested such measures in any case. He'd experienced too much brutality to take any pleasure in meting it out to others. And so he did what he would have done even without Juliana's prompting. He set a trap.

Pretending to send Eadmer to neighboring Chessmore where he could be questioned away from his family and friends, he sent the prisoner on his way with only a small escort. He let his plans be known throughout Wellesbrooke and then loudly announced his intention to search for the leader to the south. Then Gray and his knights followed Eadmer in secret.

If he was right, the stripping bandit wouldn't hesitate to snatch his minion before he could be made to confess. The bastard was bold and insolent in his moves. He'd be unable to resist making a fool of Gray. Shadows lengthened as he, Lucien, Arthur, and the others followed the escort party deeper and deeper into the forest. It had rained earlier, and the paths were thick with rain-slick leaves.

They crossed the stream near where he'd first encountered Juliana and wound their way north along the muddy track. Gray guided his horse around the mud hole that had provided him with such pleasure at her expense. Ahead the trees closed in until they almost obscured the path. He rode on until the man he'd sent ahead returned to say that Eadmer's party was making camp. Darkness would fall soon. Gray signaled to his men, and they left the path, vanishing into the trees, wraithlike and silent. By prior arrangement, they would form a loose ring around the camp and wait for their quarry to strike.

Taking up a post behind a tree near the clearing in which the guards had camped, Gray settled down to wait for darkness. Most thieves preferred the cover of night. Drawing his cloak around him, he watched the three guards he'd chosen for this task. One watched Eadmer while the other two built a fire, a big bright one that would attract attention.

By the time the shadows were at their longest and the light a deep gold, the two guards had succeeded in lighting the fire. They were standing before it warming their hands when a loud whistle and a barrage of arrows assailed the forest quiet. The bold whoreson hadn't waited for dark after all. Gray watched him ride into the clearing with several other thieves holding crossbows. Mask in place, leaning insolently on the neck of his horse, he ordered Eadmer released.

Smiling evilly, Gray dropped back from his post and ran quietly to the squire who held his horse. He heard Lucien's signal—the call of a hawk. He returned the signal, mounted, and rode back to the clearing. The bandits were engaged in forcing his guards to strip.

Once he had the thieves in sight, Gray drew his sword. The hissing ring alerted the thieves, but they were too late. Gray bellowed his battle cry, "De Valence and God!" His knights echoed it and charged.

Destriers thundered into the clearing. Crossbows were aimed, but the delay caused by surprise was enough. Lucien hurled a mace at one man, who took a blow to the head and dropped to the ground. Another didn't see Arthur's war horse until it bashed into him from the rear while the third bowman let fly a bolt that went wild. Before he could reload, Gray cuffed him with the flat of his blade. He too plummeted to the ground. In less than a minute Gray and his knights had surrounded the only thief to remain on his feet—the leader.

Gratification, triumph, and anticipation all surged in his veins as he walked his horse over to the bandit. He'd been cheated of true vengeance upon his betrayers of long ago. He'd never had the power to retaliate against those who enslaved him. But this man would never escape.

Riding close, Gray bent down, grasped the leader's mask and yanked it off his head. He looked down at a face covered in soot, at eyes set off by the blackness so that they seemed to shine like the polished steel of an Arab scimitar. His mind went blank. It was as if he stood outside his own body and watched the group surrounding the bandit. No one said a thing. His men didn't move. Not a word was uttered. The absence of speech filled the clearing with a painful void. He detected the muffled clink of a bridle, the soft snuffling of his horse, the snap of a twig under a boot. These things reminded him of the physical world, and yet his mind refused to credit what his vision revealed.

The bandit was a woman. No, not a woman, a witch with damascened eyes. He began to curse, in English, French, and Arabic.

"Holy blood of Christ, God damn you to eternal perdition." He dismounted and grasped lengths of black hair in his fist, drawing the bandit's face up to his. "Juliana."

His mind was working again, and it burned with an ugly thought—Juliana had been the one to shame him. And he had thought Saladin cruel. His knights had retreated, and they all hung suspended in silence for a brief moment. Then she spat in his face. Swearing, he thrust her from him and wiped his cheek, then grabbed her as she sprang into flight.

"Oh, no, mistress thief, you're not running away this time."

He tangled his fingers in her hair again as she tried to escape. Holding her by long tresses, he watched her struggles. God, he'd believed her lies, her tears. She'd made a fool of him before his own men, before the whole countryside. She'd stripped him naked and laughed at him. Rage burned through his mind, obliterating all else. His blood burned with it, liquid fire. A small part of him whispered warnings of actions born of hurt and later regretted. He didn't listen.

"Look," he said to his men with a nasty laugh. "We've caught a she-devil instead of a thief, a bitch masquerading as a lady."

Jeers rose up to taunt her, and he listened to them with pleasure. Juliana snarled at him and swung her fists, but he held her at arm's length.

"*Mon Dieu*," Lucien cried. "Never have I seen such a creature. Is it a man or a woman?"

"Oh," Gray retorted, "I assure you, this is a woman, when she's clean. A right lusty wench, ripe and ready."

Juliana stopped trying to hit him for a moment and gaped into his eyes. Her curses flew at him with the force of crossbow bolts, but he merely laughed at her again.

"Well, Lucien, I suppose we can't hang her, so what will we do with her?"

"*Je ne sais pas, messire.*"

Gray's eyes locked with Juliana's, and his smile widened and its evil deepened. "Ah," he said softly. "I know. A biblical punishment. 'Eye for eye, tooth for tooth, hand for hand, foot for foot, burning for burning, wound for wound, stripe for stripe.'"

She was looking at him with confusion, so he released her hair. She had been leaning away from him, and the sudden movement caused her to topple backward and fall on her rump. He planted his feet apart, put his fists on his hips, and looked down at her sputtering form.

"Take your clothes off, mistress thief."

Periwinkle

The devil had no power over those who carried the herb next to the skin, and no witchery could enter the house if it was hanging over the door. With periwinkle, wicked spirits were cast out of victims. It also eased toothache and drove out cold fevers.

• Chapter 16 •

JULIANA FELT HER JAW LOOSEN AND DROP. HER
thoughts went blank as his order resounded inside her
head. *Take off your clothes.* All she could do was stare at
Gray de Valence in disbelief.

Already confused by the frightening and miraculous
events of this day, she continued to gape at this golden
knight who stood over her like some barbarian raider,
thighs planted wide apart and straining at the leather
that encased them. He had revealed to her a wondrous
secret—that men were good for something besides cruelty, fighting, and making trouble. They, and especially
he, were good for pleasure beyond dreaming. And in the
aftermath of their lovemaking she had realized that perhaps she would never feel such miraculous pleasure with
anyone else.

She didn't understand him. He'd refused to admit that
he no longer needed the pretense of a betrothal. She was
beginning to believe he would carry out his threat to
marry her, and she didn't know what to think. Thunder
of God, this man, this heir to power and beauty, said he
intended to marry her.

But that was before she was unmasked. Why hadn't
she suspected this trickery from him? He was known for
his stratagems in warfare, and for him, this was war.

"I'm waiting, Juliana."

Thunder of God, she was still gaping at him from the
ground! She glanced around the circle of mounted men.

They'd grown quiet and were casting uncertain glances at their lord.

"Juliana," he said again.

She met his chilly gaze and found no hint of the seductive gentleness that had won her trust so short a time ago. Well, she was accustomed to belligerent men. Standing, she shut her mouth and lifted her jaw. Sticking her thumbs in her belt, she fixed him with her most wolflike stare.

"No."

She hadn't expected him to burst out laughing. She flushed as his men joined in, but maintained her defiant stance.

"By the Trinity, I was hoping you'd refuse."

He began walking toward her.

"What are you doing?" she asked as she backed away.

"I'm going to take your clothes off for you."

"Stay away!"

She scuttled backward until she hit the bulk of a knight and bounced away from him. Gray followed her while his men began to whistle and utter salacious calls. She managed to dart under Gray's swiping arms and continued her evasion. He was playing with her, or he would have caught her. The longer they played this game, the more excited his men grew. The air filled with the scent of primitive need, of lustful anticipation. Gray ignored it; Juliana feared it.

She kept her eyes fixed on Gray's. His were a dark black-green in the fading daylight and shadows of the forest. And they held no mercy. Fear turned her stomach and chilled her bones. Her hands began to shake; she wasn't going to win, not in a physical struggle. Her only chance lay in a battle of wits and courage. She stopped running.

Gray lunged at her and grabbed her upper arms. Juliana held herself rigid as he lifted her up to his eye level, then covered her mouth and plunged his tongue into hers. Forcing her to open to him, he ravaged her while his men cheered. Then he dropped her. She plummeted to the ground and stumbled, but recovered and stood erect. He came at her again, this time reaching for the shirt laces at her throat.

Her arm shot out in a warding gesture. "No, I'll do it."

His hand dropped to his side, and for the first time she saw some flicker of uncertainty cross his brow. It was quickly gone as he lifted an eyebrow and gave her an amused nod. That derisive challenge angered her as nothing else had. Her gaze impaled his. He met her defiance with equanimity, never breaking off his stare.

If it was the last thing she did, she would shatter that mocking iciness. Juliana lifted a hand, slowly pulled off a black leather glove, and let it drop. At the gesture, the men around her stopped laughing. She pulled off the second glove and threw it at Gray's feet with a sudden force.

He merely chuckled and said, "There's much more to come off, mistress thief."

Scowling at him, she unbuckled her belt. Its length unwound, taking with it a knife scabbard. She tossed it aside, and without pausing pulled off her boots. Of all the clothing she was to remove, these were the most difficult for her, so she did it quickly, lest anyone suspect.

This would be her secret victory. He didn't know she feared revealing her imperfection of limb more than the rest of her unremarkable body. That's what came of trying to embarrass a healer familiar with many bodies, sick though they might be. She would fix these thoughts before her.

The second boot shot out and landed at the feet of the French knight. Juliana straightened, settling on both feet.

Don't stop; if you stop, you'll lose your courage and whimper at his feet. Do you want that? It's what he wants. Don't stop.

He was still watching her with that mocking half-smile on his lips. She held his gaze—and dropped her breeches and hose.

Worn wool slithered around her ankles. A cold breeze danced over her legs. The hem of her tunic reached below her hips. Her bare leg kicked, and the patched material sailed at him. He blinked then, quickly, and all amusement vanished from his face. He didn't look away, and she couldn't. But she could hear several of his men suck in their breath, and one choked.

Don't stop or you'll never do it. He'll pounce on you like a rutting stallion.

Her hands lifted to her throat, drawing his attention. She began to unlace her tunic, but wavered as he smiled again. That smile signaled defeat to her. *No, don't think; don't stop. At least keep your pride.*

Laces unwound. She pulled apart the edges of the fabric, exposing the rise of her breasts. Then she lowered her arms and grasped the hem of the tunic. Slowly her fingers slid up her thighs, higher, even higher, while she looked deep into cold green eyes. Her vision filled with nothing but emerald glitter.

The black wool edged up, close to the vee at her hips. The only sign of change in him was a fine film of moisture that appeared on his brow. Neither of them would release the lock of their gazes. She had stopped breathing. Pausing, she drew in air. Then she lifted the hem.

Cold air wafted over the most intimate portions of her body. Then Gray's tall, hard body was shielding hers. Arms wrapped around her and shoved the hem of the tunic down her thighs.

"Christ's curse! Damn you, Juliana. And damn you, Lucien, all of you take yourselves off."

Noise rose up around them. She glanced around to find that his men were dragging their horses away and retreating into the thickness of the forest with their prisoners. In moments they were alone. He released her roughly. She looked up at him with a fiercely triumphant smile. Not bothering to say a word to him, she turned her back and picked up her hose.

Suddenly he lunged at her, swearing and breathing hard. Picking her up, he pulled the hose from her grasp and tossed them across the clearing. He dropped the arm under her legs so that she was resting against his chest with her legs against his. Holding her by the waist with one arm, he gripped a thigh with the other and worked his hand up, an inch at a time.

Juliana cried out and wriggled against him, but her thrashing offered him the opportunity to slip his hand around to the inside of her thigh and bring it up against the join of her leg. She screeched as he pushed against her. He chuckled and squeezed even as he foiled her attempt to shove his hand away. His fingers began to probe.

At this invasion, she cried out, grabbed a lock of his hair, and pulled. He yelped, and his hands slipped around to cup her buttocks. Juliana yanked his hair again; he swore and dropped her. Landing on her feet, she turned to run, only to be swept up in his arms again. He had one arm around her back and the other under her legs.

"Filthy sodding whoreson bastard, let me go!"

"What an evil tongue you have, mistress thief. That's another of your faults I'll have to correct. That and your stubborn selfishness and your disrespect, and your habit of trying to shame innocent knights who've done naught to warrant your evil tricks. Oh, and your unmaidenly urge to expose yourself to strange men."

"Ohhhh. Let me go, or I'll—"

"Between you and me, Juliana, there will be but one master. Understand this now, or there will be more embarrassments."

"Put me down, you pestilential churl."

"We're going home, Juliana Welles, where I'm going to drop you at your father's feet and expose your thieving sins for all to see."

She pounded his back. "As long as I don't have to marry you, I don't care."

"Oh, you'll marry me, mistress thief, but before you do, I'm going to tame that evil temper of yours. Do you think I'll endure a wife who sets herself against me and exposes me to scorn with her defiance and disrespect?"

"I'd rather marry a poisonous toad than you. Put me down."

"Not yet, my lovely thief. I think your sins merit at least one more ride across my saddle."

"By God, I'll kill you." She writhed against his back while trying to grip his belt.

"No you won't, but if you don't stop squirming all over me like that, I'm going to toss you in a pile of leaves and really take your clothes off, and that will be the least embarrassing thing that will happen to you."

She stopped struggling. Once she was quiet, Gray allowed her to dress, then picked her up again—before she tried to run away, he said. He found his men, tossed her atop his horse, and mounted behind her. Since she'd landed upright, Juliana didn't protest. Sitting between his legs, rigid and enraged, she clamped her mouth shut and stared ahead. Her men had been tied to horses and were following, guarded by knights. Her men! She'd brought calamity upon them. Gray had said he'd hang them.

"Let my men go."

"Ah, you're talking to me again."

"Only because of my men. They only did as I ordered. None of them is really a thief, you know. Thunder of God, I'm the one responsible for what's happened to you. Punish me, but let them go."

He didn't answer. She waited until her patience wore out, not a long time, she had to admit.

"Well? What say you?"

"Hush," he said. "I'm thinking. After all, there is justice to consider, an eye for an eye, and so forth."

He was delaying to make her suffer. That was it. He wanted to draw out the suspense. She bit the inside of her cheek to keep from railing at him and thus letting him know how successful his tactic was. Making fists, she dug her nails into her palms and waited.

It was dark, and Wellesbrooke castle was in sight before he made another sound, and then it was a throaty, sinister chuckle. The sound sent a chill down her backbone and made her palms go damp. He rode with his arm encircling her waist. It tightened to draw her against his hips and chest, and she felt his mouth near her ear. Warm, moist breath wafted over her cheek and throat.

"There is a way you can save your poor louts," he whispered.

"Get on with it," she snapped.

"You must promise to leave off this absurd defiance. Accept our betrothal and marriage. Become a right gentle and biddable lady. I know it will be hard for you, but it's my price, and don't snarl at me like that. You hold the lives of those men in your hands."

"Devil's spawn. Whelp of a demon. Pissant scabrous lout!"

"Then you agree to my terms?"

"Yes, you foul curse upon the world."

"Now, now, my love, you're breaking your promise already."

"Thunder of God, I'll break more than my promise. If you think I won't let everyone know it was I who stripped you of your clothes—ah!"

She gasped as he hauled on the reins sharply, causing his mount to rear. He quieted the animal while the men behind them pulled up to await his pleasure. After stroking the horse's neck, without warning, he grabbed her shoulders, lifted her, and set her sideways across his lap so that she could see his face. He drew her close, his fingers digging into the flesh of her upper arms.

"Look at me. There's plenty of light from the moon, Juliana, so look at me."

Pressing her lips together, she lifted her chin and glared at him. What she saw when she faced him made her own scowl fade. The gentle Christian knight had vanished again, to be replaced by the mercilessness of a pagan, the ruthlessness of a Godless heathen. Those eyes held the writhing of damned souls, the searing fires of hell.

"Look well, stubborn mistress," he said calmly. "See what I rarely reveal to others, and know that if you ever betray me, this is what you will face."

Strength drained from her body. Her mouth went dry, and she couldn't stop herself from looking away from that alien visage. Shaking her head, she twisted in his grip, but he shook her.

"Your promise before God, Juliana. I'll have it."

"I—I promise."

"What do you promise?"

"To stop fighting you, and—and all the other things you said. By the Holy Trinity, I promise."

He released her then with a sigh at odds with the ruthlessness he'd displayed. Removing his cloak, he settled it around her shoulders before taking his hands from her again.

Once free, Juliana turned to face forward again and tried not to tremble. What had she done? She had put herself in the power of a man more heathen than Christian, more barbarian than civilized. Only God knew what corruption and evil he'd come from in the land of the paynim. But what could she do? If she didn't obey, he would destroy Eadmer and the others. And she didn't doubt he'd fulfill his promise to hang them. Rumor attributed far worse depravities to him than simply hanging thieves.

How could she have forgotten his reputation? What happened to her when she came near him that she lost her sense and her memory? His presence seemed to cast her into disarray, wreck her ability to heed her own warnings. And that duel of stares while she removed her clothes, only now could she admit to herself that, had they been alone, she might have stripped him as well as herself.

"God save me," she muttered.

"What did you say?"

She cast around for some explanation. Her gaze caught light and movement, and she pointed to the castle.

"Look. What passes at Wellesbrooke?"

On the battlements she could see dots of light, torches held by numerous guards as they moved back and forth on the wall walk. Gray kicked his horse to a trot as they approached the bridge, and soon they were riding under the portcullis and through the gatehouse.

"Have a care, Juliana. Keep my cloak around you so that none see your thief's garb."

"I know how to conceal myself," she snapped.

He pointed back at her men. "Remember your promise."

Twisting her lips into a pained smile, she said, "Yes, my lord." *May all your glorious hair fall out.*

"Good," he said. "And in the future make your visage match the sweetness of your words."

She almost punched him, but her eye caught sight of four weary pretend thieves being herded past on foot. She bit her upper lip and held her tongue. They rode into the bailey where Gray dismounted and lifted her down from the saddle.

A rumble and scuffle signaled her father's approach. Gray's body hid her from Hugo's sight. Her betrothed shoved her farther behind his back as he turned to greet his host. His arm thrust her at Lucien, who stepped in front of her. Arthur Strange pulled her behind him, and then moved into the midst of the crowd of knights who earlier had jeered at her. In a few moments Arthur spirited her to the old keep and up to her chamber.

Alice opened the door, her face white. "Mistress, where have you been? You said you'd return before dark."

"Hush, you fool," Juliana said. She stepped into the chamber and grasped the door as she turned on Arthur. "Go away." She slammed it in his face.

Wearily she went to the bed and sat down. The folds of Gray's cloak billowed around her. Alice sneezed, causing Juliana to start.

"Thunder of God, woman, can't you be quiet?"

Alice began to sniffle. "I've had to lie to your mother and sisters for hours, saying you were ill. If you hadn't returned soon, my lady would have come in here and found out the truth. What would happen to me then?"

Pressing her palm to her forehead, Juliana sighed. "I'm full sorry. You're right, but take cheer, Alice, because I won't be playing the bandit anymore. I won't be doing much that's amusing anymore if Gray de Valence has his way. I'm to marry him."

"I know, mistress, and it's wondrous news."

"Wondrous, indeed. It's wondrous that he wants such an alliance. I don't trust him, Alice. Why does he want to marry me when he's already—um—why would he want an alliance with the Welles family?"

Alice came to stand in front of her and clasped her hands while she grinned. "He be in love."

"I have a terrible ache in my head. Don't babble foolishness at me."

"It's true, mistress. As you say, it be an unequal match, and therefore he must want you for yourself."

Juliana shrugged off Gray's cloak and scowled at it. "Great barons don't marry for such reasons. If they want a woman of lower rank, they find some illicit way to have her and marry for power."

"And since His Lordship hasn't done such a thing, he must truly want you for his wife."

Still staring at the cloak, Juliana barely listened to the maid. "He plots something. I know it. He was so mindlessly enraged at what I'd done to him, he couldn't want marriage, so what does he want . . . ?"

Love of God, he wanted to shame her as she had shamed him. Hadn't he said so? Which meant he'd most likely devised some scheme of humiliation. It was as she first surmised. He was going to shame her at the wedding, before everyone. As his cousin had. And she would have to endure it for the sake of her men.

Shaking her head, Juliana became suddenly aware of how her body ached. "Bring a tub and water, Alice. I must bathe."

"Oh, mistress, in all the excitement of your return, I forgot."

"Forgot what?"

"Edmund Strange has been found."

"Between the legs of a shepherdess?"

Alice drew near and dropped her voice. "No, mistress, in a barrel of sand, dead, stabbed to death."

"Dead?"

"Aye, mistress."

"In a sand barrel?"

"Yes, mistress."

"No wonder he couldn't be found," Juliana said. To rid armor of rust, it was rolled in barrels of sand.

Edmund Strange dead. Juliana couldn't seem to summon any response to the news. Perhaps she was too weary and too disturbed by this tumultuous day.

"Who stabbed him?" she asked.

"That be the quandary, mistress. No one knows, and your father has been ranting and bellowing for nigh onto an hour. And me, I'm scared." Alice bent and touched Juliana's sleeve. "There be a murderer about the castle, mistress, a murderer, and none of us be safe."

Betony

Betony was good for the man's soul or body and shielded him against monstrous nocturnal visitors and frightful visions and dreams. It was good for all diseases of the head and would cure them that were too fearful.

• *Chapter 17* •

JULIANA HAD TO FORGO HER TUB OF STEAMING water in favor of a rinse in a basin. Donning an old gown, she ran her fingers through her snarled hair and rushed from her chamber, her hair and Alice streaming behind her.

Edmund Strange dead, murdered. Such a thing had never happened in Wellesbrooke. Not to a nobleman, that is. Her father had hanged criminals. A peasant woman with thirteen children had killed her fourteenth newborn. A shepherd had once killed a bandit trying to steal his pig herd. These were the unhappy and rough events of life. But no knights got themselves stabbed and stuffed in barrels.

Rushing down the keep stairs, Juliana hurried to the practice yard between the east gatehouse and the armory. The sand barrels were kept in a shadowy enclosure formed by the walls of the gatehouse and armory, and a high stack of firewood. She and Alice found a crowd still gathered there. Her father's men held them back while they craned their necks to watch the torchlit proceedings.

Juliana shouldered her way to the front of the group that surged into the gap between the firewood and the gatehouse wall. In the space before her rested five barrels, one of which had been tipped on its side. Sand spilled from the open mouth of the container, and with it, a man's body. Some of the sand had been discolored by blood. Behind the barrel sat a stack of others like it. Beside these lay shovels and a stack of wooden practice swords.

Hugo and Gray de Valence were talking to a boy, one of the Wellesbrooke pages who must have found the body. The guard nearest Juliana began to argue with several curious onlookers. She took advantage of the distraction and slithered over to the group by the body. Hugo was accompanied by Richard and his steward. Gray seemed to be there in support of Edmund's brother Arthur. Hugo was expressing his sympathies to the young man.

Horrified curiosity drew Juliana to study the body of the man who almost had become her husband. When she first heard he was dead, she hadn't believed it. Seeing the body now gave her a jolt. Edmund had been a cruel and selfish churl, and she'd hated him. But even she wouldn't have designed so ignominious an end for the man—cut open and poked in a barrel like dried fish.

Edmund was dressed in a long robe, soft boots, and hose, the costume of a nobleman at leisure. His body was covered in sand, and there were several piercing wounds in his chest and one in his throat. Blood discolored the robe and its trim of gold braid. He still wore his signet ring, a silver brooch, and a fine leather belt. Beyond the corpse, Juliana could see a circular impression where the barrel must have rested. She glanced up and saw that a portion of the gatehouse tower projected out over the enclosure, thus limiting the view of anyone on the walls.

Someone had lured Edmund here, killed him, and stuffed him in the barrel unseen. A secluded spot secure from the eyes of the castle guards. Still, the murderer had risked being heard. Juliana frowned and drew closer to Edmund's body. She noted the wound to the throat and decided that it must have come first, preventing him from crying out for help.

Shuddering, she drew back as the foul scent of death reached her nostrils. Nausea caused her to swallow and wrap her arms around her waist. Someone had hated Edmund Strange much more than she. Someone had dealt him a fatal blow and yet kept stabbing him. Shaking her head, Juliana averted her glance. She'd seen people die, of wounds, of disease, from hanging, never from such malicious violence.

She deliberately turned her back on the body, returning her attention to the men around her father. Gray's voice rose above the others.

"I agree with you, Welles. We must think of who would want to kill my cousin and why. Neither I nor Arthur will rest until his killer is found."

"I've already questioned his squire," Hugo said. "The lad attended Edmund at bedtime last night and slept on a pallet in the chamber. But he's a heavy sleeper, and Edmund had shared an entire flagon of wine with him. When he woke this morn, his master was gone."

Gray glanced at Edmund's body, then at Arthur, who had said nothing and appeared to be dazed. "A foul crime, Welles. This isn't some brawl, some challenge over a slight or a feud. It's a crime of deep hatred. Only hatred makes a man attack the throat with a knife and then keep stabbing after the death blow has been struck."

"I hadn't thought of it that way," Hugo said. "I've questioned all my guards and knights, everyone who was about last night. No one heard anything."

"Then we must think upon who hated Edmund enough to want to murder him." Gray paused to glance around the small group of his knights and Hugo's. "Of those here, I can think of two with such cause—you, Welles, and your nephew."

Hugo sputtered. Richard drew himself up and launched into angry denials.

"If I had wished him dead," Richard said through his teeth, "I would have challenged him openly and run a lance through him."

Hugo pounded his chest. "Yes, I too. I should challenge you for such an insult, de Valence. If I quarrel with a man, I do it with honor."

"I know that, but who else had cause?" Gray asked.

Turning crimson, Hugo bellowed, "What cause?"

"It's one well known," Gray said, "but one about which I don't wish to speak before others."

Juliana shoved between two of her father's knights. "He means me."

"What are you doing here?" Hugo cried. "Get you back to your chamber, foolish daughter."

"Very well, Father, but you're forgetting the most important question."

Hugo vacillated between ridding himself of her interference and his curiosity. Curiosity won.

"What question? Tell me and then go."

"Who gains most by the death of Edmund Strange?"

Gray moved to stand beside Hugo and stared at her with a frown. She refused to look at him and continued.

"Who profits by his death?" she asked. The men around her were silent. "The one who becomes heir in his place."

Stunned silence filled the air. Arthur gawked at her, his mouth working. Hugo and Richard appeared intrigued, while Gray's entire body seemed to cloak itself in ice. A resentful mutter arose from the knights attending him.

Hugo cleared his throat and growled. "Juliana, you go too far, accusing a knight of such evil. Get to your chamber, girl."

Narrowing her eyes, she was about to refuse when Gray captured her arm.

"With your permission, Welles, I'll escort my own dear sovereign lady and return."

He put an arm around her shoulders with all the appearance of an attentive betrothed, and under the guise of sheltering her from sight of the body, shoved her out of the enclosure.

"God's blessing," he hissed as she resisted him, "I'll have a word with you, mistress thief. Remember our bargain."

An angry glance at Alice sent the maid scuttling in the opposite direction. Juliana yanked her arm free and marched back to the old keep. Before she reached the outer stairs, he caught her arm again and pulled her around the side between the walls of the tower and the kitchen. Losing what little patience she had, Juliana knocked his arm away and rounded on him. It was then that she noticed his expression. He was looking at her with the gravity of a priest hearing a confession he wished he could forget.

"What ails you?"

"What was in that concoction you tried to give Edmund when he first arrived?"

Avoiding his eyes, Juliana began to run her fingers through the masses of black locks that had fallen over her shoulders. "Naught."

"You and I reason alike."

Startled, she glanced up at him.

"You asked who gains from Edmund's death," he said. "I asked who had reason to wish him dead. There are profits other than riches. Revenge is one of them."

Her fingers contorted in her hair, and she whispered, "Thunder of God. You think I did it."

"Tell me you didn't, my joyance. After this day I'm not sure what you wouldn't do if you thought the cause just.

He did treat you evilly, and I know what you do to men who offend you."

He really thought her capable of this bloody violence, the fool. Let him. Offended, still furious at him for his earlier transgressions, Juliana grasped her skirts and swished away from him without a word. He ran after her, snagging her sleeve and pulling her up short.

"Damnation!" She jerked the fabric from his fingers.

"Give me an answer, Juliana, and I'll believe you."

"Oh, thank you, my sovereign lord, O great and omniscient judge of hearts. Thank you for promising to believe me if I tell you the truth."

"Now, Juliana—"

"Mother of God, you're a presumptuous arse." Breathing hard with the force of her indignation, she heard her own voice crackle with loud fury. "Of everyone in this castle, I hated Edmund Strange the most. He was a scheming bastard whose inconstancy and dishonor exacted a horrible cost from me. I wished a gut-rotting disease upon him. I hoped his man's parts shriveled. If he'd been drowning, I would have put anvils in his tunic. Make what you will of that, Sir Judge, and damnation to you."

Picking up her skirts again, Juliana noted with satisfaction the openmouthed dismay written on Gray's face. Sneering at him, she swept around the corner, up the stairs, and into the keep. Alice was waiting for her in the hall.

"Mistress, be you well? What happened?"

Juliana stomped down the hall and to the stairs of the Maiden's Tower. "Slavering devil's wight. False accuser. Witless troll."

"What's wrong?" Alice cried.

"He suspects me, *me*, of killing Edmund Strange."

Alice covered her mouth as she hurried at Juliana's side. "Oh, no."

At the dread in the maid's voice, Juliana stopped on the landing outside her chamber.

"What's happened?"

"That's why he—oh, no." Alice covered her mouth with her fingertips.

"Out with it," Juliana said. "By the reverence of God, I've no patience with quibbling."

"While you were looking at the—the . . ."

"Body, Alice, the body."

"Yes, mistress. While you were looking at it, he asked me if you'd been in your chamber last night. I said you'd been in your herb chamber. Then he asked if I was in the herb chamber too, and I said no."

"The sneaking, piss-ridden churl."

Juliana shoved open her chamber door with such violence that it banged against the wall. Stalking inside, she stopped in mid-curse to find the room inhabited by her sisters and Yolande. All three turned when she burst into the room and studied her in silence. Juliana stared back at them, her dark brows nearly meeting over her nose, foot tapping. Fixing Bertrade with a look that would have frightened a mad bear, she grew even more impatient when her sister quickly knelt before the small altar beside Juliana's bed and began whispering prayers.

"Well? What do you three want?"

Laudine and Yolande glanced at each other. Yolande nudged the older girl, who sighed and began.

"You've been ill?"

Juliana paced around the room, hands on her hips. "You know very well I haven't been ill. Do you want me to tell you what I've really been doing?"

"No, no."

Again Laudine glanced at Yolande. Yolande clasped her

hands together and rubbed one of her knuckles against her front teeth. Bertrade's prayers rose to an agitated buzz. Juliana looked from one to the other, then threw up her hands.

"For God's love, out with it. Such reticence isn't like you, Laudine."

Folding her arms over her substantial chest, Laudine lifted a brow. "Very well. We've come to ask you if . . ."

"Thunder of heaven! If what?"

Again the glance at Yolande.

"If—if you perchance quarreled with Edmund Strange and, and . . . perchance lost your temper and, and—"

"And shoved a knife into his throat?" Juliana bellowed. "By the blessed Trinity, how do you dare ask me such a thing?"

Bertrade whimpered and began chattering her prayers loudly. Yolande scurried behind Laudine, whose color was rising.

"Don't roar at me, Juliana Welles. We only asked so that we could help."

"Oh, then I suppose I should thank God for the labors my family takes for me." Juliana folded her arms over her chest and planted herself in front of Laudine. "Just because I become somewhat agitated when people annoy me doesn't mean I'm capable of murder, and it's a great heaviness that my own sisters and my dearest friend could think such evil of me."

Laudine sighed and gave Yolande a smiling glance of reassurance. "Then you didn't do it."

Tossing her head, Juliana said, "I didn't say that."

"For shame," Yolande said. "You're just being stubborn because we offended you, but we remember how you were when Edmund spurned you. You vowed to dose him with purgatives and secret herbs to make him impotent, and then you swore to—"

"I know what I said." Juliana turned her back to them.

Yolande straightened to her full height, low as it was, went to Juliana's side and touched her arm. "We haven't been allowed out of the keep since they found him, but we heard what happened. You must have been sickened by the sight of him. All that blood . . ." Yolande went on in a whisper that only Juliana could hear. "Blood in the sand, sand in his throat . . ." Yolande whispered a few more words, then covered her mouth and swayed, leaning against Laudine.

"Stop," Juliana hissed. "Saints give me patience, you're going to make me sick too."

Bertrade rose from the altar and joined them. "I pray God give you temperance and charity. We're only trying to help. Confession is the only way, Juliana."

Slowly Juliana turned around, inclining her head to the side like a hawk does when suddenly glimpsing its prey. Her damp hair swung across her face with the movement, and she fixed the three girls with a white-hot stare through its thickness.

"Holy hell!"

All three of them jumped at her ferocity. The exclamation seemed to rebound off the chamber walls. Cursing, Juliana sprang at them, and they scattered. Juliana snatched a water basin and threw it at them. It hit the wall beside the door as they retreated across the threshold.

"Interfering, faithless sows," Juliana called after them. "Close the door, Alice."

Alice had taken refuge in a corner. She obeyed and stood wringing her hands.

"Mistress, folk don't think you did the murder, do they?"

"I don't know if folk do, but that rutting, silver-haired

barbarian accused me, and you heard what my own sisters— God be merciful."

Wincing, Juliana rubbed her temples with the tips of her fingers and moaned. "Oh, all this misery has made my head ache. Heat some spiced wine, Alice, and add betony to it. I think there's some left in my healing box. And then pack for me. I'll not stay in this castle and endure suspicious looks and addled questions. It's not my fault if everyone's too blind to see that his brother had the most to gain from Edmund's death. I care not. Vyne Hill has gone too long without my attention, and I need privacy in which to think about—about . . ."

"My lord de Valence?"

Juliana scowled at the maid. "About this terrible murder."

"And your betrothed."

"No reason to think about him. I'll not marry a man who thinks me capable of murder. Now prepare that wine and speak no more of that lascivious churl."

Juliana sat on the bed, pressing her palms to the sides of her head in an effort to still its throbbing. She'd spouted brave words, but they were hollow. There was little choice for her as long as Gray threatened to expose Eadmer, Bogo, Warin, and Lambert. There must be a way to escape his grasp. She needed to think, and she couldn't think with him lurking around the castle. He would seek her out and ply her with the soft dove's-wing touch of his fingers, tempt her, lure her into succumbing—what was she thinking!

Thunder of heaven, she wanted him again. Visions of his body, the memory of his sweet breath on her neck evoked an onslaught of heat. Thick, steaming, turgid, it fed on her blood, spreading and enveloping her.

"You're an evil thing, Juliana Welles," she said to herself. "Lusting after that man when he's trapped you into marriage."

She still didn't trust his intentions, still suspected he would avenge himself on her by spurning her at the last moment. And now there was this terrible murder. It was no surprise to her that Edmund had gotten himself killed. A man with so many schemes and so much evil in his nature was bound to come to an evil end. But who could have done it? If folk really did suspect her, she would do well to try to think of someone else for them to accuse.

His brother Arthur was no doubt tainted with the same sinful nature. Perhaps he had done the deed. Gray had been incredulous at her accusation, but heirs had been murdered by jealous brothers many times. Hugo's days would now be spent in search of the murderer, but with Gray unwilling to suspect Arthur, the search might be futile.

How badly did Gray wish to protect his friend? He hadn't voiced his suspicions of her before others, but she knew how ruthless he could be. If he had cause, might he accuse her to save Arthur? No. She didn't want to believe that. Yet he had suspected her, accused her.

Alice handed her a cup of hot wine. Juliana sat back against the pillows, sipped the potion, and wished it would banish her confusion along with her headache. She was afraid. Not of being suspected, but of falling in love. No, that wasn't right. She was afraid that it was too late to stop herself from falling in love.

Gray de Valence infuriated her, insulted her, bullied her, and she wanted to kick him in his flat, hard stomach. But beneath all the fury and ill will lurked timorous, uncertain, and yet thrilling feelings; wide-eyed, fluttery, soft feelings. And searing, hot-breath, churning feelings that left her with an urge to claw his back and rake her teeth along his bare chest and belly. If only she could be sure of him. But how could she when she hardly knew him, despite their intimacy.

Pressing the cup against her forehead, Juliana sighed. She had committed a woman's most terrible sin, one of them anyway. The church condemned fornicators. If Clement knew, he would say that she should wipe out the sin by marrying Gray, but it was beyond her imagining that a man as wondrous as Gray de Valence would truly want to marry her.

"What am I going to do?"

"Mistress?"

"Oh, Alice, are you still here?"

"I be waiting to prepare the bed, mistress."

Juliana left the bed and huddled in the chilly window embrasure. It wasn't like her to be so confused. Everyone knew how strong-willed she was. She always knew what choice to make, never faltered over decisions, gave orders without hesitation. But all her decisiveness seemed to have vanished. No longer certain of her judgment, she feared she had fallen in love with a man who was secretly bent on destroying her. How was that possible? Perhaps it wasn't. Could she have lost all her wits? No. She hadn't suddenly lost her ability to judge men's character. Gray was annoying and ruthless, yes, but not vicious or evil. Was he?

"You're confused," Alice said as she pulled a gown from a chest at the foot of the bed.

Juliana gave her a rueful smile. "Yes, most confused."

"It's because he be a match for your famous temper, mistress."

"What are you talking about?"

"He stands up to you. Gives blow for blow and returns for more. When you two clash, the heavens be racked with thunderbolts. I always knew you'd never marry a man you could beat."

"Are you saying he's won?"

"No, but he hasn't lost, has he?"

Juliana began removing her gown with quick, agitated movements. "I'll never lie down under his boot, and don't you say I will."

"Never did."

"He hasn't bested me yet."

"No, mistress."

"And he won't."

"No, mistress."

"If he thinks he can make me do his bidding, he's got the wits of a mayfly. Gray de Valence isn't going to make a spectacle of me with his pretense of a betrothal and his foul suspicions. Go to bed, Alice. We'll start for Vyne Hill before dawn."

"Ah, then he's given you permission to go."

Juliana grabbed a pillow and hurled it at the maid. "Donkeys will sing and priests fly before I ask that Viking's permission. Get out."

The door shut. Juliana glared at it while she tried to strangle the covers. Then she got up to retrieve the pillow. Crawling into bed again, she lay on her back, arms folded, fuming. Even if Gray hadn't voiced his suspicions of her, even if he hadn't shamed her in front of the entire demesne of Wellesbrooke, she wouldn't marry him. Why? Because the rutting knave had ordered her to marry him, ordered.

No one commanded Juliana Welles, especially not some conceited rooster knight used to women quivering and swooning at the sight of him. She was going to show him that Juliana Welles submitted to no man.

Rue

Rue warded off disease, insects, witches, and all manner of evil things, including feebleness of sight and headache.

• *Chapter 18* •

THERE WAS A MURDERER LOOSE IN WELLES-brooke castle. Gray ran his fingers through his hair while he walked the length of his pavilion. Seated on folding stools, Arthur and Lucien were talking quietly while Imad prepared a late serving of wine and bread. Arthur's voice rose in distress, to be quieted by Lucien's soothing tones. Knowing the brothers' past, Gray hadn't expected his cousin to regret Edmund's death, but Arthur seemed genuinely grieved. Perhaps he sorrowed more for what he wished his brother had been than for what he really was.

And perhaps God had blessed the Strange family by replacing the older with the younger. Or perhaps Satan had taken one of his own to hell. Whatever the case, there were mundane tasks to be performed. Edmund's body had been moved. He would be buried quickly, to-morrow night, before the corpse could decay further. No time for ceremony, no time to bring the rest of the family here. His funeral would be as irregular as his character.

He should have been distressed for his aunt, Edmund's mother. He should have been consoling Arthur or search-ing for the culprit, but all he could do was pace and worry about Juliana. Gray spun around and stalked back to the other end of the pavilion. His route took him past the hangings of peacock green and blue, past a candle stand almost as tall as he was, past a table bearing the treasures with which Imad insisted he travel—a covered ewer of agate mounted in silver, ovoid gilt flasks for wine and water, enameled silver spoons.

Outwardly he appeared as hard and smooth as the surface of those utensils. Inside he still felt dazed with the discovery of Juliana's secret. And he was aghast at himself. On the ride back to Wellesbrooke with her in his arms his rage had faded. He had tried to keep hold of it, but he was holding Juliana, and her warm body and soft hair seemed to have a greater power than his anger. He had fought against this loss of rage, trying desperately to reject the idea that, in spite of his hurt, he couldn't endure the thought of not having Juliana. And she still wanted him, something he was sure she'd never admit.

It was still hard to believe that she was a bandit. Not an ordinary bandit, but one who—according to gossip—preyed on vainglorious knights in need of humbling. He had to admit that her victims included knights who were the embodiment of arrogance and pomposity. He could imagine what she must have thought of their strutting, puffed-up pleasure in their own existence.

He smiled to himself. He could think of a few men in need of Juliana's remedy for presumptuousness. His pacing had taken him to the corner where Lucien and Arthur sat. Arthur had lapsed into brooding silence.

"Lucien, you've reminded everyone not to reveal Mistress Juliana's little habit of playing bandit?"

With a glance at Arthur, Lucien stood and came over to Gray. "*Oui, messire,* they've been sworn to silence."

Gray closed his eyes and pinched the bridge of his nose and sighed. "I was furious with her, but . . . What Edmund did to her, she must have been deeply hurt." He sighed and glanced at Lucien. "I suppose I should be grateful that her vengeance upon all those men was as mild as it was."

Lucien snorted. "She should thank *le bon Dieu* you've stopped her before she came to harm."

"She's not thankful, Lucien."

"No, *messire.*"

"Now, what have you found out?"

The knight glanced at the silent Arthur, who appeared to be lost in his own thoughts. "Pardon, *messire*, but the news isn't good. Already talk has spread, rumor and speculation feed each other."

"What rumor?"

"That the one who hated Edmund the most was—"

"Juliana," Gray said. "Go on."

"Folk speak of her rage at him, of how she lets nothing and no one deny her will, of her promise to avenge herself upon him one day. She spoke of it—no, shouted it—after he spurned her. The talk is spreading rapidly, *messire*. The whole barony will be whispering the rumors by week's end."

"Curse it. She fed the gossip by lurking around the body and calling attention to herself." Gray threw up his hands. "And did she swoon or cry out like a gentle demoiselle? No, she made herself conspicuous by accusing my cousin of murder, thus making more than a few people think she had reason to divert suspicion from herself."

Arthur sighed, left his stool, and joined them. "She was right. I might have been the killer."

"Don't be a fool," Gray said. He studied his cousin, whose color wasn't good. "You should go to bed."

"I can't sleep, and you should realize how difficult our position is, cousin. Everyone was asleep last night when my brother was killed. I could have stolen out of my tent and killed him."

"So could anyone," Gray said. "So could Juliana."

"I regret to say, *messire*, that it appears that the lady's father is also fearful of just that possibility." Lucien shrugged. "The castle is brimming with such rumors."

"Hell's fire!" Gray pounded his fist against his thigh. "Her maid says she spent the night in her herb chamber, whatever that is. But no one saw her, so no one can vouch for her innocence. And her contrariness only adds to her appearance of guilt."

"She does have a fire-and-brimstone temper," Arthur said.

"*Oui*," Lucien said. "I've never seen such an adventurous demoiselle. *Mon Dieu*, when I think of how she robbed you of your garments and sent you back to the castle, er, most ungentle of her. Most un-Christian."

Gray fastened a chilly stare on the knight. Lucien covered his mouth, but Gray heard a snigger. He thought he heard a titter and glanced over his shoulder at Imad, who was placing wine on a serving tray. The youth's face was placid, immobile, but he avoided Gray's eyes.

Imad came to them bearing the tray. The flagon was of porphyry mounted in gold; the drinking vessels were mazers of silver-mounted boxwood. Imad refused to travel without such luxuries, insisting that Gray's position required them, and that having to serve from plain ceramic or wood was beneath him. Gray watched the youth closely for traces of amusement, but could find none in those almond-shaped black eyes. His thoughts returned to the dilemma of Juliana.

"Of course, she couldn't have done it," he said as Imad poured wine into his mazer.

Lucien and Arthur exchanged looks. "Of course," they said together.

"She was being obstinate when she ranted at me about how much she hated Edmund. She did it out of spite, but still . . ."

"Her manner is unfortunate," Arthur said.

Lucien swirled wine in his cup and nodded. "Indeed. If she remains silent about where she was and becomes furious if questioned, she appears guilty. Especially since her hatred of Edmund has been bruited about the countryside for months."

"Her willfulness and bitchy temper will ruin her," Gray said.

He frowned into the bowl of his mazer. How was he going to protect her when she didn't want his help? God, he was weary. This murder was the culmination of a day crowded with momentous happenings. He was still reeling from that encounter with Juliana in the cave—that explosion of pleasure in a sightless void—followed by the discovery of her foul offenses against him as the bandit. He'd made her pay for her transgressions, he would continue to do so, but he didn't want her falsely accused of murder. The thought of her in danger near drove him mad. And if she continued to go her contrary way, she would end up in some dungeon.

"Gray?"

"What? Oh, I'm sorry, Arthur. I was thinking."

"It's late. We should all take our rest. Good e'en, cousin."

He bid good night to Arthur and Lucien. Imad came forward to take his mazer.

"You haven't eaten, master."

"Not hungry."

He went to the arras that divided his bed from the rest of the pavilion and brushed it aside. Imad had fashioned his idea of a proper sleeping arrangement—a couch upholstered in Arabian silk, cushions and covers of brilliant hues, the finest of Stratfield furs, miniver and fox. He sank down on the couch, then got up and shoved a pile of pillows off it. Imad had followed him and knelt to retrieve the expensive cushions. Gray sighed and tugged on a lock of Imad's black hair. He could talk to the boy as he could to few others. They had shared a place in hell. When he first met Imad, he had vowed to save him from destitution and slavery as he himself had not been saved.

"You're feeling well?" he asked gently.

Imad looked up at him, his arms full of pillows. "Yes, master. Mistress Juliana has taken excellent care of me. Did you know she even gives her herbs to passing beggars and peddlers? This unholy land allows its women too much liberty."

"Mistress Juliana would physic the devil himself if he came to her door. I'm worried about her, Imad. Everyone will forget her kindness. Do you think they'll remember how she drags herself out of bed and into the dark, no matter how cold, despite storms or snow, to care for sick peasants? The whole barony has benefitted from her skills, but will anyone remember that once these rumors take hold?"

"That is a danger, master." Imad stood and set the pillows aside.

"Damnation, she's going to make her own ruin."

"Yes, master."

"I've sworn my men to silence, but if anyone finds out she's this stripping bandit . . ."

"A most unhappy possibility."

"If it becomes known, then everyone will realize that she can handle weapons better than most women and steal in and out of guarded places, and folk will say how fierce she must be to behave so."

Imad knelt in front of him and gripped one of his boots. Out of habit Gray let him pull it off.

"And she grows more and more peevish, damnably irritable, thus fostering the appearance of guilt. The talk will get worse."

"When the truth is that Mistress is mostly annoyed with you."

Imad pulled off the other boot and set it beside its mate. Gray stared at him.

"How do you know that?"

"I have seen it in the stars, O master. Fate has ordained that your constellations meet and merge. Even though you're both unbelievers. You and Mistress are like the fire stars that clash in the heavens and rain showers of gold upon the earth."

"You mean we fight all the time. But it's her fault."

"Of course, master."

"It is! I would have been generous, sweet-tempered, chivalrous, but she has been obdurate from the beginning, the very beginning. Remember, she threw mud at me."

"I remember, master."

Gray glanced down at Imad suspiciously. "And now her evil temper and spiteful ways have put her in danger. She has to be protected from herself."

"Women are always in need of guidance."

"Especially this one," Gray said.

He rested his forearms on his knees and thought in silence for a while. Imad arranged the covers on the couch and began extinguishing candles.

"Imad, before you retire, tell Lucien and Arthur we're rising early tomorrow morn. Have them prepare to leave Wellesbrooke quickly and quietly, before dawn." He lay back on the couch and propped one leg on his knee. "I have to make her tell me the truth, make her see she has to stop behaving as though she's capable of murder."

"Yes, master."

"She must be stopped, Imad. She can't skulk about the castle and the demesne alone with a killer abroad. She's going to learn the manners of a gentle lady, and I think she'll take her lessons better at Stratfield, away from her servants and the protection of her father."

"But master, her father will come after you."

"Not if I marry her."

Imad inclined his head. "Thy wisdom is unbounded, O great master."

"You won't think so for long," Gray said. "You're coming along this time."

"Me? In the wilderness? Oh, master, you know I hate rough travel. I can follow with the baggage, at a sedate pace that doesn't kick up clouds of dust and jar my bones."

"You're coming, so be ready. Mistress Juliana is going to be furious, and I'm counting on you to keep watch over her when I can't. Otherwise I'll find myself standing in front of the priest with no bride."

He stopped at the sound of a hail. Imad went outside; Gray rose from the couch and emerged from the sleeping enclosure when the servant returned with Hugo Welles. Concealing his surprise, Gray offered wine and a cushioned stool, both of which his host refused. Hugo planted himself in the middle of the pavilion, thick arms thrust behind his back, his jaw thrust forward like a belligerent hound and proceeded to make courtly conversation. He talked of the hunt, of hawking, of the young king's health, until Gray set aside the mazer of wine he'd been nursing and confronted him.

"Is something wrong, Welles?"

The jaw jutted like the head of a war axe. "Wrong, wrong, wrong? What could be wrong? A knight has been murdered while under my roof. Naught is wrong. Of course something's wrong. Er—you were gone a long time today."

"Yes, chasing that bandit."

"Thought you caught that fool Eadmer, didn't you?"

"A misunderstanding by my men." Gray eyed Hugo, whose gaze slid away from his. "You're not concerned about bandits."

"Juliana was in her chamber all day. Her maid said she was ill, and the night before, she was in the herb chamber. But no one saw her. Even Juliana doesn't usually lurk in dark corners so much. I wish . . ."

"Yes?"

Hugo slanted his gaze in Gray's direction. "The whole demesne is full of talk about you and my daughter."

"No doubt they're right glad for our happiness," Gray said in his most courtly manner.

"You're a young man, de Valence. Young and full of vigor. I know what it is to be a young stallion in need of a mare. Now that we've arranged the betrothal, I can be tolerant."

"Welles, what are you talking about?"

Gray watched Hugo's face turn burgundy. "The devil take you, de Valence. I'm talking about my daughter's absences. No! Don't say anything. I don't want you to speak, and I especially don't want you to deny anything. I'm telling you that I think that, for my daughter's sake, I'll be tolerant." Hugo rocked on his heels and glared at Gray. "As long as the marriage takes place, I'll keep silent about it. I don't want to know where she went with you today—*or last night*. Do you understand?"

"But last night I—"

"Hold your tongue!"

Gray looked at Hugo closely, then whispered, "You think she did it."

"I don't understand you, and don't wish to speak of it."

"You're so afraid, you're trying to divert suspicion."

Hugo drew himself up. His brows crashed together as he said, "I would never engage in such a dishonorable course. Are you saying you haven't pursued my daughter after the antics I've witnessed?"

"No."

"Are you saying you haven't had intimate encounters with my Juliana?"

"You're right, Welles. I should hold my tongue."

"Then I'm right. Juliana spent much of her time today with you."

"Aye."

"And last night as well."

Gray turned away and began pouring more wine into his mazer. "Perhaps." He was surprised when Hugo strode swiftly over to him and placed a wide hand on his arm.

"You're betrothed to her, de Valence. Therefore Exodus doesn't quite apply. You know, 'And if a man entice a maid that is not betrothed, and lie with her, he shall surely endow her to be his wife.' So long as you marry her . . ."

"You're afraid for her," Gray said quietly.

"I've said nothing, nor will I." Hugo's complexion had regained its customary ruddy hue. "Just marry her, quickly, and take her to Stratfield."

"I was thinking the same thing."

"Then we're agreed."

"But what if she did mur—"

Hugo bellowed at him before he could finish. "By the Trinity! Hold your tongue or I'll cut it out."

He was wine-colored again. Gray drew away from him and favored his host with a remote stare.

"You should labor to curb that temper. Someday you're either going to bellow yourself into a fit or annoy someone without my Christian restraint. Oh, don't bother to argue with me. Due to this evil occurrence I was considering speeding up the marriage plans. However, Juliana is as inflexible as ever."

"God's curse on her. You're right." Hugo began to rock on his heels again. "I'll order her to consent."

"How often does she follow your orders?"

Rubbing his chin, Hugo seemed incapable of words.

"I may need to use—persuasion," Gray said.

Their eyes met in understanding, and Hugo grinned.

"I knew you were the match for my Juliana. By the reverence of God, de Valence, that girl has been a trial to me since she was born. She was stubborn in the womb. Refused to be born. Three weeks late she was, and when she was little, she used to wheedle and coax me into allowing her treats. But then when she got older, whew! The longer she remained unwed, well, the more she went her own way. I was remiss in not making her accept another husband before now. Perhaps she wouldn't have become so headstrong."

"Some arse would have tried beating her, and she wouldn't have tolerated that. She would have . . ."

Neither of them wanted to complete the thought. They looked away from each other. Hugo cleared his throat.

"Yes, well, then we're agreed."

"Tomorrow morning we'll go to her together," Gray said. "We'll put it about that I fear for my betrothed's safety and thus want to put forward the marriage date."

"She'll refuse."

"And we'll argue, but everyone's accustomed to that, so when I toss her over my shoulder and carry her off, it will surprise no one."

"Carry her off? What need is there for such a display? I but asked you to—"

"Welles, I'll only carry her to Friar Clement's cave. He can marry us. I've already talked to him about Juliana.

Besides, I have a method of persuasion that will work with your daughter."

"What is it, by God? I have need of such a method."

"It wouldn't avail you."

Hugo sighed, but didn't inquire further.

"After the marriage, I'll take Juliana to Stratfield. Once she's left Wellesbrooke and ceased to call attention to herself, all this evil talk will fade."

"Not if I don't find a murderer," Hugo said as he shook his head.

"I've been thinking about that." Gray glanced at Hugo out of the corner of his eye. "You have been plagued by this foul stripping bandit of late. He and his minions are the most likely criminals about. If Edmund discovered him engaged in some act of thievery, and they fought, he could have killed my cousin to save himself."

"But the stripping bandit has never even wounded anyone."

"Do we know that for a certainty?"

"No, but he's never come into the castle either."

"He was growing more and more bold as time went on, or he wouldn't have risked robbing me."

"True."

"So it only makes sense that the real culprit might be this stripping bandit, and that he's already fled the barony in fear for his life."

Hugo gave a loud whoop and clapped Gray on the back. "Right wondrous, de Valence. A noble course of reasoning, and so much more believable than all this foolish talk about, well, all this foolish talk."

"I thought you'd like it."

Rubbing his hands, Hugo strode toward the tent entrance. "I'll consult my steward and my marshal at once. They're sure to agree with you. I knew there had to be an answer. I knew someone else was responsible."

"Good e'en to you, Welles."

"What? Oh, yes, God give you rest." Hugo disappeared, but Gray could still hear him.

"Why didn't I think of the bandit? Of course. A most convincing explanation. The bandit, of course."

Gray allowed his shoulders to slump once Hugo was out of sight. Sinking his head in his hands, he thought about what had just happened. Hugo Welles suspected his own daughter of killing Edmund. Was it just suspicion, or had he discovered proof of Juliana's guilt? After all, she wasn't the only one to be spurned by Edmund. No one had suggested that little Yolande might have killed him.

Juliana couldn't have done it, not the loving, innocent firebird he'd made love to in that cave. Hugo was making the mistake of thinking that because he and Juliana shared quick tempers, they also shared blood thirst. Surely that wasn't true. Women could be fierce, and Juliana was one of the fiercest. Women guarded manors and defended besieged castles against armies. This he knew. And Juliana had already taken up arms, but not in defense.

He hadn't been serious in suggesting that the bandit was guilty, only hoping for a temporary distraction. But Hugo had jumped on the opportunity to offer a credible substitute for his daughter, a known thieving knave. Even now he was probably announcing the bandit's guilt to his knights. Gray stared at the flap through which Hugo had vanished.

"Yes, Welles, that's what I fear the most—that it was the bandit who killed my cousin."

Rosemary

The flowers put in a chest among clothes or books prevented moths. Rosemary leaves boiled in white wine and applied to the face made it fair. Leaves under the bed's head delivered a sufferer from evil dreams.

• Chapter 19 •

BEHIND THE MANOR HOUSE AT VYNE HILL, THE kitchen garden was flooded with sunlight, and for once the cold wind had died down and allowed the air to warm. Women hoed and weeded in rectangular planting beds while several girls watered. Juliana walked along the rows of plants while consulting a journal in which she'd listed the proposed contents of the garden. Alice followed with a box containing quills, ink, and water, sneezing periodically.

Juliana walked down the path between two rows of beds, then turned and surveyed the garden. A fat black and yellow bee flew by; its buzz harmonized with the women's chatter. Making a mark by an item on her list, Juliana ran the feathered end of her quill down the page.

"I think we've got all the cooking herbs either planted or stored for sowing. Let me see, anise, basil, dittany. Did we bring mallows? Ah, yes, now I remember. And the tansy of course. Yes, that's everything at last. Did you set out those pots of rosemary, Alice?"

"Ah—ahchoo! Oh, yes, mistress."

Juliana closed the journal and handed the quill to Alice. After arriving this morning, she'd tried to avoid thinking about her predicament with Gray and Edmund's murder by keeping herself busy. But in brief moments between giving orders or while supervising repairs, confusion brimmed to the surface. She was furious with herself, for some time during the night she'd accepted her love for Gray without really understanding it or him. She hardly knew the man. Her heart was perverse, her body a traitor to her will.

She was furious with herself for joining the ranks of weak-kneed damsels who sighed behind kerchiefs whenever Gray de Valence appeared. She was furious at herself for longing for the touch of a man whose heart was full of deceit. She was furious at herself for loving him when he treated her like a—a milk maid in need of a tumble. And most of all she was furious at him for getting the better of her.

"Alice," Juliana said as she glared at a discarded hoe. "I won't be trampled beneath his boot."

"Whose boot, mistress?" Alice covered her nose with a kerchief and stifled a sneeze.

"He's worse than Yolande and my sisters. I cannot believe he suspected me of—" Juliana glanced around at the women in the garden and lowered her voice to a whisper. "Of murdering Edmund. The evil-minded lout. I was as confounded as everyone else when I found out, but no doubt he thinks I should be as whimpery and pale as Yolande at the idea."

Behind the kerchief, Alice murmured some comment, but Juliana was lost in recalling Yolande's distressed remarks. At the time she'd been too furious to do more than rant at the three girls, and Yolande deserved the chastisement most of all for being such a coward. She had nearly swooned when she described poor Edmund's body and how the sand that had spilled into the wound at his throat had been dark from his blood.

"Humph." Juliana kicked a clod of dirt. "Weak livered and witless. Why, I saw the body myself, and I didn't grow all jittery and addled like a . . ." Juliana's voice trailed off. She stared past Alice at the brick wall around the kitchen garden. "I don't believe it."

"What, mistress?"

She blinked and dragged her gaze back to Alice. "Oh, naught. Now, um, let me see . . . where is that list of repairs?"

Someone called her name. Eadmer ran across the garden and skidded to a stop, nearly slipping on the gravel that had been laid on the path.

"Mistress, little Jacoba, she be taken ill again." He paused to catch his breath. "Her mother begs you to come."

Taking time only to fetch her healing box, Juliana ran to the village; it was quicker than waiting for her horse to be caught and saddled. Little Jacoba had gotten better since Juliana had sent remedies for her. What had happened?

Jacoba's parents lived in a house near the old Norman church. Juliana hopped from stone to stone across the ford in the stream and hurried down the dusty track between a row of houses until she came to the church and its graveyard. Children scurried out of her way, and she nearly collided with a farmer and his hay cart. Beyond the church lay a thatched house sheltering beneath the branches of an apple tree. A small crowd of women and old men had gathered in front of the house. A woman hovered at the door and waved to her. Jacoba's mother.

"What's wrong?" Juliana asked as she pressed by the curtsying woman and entered the dark cottage.

"Oh, mistress, I tried to keep her quiet, but this morn she started chasing the chickens, she did. High spirits, that's what did it."

Jacoba lay on a pallet near the central fire. The house was large, but had only one room in which the family slept, ate, and worked. Other pallets were rolled up and stacked in a corner. Tools hung on the walls while sacks of grain huddled beneath a rickety shelf. From the fire, smoke curled up toward a hole in the roof, but much of it remained in the room. The mother began waving her apron to keep the smoke away from Jacoba. The child was coughing violently.

Kneeling beside the girl, Juliana opened her healing box and plucked a ceramic bottle from it. She pulled out the stopper, waited for the coughing to ebb, then held the vessel to Jacoba's lips. She kept it there until the bottle was empty. Jacoba swallowed the last of the potion, coughed, and licked her lips. Dark brown hair was plastered to her brow. Her skin was almost transparent while her cheeks were flushed. Only four, she was one of those children whose eyes seemed too large for her head. She began to cough again.

"Come, little mite," Juliana said. "Let me help you sit. There." Looking around, she saw a stool and brought it to the child. "I want you to sit before this stool and prop your arms on the seat. That's good. Now, rest your head on your arms. You see? That feels better, doesn't it?"

Jacoba smiled weakly and nodded. Juliana stroked the child's hair while she waited for her potion to begin its work. Gradually the coughing eased. When Jacoba seemed calm, Juliana rose, picked up her healing box, and went outside with the mother. Retrieving a bag from the box, she handed it to the woman.

"You were right. She's an active child and hasn't rested enough after her illness. This is elecampane, horseheal. I've already prepared it, so you may mix it with watered wine. I'll send some from the manor. It will help get rid of the foul humors in her chest and lungs." Juliana handed the mother another bag. "Make rosemary tea for her. It should—"

A sudden rumble distracted her. They both turned and looked toward the ford in time to see a destrier plunge into the water and send a great fan of water spraying into the air. Through the spray of water Juliana saw a flash of emerald-green pennant blazoned with a gold dragon. She groaned.

"Not him again."

Hooves thundered, armor and weapons set up a din as the riders galloped down the path. At their head rode Gray de Valence, resplendent in emerald and silver surcoat over light mail. He had shoved back the mail cap from his head, and the sheen on his armor was almost as bright as his hair. Juliana watched him toss his head to shake a lock from his eyes. For a moment her imagination summoned visions of this man—wearing animal skins and iron instead of silk and steel—sailing a long ship with a high, curving prow and square sail.

Setting her jaw, she quelled the shiver of excitement that darted through her and banished the barbaric vision. How could she allow herself to lose all composure merely at the sight of the man riding his damned horse? She marched to the low fence that surrounded Jacoba's house and stopped at the gap at the front; she set the healing box on the ground and straightened as Gray rode past.

He saw her, shouted, and wheeled his mount. Leading his men in a circle, he rode to her, hauled on the reins, and slid from the saddle before his horse had stopped. Juliana sneezed as dust billowed up. Waving the clouds away, she kept her gaze fixed on him while he stalked over to her. She glanced behind her to see that the group before the house was staring at him and whispering. Turning back, Juliana was about to launch into battle with him when Gray suddenly grasped her hand and bent over it. All she could do was stare when he kissed her fingers.

"God be thanked that I've found you, Mistress Juliana," he said loudly enough for their listeners to hear. "Are you well?"

Juliana stared at him without speaking. Keeping hold of her hand, Gray stepped closer and gave her a smile so unctuous and solicitous that it banished whatever words she'd summoned as an answer.

"My dear sovereign lady," he said in that same loud and attentive tone, "your father and I went to your chamber to speak with you this morn and found you gone. You have caused your family and me great distress by leaving so precipitously when there's a murderer about."

Lashes fluttering, Juliana looked down at their joined hands, then recovered herself. She tried to pull her hand away from his, but his fingers tightened, and he slipped his free arm around her shoulders. Each struggled to gain the advantage while attempting to conceal their efforts from the onlookers. He kept his smile plastered in place even as she elbowed him in the ribs.

"Dear Mistress Juliana, have no fear. Your father has sent me to keep you safe while he searches for the one who killed my cousin."

"What?"

Her voice squeaked, and she went still.

"My men will search the area around Vyne Hill. Your father is convinced that the culprit is that whoreson stripping bandit who's been preying on the barony for so long."

"Thunder of heaven!" Juliana began to pull on her captured hand again. "What have you—"

"Have courage, my sweet demoiselle," he said as he pulled her close to thwart her struggles. Once they were close, he hissed at her. "Saints and sinners, woman, be quiet, or do you want Vyne Hill to suspect you of murder too?" Aloud he said, "Come, we must speak of how your father discovered the guilt of this evil knave."

Gray inclined his head in the direction of the villagers. "God save you, good people."

"God save your lordship."

"God curse you," Juliana growled, but her imprecations were cut off when he suddenly mounted his horse and pulled her up into his lap. He launched into a gallop that nearly unseated her. Her arms flew out and then clutched at him.

"Hold on, or you'll end up in the dirt," he said, that same obsequious smile lurking about his lips.

She had little choice, so she gripped his belt and the horse's mane until they reached the manor courtyard. His men barreled after them, sending geese and chickens fluttering and honking in all directions at their thunderous invasion. All at once Juliana found herself lifted and dropped to the ground. She landed on her feet with a jolt. Gray dismounted and snatched up her hand. No longer smiling, his air of solicitous concern gone, he walked into the hall so rapidly that she nearly had to run to keep up. Inside he paused by her steward.

"Where is my lady's chamber?"

Piers's jaw worked soundlessly, and he pointed up the wooden stair at the other end of the hall. Before Juliana could protest, Gray pulled her after him up the stairs. She was too busy fumbling with her skirts to keep from tripping to protest. He opened the door to her room and plunged inside. A few more of those long-legged strides brought them to the bed. There Gray stopped and gently swung her around so that she bounced against the mattress and sat to catch her balance.

By now Juliana's hair had come loose from the caul that held it and tumbled about her face. She blew and clawed at it with her fingers. She stood up, but he touched her shoulder with one finger, which was enough to tip her back on the bed. Hands on his hips, legs planted apart, he stood in front of her. He still wasn't smiling, and when he spoke, his voice was silky and cool, like the skin of a viper.

"We had an agreement."

Juliana glared at him even as she felt an internal shiver. This man looked as if he could chop her neck with a war axe and sing while he did it.

"You had an agreement. I was forced." She gasped when he poked her chest with a forefinger.

"You gave your word, you faithless obstinate." He straightened and looked down at her as if she were a piece of muck among the floor rushes. "Do you know what you've done? No, because you never think about the price of your headstrong, peevish behavior. Your father and I went to your chamber and couldn't find you. The whole castle knew about it in moments, and do you know what everyone thought? They thought you'd fled because you killed my cousin."

Juliana gaped at him.

"What, no words, no curses? What a marvel. If your father and I hadn't put about a story about the stripping bandit, news of your guilty flight would be spreading throughout the demesne by now. Don't you realize that your hatred of my cousin is well-known?"

"He was a—"

"Holy hell."

The words were said softly, like a verbal caress, and they frightened her. Juliana bit her lip and peered up at him through a screen of black hair. Her father's rages didn't compare to the wrath she now witnessed. Wolves don't make a great noise when they stalk for the kill. That was it—Gray's quiet iciness signaled an intent far more threatening than any she or Hugo could manage with their shouting. Without saying a word, Gray conveyed a menace she was sure he would fulfill. And she could have sworn he grew taller. His long fingers strayed to a dagger shoved into his sword belt. They caressed the shining gold hilt.

"You listen to me, Juliana Welles. And I mean listen. I don't want to hear one word from those pretty rose lips. Even your father suspects you of killing Edmund. Ah, that shocks you. Good. Rumors have spread that you threatened my cousin's life."

Juliana swore at him and tried to stand, but he planted a knee beside her hip and nearly straddled her as he grabbed her shoulders and brought his face close to hers.

"By God, you're going to tell me the truth."

The words were said calmly, as though he'd seen into the future and was merely telling it, but his rapid breathing and that gaze that seemed transfixed on her lips disturbed her. His hand left her and strayed to his dagger again. Swallowing hard, she watched his fingers stroke the weapon. Then they strayed to her temple. They fluttered and skimmed down her cheek to her throat like a gentle summer breeze. Unable to move, Juliana realized that she was having trouble summoning the strength to breathe.

He was so close that his breath disturbed the fine wisps of hair at her temples. "Did you kill my cousin, my joyance?"

At the endearment, Juliana's brows drew together, and at last she woke from the daze into which his very nearness had cast her. Gray saw her expression—and chuckled. Unable to believe what she heard, she was caught off guard when he bent her backward and pressed her to the mattress. His lips brushed her cheek and trailed down her throat.

Before she could push him away, his teeth raked a path from her shoulder up the back of her neck. Stings of arousal jabbed through her, robbing her of reason and speech. He murmured another demand, but she couldn't find her voice because his teeth were skimming down her neck and his hands had captured her breasts. The onslaught was so sudden and so complete she had no chance to defend against it.

He said something to her, but blood was rushing in her head and ears. His fingers pinched her nipples, and she made a sound at last, a cry that made him capture her mouth and plunge inside it. She sank into a well of bright, hot arousal. Her hands ran over his body only to meet cloth and chain mail. He must have sensed her frustration, for he clasped her hands and brought them to his hair. Her fingers tangled in soft locks.

Gray seemed bent on kissing the soul from her body. He tasted of wine and smelled of leather and horse. The air seemed to grow thicker and warmer the longer they kissed. When his hand strayed between her legs, she groaned. Her gown was up around her hips. Holding himself so that he didn't crush her, Gray kept her mouth busy while he loosened the ties of his clothing. She felt him shift briefly, using his formidable strength, but his long hair was in her eyes and his teeth were biting her lips.

He lowered himself again, and this time she felt his heat between her legs. Rigid strength touched her, slid against her, drove her. She clawed at his back. Her fingers worked in the fabric of his surcoat as he gently rubbed against her.

Finally she lost all patience, clamped her hands on his buttocks and rammed him to her. He understood. Rising slightly, he shifted his hips and plunged into her, rocking and stabbing with sharp, short movements. Juliana pushed back while shoving him into her. They worked together, grabbing pleasure and gorging themselves on it until first she and then he cried out at its churning culmination.

He gasped and strained against her, then collapsed on top of her. Juliana felt his hot cheek against hers, and stroked his hair. Gradually their panting ceased. She could feel him inside her, still hard and twitching, when he lifted his head and looked down at her.

"Now, my joyance," he murmured. "Tell me you didn't kill my cousin and then I'll set about marrying you."

Her cry of outrage originated deep in her belly and rebounded off the walls, making him wince and take in his breath with a hiss.

"Don't squeeze me like that."

Juliana bucked beneath him. He hastily pulled free of her, rolled away, and stuffed himself back inside his clothing. She shoved her skirts down, feeling wet and sticky. Scrambling to the floor, she picked up a pitcher and hurled it at him. Gray ducked, and it crashed against the door. Shards flew in all directions, but Juliana paid no heed. She was already throwing the basin that had sat beside the pitcher.

"Juliana, you stop that at once!"

He dodged the flying basin, which nearly hit his head as he backed toward the door. He reversed his course but stopped when she picked up a stool. As she raised it over her head, he danced away from her and opened the door.

"Evil-tempered shrew."

"Lying seducer!"

Juliana hurled the stool at him, but all it hit was the door as it closed behind him. She picked up a candlestick and its holder and raced to the door in time to hear a click. She jiggled the latch. It wouldn't open. Using the brass candlestick holder, she pounded the oak panels.

"Gray de Valence, you open this door," she shouted.

"Verily, I will. Once you've curbed that witch's temper

of yours. Remember our agreement, my joyance. You're to adopt right gentle and biddable ways as befits my betrothed. Prove to me that you have, and you can come out. Until then, you'll remain in your chamber. It may take a while, but you and I are going to come to an understanding about how a wife behaves to her husband. Then I'm going to send for Friar Clement, and we'll be married. Fare you well for now, my love."

Uttering the loudest bellow she'd ever managed in her life, Juliana pounded the door until the violence of her blows caused her to lose her grip on the candlestick. It flew out of her hand and clattered across the floor. Breathless, hot, and helplessly furious, she watched it roll in a circle. After a while she noticed that her hands were stinging. She looked down at them. They were bruised and bleeding.

She studied the door; he was gone. He had locked her in her own chamber in her own manor. And he was going to make her marry him. God, he'd exploited her desire for him and then asked her if she'd killed a man. If she married him, she would spend her life trying to escape the dominance of his will and his body. She'd never win against both.

To think only this morning she had been wavering in confusion over her desire for him. But no more. She'd rather spend her life alone than on her knees before Gray de Valence.

Yarrow

This herb was used to stop the flow of blood from wounds, for headaches, for heartburning, and for he that could not hold meat.

• Chapter 20 •

JULIANA STRODE ABOUT HER CHAMBER, HER pace quick with agitation, rage, and regret. God was punishing her for her sinful lust. Did not the Bible go on and on about temptation?

"'Abstain from fleshly lusts, which war against the soul,'" she muttered.

Her route took her around the bed past a long clothes chest at its foot. She paid no attention to her surroundings until she kicked something on the floor and it rolled —the rounded bottom half of the pitcher she'd thrown at Gray. She stared at it and blushed even in her anger as she remembered the way his lust had vanquished his resolve to question her. Lust. To think she inspired lust in such a magnificent man. And how quickly he regained his domineering manner once it was slaked, the false-hearted craven. Magnificent, yes, but deceitful.

There was a noise outside, the sound of a key turning in a lock. Juliana cursed and glanced around the room. She'd destroyed most of the objects useful for throwing. Snatching up the fragment of the pitcher, she heard Gray call her name and hesitated. *He's coming back. What if I succumb to sin again?* Without thinking, she raced to the clothing chest, lifted the lid, and jumped in on top of some of her best gowns, the rounded shard still clutched in her hand. She lay on her side and was peeping through the crack between the lid and the chest when Gray came in.

He'd changed into a crimson tunic held in place by a black leather belt. Hose and kid boots encased those long legs, their strength evident in the play of muscles beneath their covering. In these simple garments he looked more the noble knight than many men in their expensive gowns bordered with fur and gold embroidery. Why couldn't he appear as evil as he behaved?

Gray was looking around the room. Then he smiled, leaned his back against the door, and folded his arms while shaking his head. "I know you're furious with me, but just how many places are there to hide in this chamber? Come, Juliana, it's not like you to be so witless."

Her face burned as she heard the condescending tone in his voice. After debauching her in her own manor while suspecting her of murder, he was treating her like a child! Her hands tightened into fists, but the one in her right hand closed around ceramic smoothness.

"Come out," Gray said. "If I have to search under the bed and in the chests, I'll turn you over my knee when I find you."

Juliana lost what shreds of her temper were left. Shoving back the lid, she sprang from the chest, the fragment gripped in a cocked arm. As she rose and drew back her arm, there was a knock. Then everything seemed to slow down. Too late she saw Gray turn to open the door; at the same time, she tripped on the hem of her gown, throwing off her aim. Too late she realized what would happen. She was already throwing the shard.

"No, don't move!" she screamed.

Gray's arm stretched out across the door panel, and the shard cracked against the wood next to it, splintering and sending a flake stabbing into the back of his wrist. Horrified, Juliana stood in the chest, unable to move as he cursed and jerked his hand from the door. He pulled out the flake. Its point was crimson with his blood. Gray ignored the wound as Imad darted into the room, glanced at them both, muttered something in Arabic, and then said, "The mistress left this in the village." He set down her healing box and lifted Gray's hand.

"A small cut, master."

While Imad searched for a bandage from her healing box, neither of them spoke. After glancing at Imad, Gray raised his jewellike gaze to her.

"Wait there, my joyance. That chest will make a good seat when I turn you over my knee. Oh, don't look so shocked. I'll send Imad away before I lift your skirt."

Her blood heated and shot in boiling waves to her face. Juliana vaulted out of the chest, slammed the lid, and rounded on him, her voice shaking.

"By all the demons in hell, I'll not endure this. You seek to make me your slave."

"What?" His tone was at once startled and bewildered.

She rushed on, impelled by the need to rid herself of this pain with words. "I'll not have it, do you hear? I'd sooner marry a leper than spend my life groveling at your feet or enslaved and—and performing for your pleasure."

His lips moved, slightly apart, and his gaze shifted, lowering to his wrist. Imad had been pressing a bandage over the cut but had frozen at their exchange. The length of cloth dropped to the floor. In the stillness Juliana felt the sudden change in him without understanding its cause. Then he looked up at her.

His gaze was filled with astonished hurt. He shook his head and spoke in a broken voice. "*Enslave*, you think I'm capable of such a thing when I— I thought there was more between us than . . . than desire. I thought you understood what I am. But I was a fool to think you looked beyond the outward guise—and simply liked me."

In but a moment Juliana's righteous anger disappeared. The unfortunate choice of a word had wounded him as no sword or dagger could, and she had been the one to hurt him. Pain stabbed through her as she realized what that one word must mean to him, the degradation and suffering, the shame.

"No," she whispered as tears blurred her sight. "I didn't really mean . . ." She lost her courage in a wave of remorse.

"Um, if you put yarrow on the wound . . ." She tried to begin again, but he was gone, quietly slipping out the door and closing it with elaborate care. Juliana was left to plead with the polished oak. "I didn't mean it."

That look, it haunted her. All composure, all mastery, even his chill reserve had been ripped from him, laying bare tortured and suffering radiance. She'd wanted to win against him, not shred his soul. It had never occurred to her that she held the power to do it.

She was still standing beside the chest, oblivious to anything but her misery. How could she have been so reckless? She should have understood what that word would do to him. A clatter distracted her, or she would have burst into tears of regret. Imad had closed the healing box and was setting it on a table. Straightening his flowing robe, he came to her, held out his hand, and guided her away from the chest. Juliana covered her face with her hands while he set about clearing the chamber of broken pottery and upset furnishings, his expression impassive. She was crying silently when he spoke.

"He saved my life."

Juliana stopped crying and peered at the youth through her fingers.

Imad knelt on the floor and plucked shards from beneath the bed. He kept his eyes lowered, his tone flat. "I was surviving by thievery on the streets of Alexandria, a scrawny, filth-ridden little asp. I tried to cut his purse, and he caught me. His guards would have beheaded me, but he forbade it and begged Saladin to allow him to keep me. I wasn't grateful until later, when he persuaded the master not to sell me to a brothel. He still won't tell me how he did it."

"I can cure scores of ailments," Juliana said. "But I can't cure myself of my evil temper. In truth, no one has ever made me so angry."

Imad straightened and sat back on his heels to regard her with solemn black eyes. "I have remained silent by his command, O divine mistress of beauty. But you and he are like two lions, each with majestic temperament and deadly claws. He had begun to sheathe his, or he wouldn't have concocted this tale of the bandit's being the murderer."

Juliana felt a muscle in her jaw quiver. "I didn't kill him."

"He knows that, O light of the world, in spite of your pretense otherwise. But you don't know what a battle he fought to put aside his rage at having been stripped and paraded before strangers at your hands. Did you never think that such a thing would repeat the humiliations he suffered as a slave?"

Juliana's knees turned to water. She sank down on the chest at the foot of the bed. "Oh, no."

Imad began putting shards on a tray while she contemplated the evil she'd done to Gray's pride. He carried about him such an air of stately composure; it concealed wounds of shame barely healed, and she'd ripped them open.

"Tell me what happened to him," she said.

Imad rose smoothly and put the tray on the bed. "I cannot, mistress. If I did, he wouldn't hurt me, but he would send me away, and suffer great sorrow at my betrayal. I would never do that to him."

"Is it so terrible?" she asked.

A long silence followed. Imad touched the shards on the tray, then came to kneel before her. His movements fluid, he sank to the floor and lowered his forehead to touch the tip of her boot. Then he sat up.

"A slave has no dignity, no privacy, no will of his own. For him there is no justice, no appeal, no relief. There is only abject debasement, invasion of body and spirit, subjugation, and shame. I do not have to describe for you what this would mean for a young man of such fire and so wild a spirit as my master."

"No."

"And as a healer, I think you have great sense. Sense enough to offer solace without the pity that would destroy him."

Juliana's shoulders slumped. "I should have talked to him instead of losing my temper."

"Yes, mistress, but he wouldn't have told you what you really needed to know."

"Prideful."

"Yes, mistress."

Then she remembered being hauled to her room and seduced. Her eyes became slits. "But he's at fault too. At fault, ha! He tries to drive me like a sheep. I shouldn't have used such a mean word to him, but he has been as careless of my feelings and desires."

Imad lifted a hand, causing her to shut her mouth and give him an irritated stare.

"And do you know what causes him to behave like this Viking to whom you compare him?"

"Oh, you heard about that?"

"Yes, O flower of divinity. And I will tell you one thing, though the master would never wish me to. His tyranny arises out of fear."

Juliana heard her quivering voice. "Fear. Fear? Gray de Valence is afraid? Of what?"

Imad slipped his hands in the sleeves of his robe and lifted jet-dark brows. "Why, fear for you and fear of you, mistress. He fears your temper will ruin you, and he fears his own feelings for you."

"Are you certain?" She dared only whisper the question.

"As certain as Allah is the light."

"Curse it, then why hasn't he said this to me?"

"Have you spoken of your fears to him?"

"Oh."

She subsided into thought while Imad waited, undisturbed by her long silence. She remembered Gray's wild fury at her refusal to declare her innocence. She remembered the way he touched her—as if he couldn't resist the compulsion—even when his purpose was to drop her in a washtub. Now memories came quickly to her. The desperation in his eyes as she plummeted toward him down that hillside above Clement's cave. The angelic gentleness of his touch in the blackness of that same cave. And finally, after they'd made love, the tremor in his voice as he admitted that he was enslaved.

She had been too caught up in her own fears to perceive the gravity of those words or what it must have cost him to utter them. What had she done? Cold, unremitting fear invaded her; this cursed temper of hers might have cost her this incomparable man.

"God give me grace," she whispered to herself. Then she looked up at Imad. "Do you think he'd forgive me?"

"The master follows the word of God. The Prophet has written that He won't take you to task for vain words, but for what your heart has amassed."

"That doesn't sound good for me."

Imad laughed. "But it is, O kind and generous lady."

"I'm not kind. I've a tongue like a dagger and the

temper of a wounded stoat, and look what letting them run rampant has done to Gray."

"There is a shadow on the sea, but a good breeze will send it flying."

"Are all Muslims so circuitous in their language?"

"I know not what you mean, mistress."

Juliana hopped from the chest and began touching her hair and clothing. "Thunder of God, I must look like a devil's crone. Er, um, Imad."

"Yes, O divine lady of light."

"He really did mean to marry me?"

Imad cocked his head to one side. "Of course, mistress. He cast aside this preoccupation with vengeance, this crusade for belated justice, all in pursuit of you."

"Then perhaps it's time that he found out what it's like to be pursued."

"Many women have pursued him, mistress."

"Not like me, Imad. I assure you, not like me."

Gray sat on a bench in one of the sparsely furnished manor chambers. His squire and Lucien had found him there. He paid no attention when, upon seeing the tiny dots of blood on his sleeve, Simon had begun to mutter and removed his tunic. When he didn't resist and continued his blank perusal of the chamber walls, Lucien pointed to the bandage on his wrist and asked the origin of the cut. Gray's glance barely touched the wound as he explained without revealing details.

"*Mon Dieu, messire.* She could have put out your eye."

The wound was nothing, a little puncture unworthy of a child's notice. But the words, her words . . . Those had ripped through him as though a jagged shard of steel had pierced his chest. That she could think him capable of acts such as those of Saladin, of that terrible lack of compassion for the helpless . . .

His mind reeled anew under an assault of memories that made him feel dirty. Again he felt the hands of strangers on his bare skin, felt the gaze of a master upon his unclothed body. And yet Juliana thought he, the former slave, was like the slavemaster. In her eyes he was an animal, a brutish thing with yellow fangs and ungovernable lusts. The possibility that she might revile him the way he did Saladin made him want to howl.

Gray closed his eyes. More than to anyone else in the world he'd given himself to Juliana. He had been on the point of baring himself to her, uncovering his soul. And what frightened him near to tears was that even now, in spite of how she'd turned on him, he still loved her.

He'd known slavery of the body, but not this all-encompassing slavery of the heart. Against it he was more helpless than ever he'd been against Saladin. He was lost to her, and that evoked terror, terror that there was nothing he could do to save himself, and that, in spite of their fleshly desire, she might not return his love.

A small, secret part of him wanted to moan. He could feel it, deep in the narrowest, blackest cavern of his soul. Small, lost, cowering, that part of him he kept hidden, protected. That small, pale ghost of his lost innocence was in pain. And the pain was growing, no matter how he tried to master it. Soon he wouldn't be able to conceal it. Perhaps he'd failed already, for Lucien was staring at him.

The knight dismissed Simon and drew near. "You're as pale as the white walls of Wellesbrooke, *messire*. What has happened?"

Gray shook his head, but Lucien repeated his question. With each query, that trembling gray wraith within him grew stronger, more substantial, and threatened to overwhelm him. He muttered something, part of the truth. Lucien must have guessed at the rest, for he touched Gray's arm and spoke in a whisper.

"*Sacré Dieu*, what has she done to you?"

Each word stabbed into him, carving slices into his already bleeding heart. Abruptly Gray shoved Lucien aside and thrust himself off the bench.

"Enough, Lucien." He raised his voice. "Simon! Simon come back here."

He waited impatiently while Simon returned and helped him don a clean tunic of soft forest-green wool. He fastened his own sword belt only to be distracted by the sight of the white bandage on his wrist. His fingers touched the cloth gently. Then he heard Lucien swear again.

"Go away, Simon," the knight said.

Gray looked up from his wrist to find himself alone with Lucien. His friend stood before him, fists planted on his hips.

"Never have I seen you beaten to your knees, sire. You mustn't let her do this to you. Cast this demon-tempered creature aside before she destroys you. Choose a lady more noble, more worthy of your hand."

Gray rammed his sword into its sheath so violently that he grimaced at the jar to his cut. "By Satan's staff, be silent!" He stood there breathing hard and scoring Lucien with his stare, his voice throaty and rough. "I have no choice. Don't you understand? I. Have. No. Choice."

Whirling from the knight, Gray rushed from the chamber. His pace quickened until he was running. Down the stairs, across the hall, into the courtyard, and around to the stables. His mind burned, his lungs heaved. He didn't remember saddling his hunter, but soon he was astride the bay and clattering across flagstones, beneath the portcullis, and out of the manor. He heard shouts behind him, but only kicked his horse into a gallop. The shouts faded, but the pain remained with him.

Harder and faster he rode. Clods of dirt flew in his face. The mass of muscle and sinew beneath him pounded across fields, leaped across logs, hedges, streams, plunged into woods. Bending over the horse's neck, he urged the animal on, gripping with his knees, straining forward. The hunter sensed his desperation and lengthened his stride, clawed the ground, and surged over the landscape. Soon they were both sweating, but still they charged on, careening down winding trails.

His desperation only increased upon encountering the river Clare. A lunatic plunge across it, and he was climbing hills. He only woke from the madness when his horse almost toppled backward down a near-vertical slope. The hunter's scream of terror jolted him back to his senses. Hauling on the reins, he rode the horse back down the slope and dismounted. He stood beside the animal and sucked in huge breaths. He and the horse sweated and trembled together.

After a while he heard running water. Pulling on the reins, he led the horse to a stream that tumbled down the hillside. They drank deeply, then Gray removed his tunic. He cupped his hands and splashed water over his head and torso. Then he tended to the hunter, removing the saddle and wiping the animal down with fists full of grass.

Exhaustion numbed him, blanked out his thoughts except for the need to care for the horse that had served him despite his carelessness. When he'd done, he was shivering, but this time from weariness. He put on his tunic and belt again, and at last took stock of his surroundings.

He was in a ravine between two hills thick with trees and brush. The stream danced over the rocks that its rushing water had exposed and plunged over an outcrop in a small waterfall that fed the pool in which he'd bathed. Afternoon sunlight formed golden splashes of light on the water while shadows formed by overhanging branches leaped in and out of the brightness.

Gray looked up at the sky. Fat white clouds sat in the sky, unmoving, distant. The sky still held the last vestiges of crisp winter cleanliness. The screech of a hawk pierced the deserted silence. He stood beside his horse and looked east, in the direction of Vyne Hill. In spite of his rank, his possessions, what did he have to give? A body and soul corrupted, used, degraded. She was so quick to anger. What would she think if she ever found out how soiled he was? If she ever found out, how could he face her?

Gray closed his eyes and turned around. Lowering his head, he sighed and took up his horse's reins. He hopped across stones, tugging the animal behind him. Without glancing in the direction of Vyne Hill, he plunged deeper into the wooded hills.

He couldn't go back. Not yet. The pain was still too great, his fear too strong. Would it not be safer to take a woman for whom he cared not at all? Then, if she scorned him, turned on him, looked at him with disgust, he wouldn't care. If he married a less admirable woman, one he didn't desire, he would risk no pain. He wouldn't risk enslavement. His heart would remain inviolate, free. No, it would never be free. Juliana held it in her hands, wore it on her girdle with all those damned keys she carried, pinned it on her cloak like a brooch.

These thoughts drove him deeper and deeper into the hills. The farther he climbed, the more frustrated he grew, for he couldn't escape the feelings. They climbed with him, or, rather, they skipped and flew with him, like gnats swarming around his head. He went faster, tugging the hunter behind him as he climbed, to no avail. When he stopped again, out of breath and in as great a misery as when he started, he began swearing and kept on until he had no breath left to speak.

Then he looked around and noticed his surroundings again—and realized he was lost. The sun was dropping behind a knobby hill to the west. A chill crept into the air. He should go back. It was dangerous to be out alone in the hills at night. There were wolves, perhaps even bears. As it was, he would have to take shelter at Welles-brooke. He wouldn't be able to make Vyne Hill before nightfall.

He should go back. He kept telling himself to start, but he remained motionless, staring at the halo of gold behind the hills that signaled the sun's descent. He couldn't seem to summon the will to move or to care whether he risked the dangers of the dark wilderness. Spending the night fighting off wolves was a far more palatable alternative to spending it fighting off a loathing of oneself. Far more palatable, indeed.

Marigold

 Looking at marigolds drew out evil humors of the head and strengthened eyesight. Marigold was used against poisoning, intestinal trouble, and angry words.

• *Chapter 21* •

WITH IMAD'S HELP, JULIANA DISMOUNTED AT the foot of the hill that concealed Friar Clement's cave. Lucien was climbing down the slope. She tossed her reins to the squire Simon and went to meet the knight with Imad at her side.

"You're certain he went to the friar's cave?" she said.

Lucien gave her a cursory glance before fixing his sunset-blue gaze on some point over her shoulder. "*Oui.*"

Raising her brows, Juliana put her hands on her hips and moved so that she blocked Lucien's view of the tips of her mare's ears. "Look you, sir knight, I've admitted my fault, and I'm trying to amend it. I've behaved in most hasty wise, and it's a great heaviness to me. But put yourself in comfort. I'm going to make an end to this—this havoc wooing. If I've ruined myself with your lord, I pray God will give me the grace to withdraw from him in a gentle and Christian manner, no matter the cost to myself."

Lucien studied her while she spoke, and when she finished, a look of reluctant esteem crept over his features. "Such a course works to increase your honor, demoiselle."

"I'd rather have Gray de Valence than all the honor in the kingdom."

A smile brightened Lucien's dour expression. "I want whatever makes *messire* happy, as do all of us. I only wish

Arthur had been at Vyne Hill when you quarreled. He might have been able to reason with his cousin."

Juliana was busy rearranging the folds of her cloak. She wasn't going to let this mocking Frenchman know her opinion of anyone who bore the name Strange. "Where is he?"

Imad came forward, tucking his hands in the wide sleeves of his robe. "Sir Arthur is hunting that murderous bandit, O great mistress."

"Hunting the band—" Juliana eyed Imad, then Lucien, both of whom returned her look with amused eyes and placid expressions. It was clear they had never considered that Arthur might be the killer or that they might be sending a murderer to hunt an innocent man. "I suppose my lord thought such a mockery was necessary."

"*Oui, demoiselle.*"

"I trust verily that the poor man will be allowed to give up the chase for this—uh—bandit soon." Juliana bit her lip against further comment about how much Arthur had benefitted from his brother's death. She would talk to Gray privately about her suspicions. Turning away from the men, she pulled off her boot and emptied it of a pebble and replaced it. Then she picked up a bundle containing a blanket, food, and drink, and slung it over her shoulder. "I'm going now."

Lucien held out his hand to assist her, but she shook her head. "You and Imad will camp here. I'll not have you looming over me when I find my lord."

"*Mon Dieu*, he'll have my head on a pike if I let you wander these hills alone."

Imad nodded vigorously, and Juliana could see a look of resolution on Lucien's face. She folded her arms and sauntered over to the knight.

"Very well, but I should warn you that I intend to go directly to the cave and throw myself in my lord's arms, and when I do that, he won't thank you for lurking about and gawking at him like a pair of milk cows."

"We will stay far enough behind you to prevent such an unfitting occurrence, O beauteous mistress of the sun."

"Imad, if you and this French knave follow me, I'll lead you such a chase that you'll end up spending the night in a bramble patch. I've been climbing these hills since I was a child and need no escort, but if you don't stop arguing with me, I won't reach the cave before dark."

Lucien sighed and shook his head. "As you wish, demoiselle. We'll escort you halfway and return here to make camp. But upon the morrow we'll seek you out." He gave her a sly glance. "If *messire* doesn't toss you back down the hill before then."

"I'll try to prevent that with my uttermost power."

She set out without further argument from Lucien. Imad clambered after them, cursing each rock in his path and lamenting his fate at having to leave the shelter of civilization for savage country. True to their word, they left her halfway up the hill. Juliana watched them until they vanished down the slope, then made her way up the hill to the friar's cave.

She'd discovered that Gray had quit Vyne Hill when his turbulent departure created a tumult among his men. Knowing that a large party following him would invite their lord's wrath, only the squire Simon had pursued his master with Lucien not far behind. The Frenchman had refused to wait for Juliana, but she soon caught up with him with Imad trailing after her. Simon had shown Lucien their lord's whereabouts and been sent home.

Sunset was almost upon her when she reached the clearing before the cave. She hid behind a tree that offered a view across the open space to the mouth of the cavern. At first she was dismayed at not seeing Gray, but then she saw his hunter unsaddled and tethered nearby.

The journey into the hills had given Juliana time to consider ways in which to atone for her miserable actions. Looking back on her behavior toward Gray had been an unpleasant task. Her attitude embittered by her past, she'd belabored him with insults and suspicion from the beginning. Without bothering to get to know him, except through her unconquerable and sinful desire.

If she hadn't been so busy wallowing in craven fears, she would have talked to him as he'd asked. Then she might have learned from him the things Imad had told her. Or perhaps not. She wasn't the only one filled with reluctance to confide, to bare her innermost secrets. Well, the past was past. Her task now was supplication. But she knew Gray de Valence. He wouldn't believe pretty apologies. Mere words wouldn't hack a path through the ice fortress he'd erected around himself by now.

And she had to reach him, for that look on his face when she had wounded him had stripped away that exotic and glamorous façade to reveal something she never hoped to find in him, something that even now she dared not name to herself. She wouldn't name it, but she would have it, and him, no matter the cost.

Bold and valiant measures, that's what she needed. She would have to startle him, deny him the opportunity to rebuff her outright. She had searched her soul for the way, for the right answer, the key to his maltreated heart. And she'd found it. The question was, did she have the courage to use this most unusual key?

Glancing around the clearing, she decided that Gray was either deep inside the cave or had left for the moment. A fire before the cave entrance signified his intention to remain the night. She ran to his horse, untethered it, and took it deep into the trees. If Gray tried to leave before she could speak to him, he'd have to do it on foot. She was walking back to the clearing when she heard the crack of twigs under a boot. She crept back to her tree and peered around it.

Gray had returned with an armload of wood, which he dumped near the fire. He stood up, then turned quickly to look at the place where his horse should have been. Swearing, he clamped his hand to the sword at his side, rushed to the spot, and studied the ground. He knelt for a moment, then lifted his head and stared at her.

"Come out of there," he said in that wintery tone that so frightened her.

Juliana Welles, don't let him intimidate you. It's what he wants. He's afraid he's revealed too much. Thunder of God, remember what he feels like beneath those lordly garments. Remember how he moans when he's inside you. This is that same man.

With such thoughts racing through her head, Juliana left the shelter of the tree and took several hesitant steps that brought her to the middle of the clearing. He watched her the whole time, his expression blank, his eyes like new leaves encased in frost. Juliana stared into that chilly gaze as she stopped, and her legs began to feel as if they were turning to slush. Her tongue darted out to lathe her lips.

"I—I've come to beg you to forgive me."

He gave her a stately nod, the mighty lord enshrouded in the formality of chivalry.

"No," she said, her voice faint. "Not with words. Through my hell-cursed temper I've almost destroyed your—your affection for me, and I must atone. I have to show you—"

"That is unnecessary. I forgive you. Now go away. I trust you've come with my men. They wouldn't have let you make the journey alone. Good e'en to you." He turned to go.

"No, wait!"

She watched his shoulders go rigid, his back stiff, but she didn't move.

"You didn't let me finish. I have to show you that I'm sorry. I was afraid, like you."

He faced her again, this time chuckling, although the sound held little merriment. "I assure you, mistress. I've never been afraid of you."

"No? Well, I've been afraid of you, and I've been evil to you."

He was turning again, his body and heart removed from her.

"If you're not afraid, why are you leaving?"

That stopped him. A flicker of annoyance broke through the frost of his gaze. Now, now was the time. Juliana held his gaze with hers, dropped her hands to her girdle and unfastened it quickly. Casting it aside, she drew her gown over her head and discarded it as well. She heard a curse.

"What are you doing?"

"I'm going to do something that requires more courage than anything I've ever done. It's the only way I can prove to you that I didn't mean to hurt you."

"I told you—put that back on!"

Juliana tossed her undertunic aside as Gray leaped to her.

He picked up the garment and threw it at her, all aloofness gone. "Blessed God, you're cursed bold for a maid."

Pulling the undertunic from where it landed on her shoulder, Juliana let it fall to the ground. Gray watched it slither down her bare breast, past her hips. His gaze caressed her legs and lingered over the stockings and boots she still wore. A crimson flush spread up his neck. His breathing grew short and sharp, but he took a step back from her.

"Aye, you've the courage to do this, but all it will prove is that I desire you, and that you can't resist me. This I already know."

Whirling quickly, he strode toward the mouth of the cave.

Trembling, Juliana raised her voice. "Arrogant man, baring myself isn't what I meant."

He looked back at her in surprise, and when she had his attention again, Juliana bent and removed her boots. Her fingers were cold and they shook, but she managed to take off her stockings as well. Throwing them out of the way, she forced herself to rise and stand before him. He was glaring at her this time, but she knew why. It was because he was aroused and didn't want to be. But what she feared most was that he'd forget desire as soon as she began to walk. Waves of fear broke over her, and her whole body shook.

Do it. Do it before you lose all courage. Do it and end it, now.

Juliana took a step, and then another. Her body shifted, slightly off balance, her gait uneven. Slowly, she crossed the space between them, giving him time to see what she never allowed anyone to see—her shamefully ungainly, misshapen walk. She kept her gaze fixed on his, certain that his anger would turn to disgust. One last step, and she would be within arm's reach of him. She took the step, lurched to a halt, and his rage burst upon her. Grabbing her shoulders, he jerked her close.

"By the curse of Satan, you'll not trick me with my own lust!"

Pushing against his chest with both hands, Juliana winced at his painful grip. "Lust! Did you not see?"

"See what, damn you?" He was shaking her now. "See your body, your pink and white body? See those black curls winding around your breasts? I'm not blind, Juliana, nor am I a eunuch."

Juliana thought her head would rattle off her body with the force of his shaking. "No, no, no, no."

The shaking stopped, but his anger didn't. His hand fastened around her neck, and he yanked her so close he could have kissed her.

His voice rough, his breathing harsh, he whispered to her. "See what then, how I burn and swell the moment your flesh escapes the folds of your gown? By God, I'll teach you the cost of playing with me."

His mouth swooped down on hers, violent and ruthless. Juliana tried to speak, but her lips were buried beneath his. She twisted her head, slipped away from that ravaging mouth. At the same time, she drew back her fist and jabbed him in the stomach. He gasped, but didn't release her.

"Oh, now look what you've done," she cried.

"I!" He pulled her close. One hand slipped down to squeeze her buttocks. "God, you're begging for chastisement."

If she didn't stop him, they'd end up wrestling on the cave floor. Juliana reached up, grabbed handfuls of his hair and wrenched his head up, pulling his lips from her shoulder. Then she shouted, her nose nearly touching his.

"You didn't pay attention! Didn't you see me walk? Thunder of God, didn't you see the way I walk?"

His breath coming fast, still gripping her neck and buttock, Gray said nothing. His brows drew together, then his grip loosened.

"Your walk," he repeated in a dead tone before he lapsed into silence again.

After a moment, his lips parted, and a faint "Oh" came on a sigh. Then he looked at her. Heavy silver locks swung forward as his head moved. Juliana swallowed and made herself look into his eyes, only to find the sweet warmth of a summer wind as it skims over grass-covered hills. A musing smile parted his lips, and he bent to whisper close to her ear.

"You thought I would turn from you in revulsion, didn't you, you foolish maid?"

It was her turn to stare with her mouth open. "You didn't even notice. Why didn't you notice?"

"Because, my joyance, you limp, slightly. It's only in your own eyes that you stagger like some misshapen monster. In my eyes, you glide like a falcon soaring on the unseen winds."

"No I don't, I hobble, stagger, and—"

"Mother of God," he said in a wondering voice. "You think yourself so distasteful, and yet you bared yourself to me."

"I told you I wanted to show you how much I regretted my foul temper. And it was callous and stupid of me not to realize how terrible it would be for you to be stripped."

A stream of war-camp curses interrupted her. "I'll beat Imad until he bleeds."

"That you would never do."

"I'll think of some evil punishment."

Juliana cleared her throat. "I—I give you leave to withdraw from our betrothal."

She was proud of that dignified statement until he threw back his head and laughed.

"Arrogant Viking."

"I can't help it. You're such a law unto yourself that you imagine that your father would allow such a thing, and that I would let you go."

"You won't?" She glanced up at him briefly, but was too cowardly not to drop her gaze.

He lifted her chin so that she was forced to meet his eyes. It was like staring into emeralds set afire.

"My own dear sovereign lady, my joyance, my life. You made me forget vengeance and duty, and then tried to martyr yourself. I might as well have been a lion and you a Christian."

Say it. Say it now. "Gray, I love you."

His head turned to the side and lowered. His eyes closed. "Don't say that until I've told you what it is you love. No, don't stop me."

For once Juliana kept her mouth closed and listened. She stood naked in the circle of his arms and listened to that quiet, throaty voice tell a tale of betrayal and shame, listened as the voice broke, strangled on unshed tears. Pain shot through her heart at the telling, but she knew better than to give in to it. She wouldn't intrude her own sorrow upon his. She contented herself with touching his shoulder where the brand had seared him. And when at last that rough whisper fell silent, she felt the brush of a curtain of silken hair as he turned his face from her.

She stopped him, her fingers touching his jaw, turning it back to her. Then, standing on her toes, she covered his mouth with hers, and said with her body what words seemed too meager to say.

Black Hellebore

 The root of black hellebore was used in a mixture to kill wolves and foxes. It was also said to cure gout, scruff of the head, and scabies.

• *Chapter 22* •

GRAY WOKE TO FIND THAT THE FIRE HAD DIED down. Juliana was sleeping in the curve of his body, the top of her head barely visible beneath the blanket. He was tempted to nuzzle into the depths of her hair and find that sensitive spot on her neck, but he decided not to disturb her. Making love thrice in one night had wearied her.

He was glad there wasn't anyone to see the bemused smile he wore. Never had anyone valued him so greatly as to risk what she had risked. He would never forget the proud lift of her chin or the love in her eyes as she walked across the clearing to him, naked and certain of her deformity. That slight limp, it only made her more unique to him, more precious. And she had thought he would find her repulsive.

Juliana had offered him her soul, and given him back his own. He was so happy he was certain disaster was about to strike, for such happiness was unnatural. In his experience, life offered more misery than delight. Surely he would have to pay for this felicity. But not tonight.

Rising carefully so that he didn't disturb Juliana, he searched for his cloak. They had dressed after lovemaking, for the night was cold. Gray fastened the garment and went outside to the pile of wood he'd discarded near the entrance. The moon had vanished, and a breeze sent black tree branches dancing. Limbs creaked and whined as he filled his arms with logs. He got to one knee and was standing up when something crashed against the back of his head. Pain rammed through his skull just before he collapsed.

His next perception was of being dragged by his legs. His head banged over the ground, his cheek scraping against pebbles. Suddenly he glimpsed firelight, and he was thrown against the rock wall of the cave. Still dazed, he gasped when his head hit stone. He could only see a blur of light and dark for a few moments, while voices around him blared so loud he couldn't understand them.

He had to regain his senses. If he lay still as if unconscious, his attackers might leave him alone long enough for him to recover. Moments passed in which his vision slowly cleared and his hearing grew more distinct. Finally he was able to see through his lashes.

A cloaked figure stood over Juliana, its back to him. Juliana was sitting by the fire, hands and feet bound. She spoke to the figure, but Gray was distracted by the crunch of a boot on dirt near his feet. He looked down and saw what he would have seen sooner if he hadn't been so dazed. A sword point rested over his heart. A man-at-arms held the blade, but he was looking at the two by the fire.

Gray thanked the Holy Trinity he hadn't moved; he would have ended up with the sword in his chest. Biding his time, he turned his attention back to the cloaked figure. A sweet, high voice issued from it, nearly causing Gray to open his eyes in astonishment.

"I'm sick of enduring you and your family," Yolande said as she brushed back the hood of her cloak. Her voice was whispery and dulcet. "Through with giving place to those beneath me, sharing with you and your sisters, obeying when I should command. And I'm done with loneliness. No more being shut up in towers so no man can reach me, no more longing for a companion who will treat me as I should be treated. Gray was doing that until you seduced him."

"You killed Edmund," Juliana said, her eyes wide.

"Oh, yes, Edmund. Well, I waited for you to do it, but you didn't."

Wide-eyed, Juliana said, "Why? Why did you kill him?"

"Oh," sighed that faint, chimelike voice, "I couldn't allow him to go unpunished for spurning me before the world. I am Yolande de Say, and no one deals me an insult. I could understand Edmund not wanting to marry you when he could have me, but then he threw me aside for some ugly hag with more castles and lands."

"But—"

"I didn't like all the blood, though." Yolande began to wipe her hands on the front of her gown, rubbing them ceaselessly. "Such a lot of blood, it soiled my gown, and I had to burn it, but at least I assured myself that Edmund paid for what he did to me, just as you will pay for taking the Sieur de Valence from me."

"I didn't take him. Neither of us planned what happened between us."

"You see," Yolande continued. "I know God has a plan for me. I'm to be a great lady, the greatest in the land. You and your family never understood my rank or what was due me, but now I'm old enough to order matters as I see fit. That's why you must die. With you gone, I'll have Gray."

Juliana shifted her weight so that she was sitting on her heels. "But he loves me."

"You'll be dead, and men are fickle. Didn't Edmund prove that?" Yolande said. "And in any case, if he spurns me again, I'll kill him and take Arthur, who is his heir."

Yolande knelt and rummaged among the remains of the meal Juliana had brought with her. She found a bottle of wine, opened it, and produced a packet from a purse suspended from her girdle. While she busied herself with the wine bottle, Gray stole looks at the man-at-arms. He was a big man, built like an ale vat, with scarred hands and yellow teeth. A man not easily subdued.

Movement by the fire caught his attention again. Yolande was pouring a fine, dark powder from a jar into the wine bottle. Replacing the stopper on the bottle, she shook the contents vigorously.

"I thought I would like killing Edmund with a knife, seeing him gurgle and bleed," she said as if she were discussing a round dance. "I did like the gurgling, but the mess was disgusting, and I don't want to ruin any more gowns. So I stole your mother's key to the herb chamber and read your herb journal."

Juliana shot a quick glance at him, while she addressed Yolande. "What's in that powder?"

"It was clever of you to make a list of dangerous plants, and even more clever of you to put those plants aside in a chest. But you never said which of them was the most poisonous, so I used some of each."

Gray went cold. It was all he could do to keep from lunging at Yolande.

"All?" Juliana said in a faint voice. "You used all of them?"

"All that I could find. You must have used up some, for there were several empty jars. But I did find henbane, larkspur, monkshood. I remember there was black hellebore and nightshade, and cuckoopint. I thought cuckoopint was for swelling and for making the skin white and clear."

Juliana glanced at him again. This time he risked opening his eyes and meeting her gaze for a brief moment. The guard didn't notice, but Juliana almost ruined them by gasping.

"Oh! Oh, yes, cuckoopint. It's only meant for poultices and such. Thunder of God, Yolande, the whole plant is poisonous, the berries, leaves, flowers, even the roots."

"I know. I read it in your herbal." Yolande held out the wine bottle. "Here. Drink, or Osbert here will kill Gray."

He tensed and stole a glance at Osbert. The fool was engrossed in the scene between the two women and wasn't even watching him. Gray looked back at Juliana, who had grasped the bottle. She didn't look at him again, and brought the vessel to her lips. Yolande stood over her with an expression of quiet beatitude while her eyes took on that soulless vacuity that so reminded Gray of a crocodile.

Osbert shifted his weight from foot to foot and looked at him, then shifted his attention to the women. Gray lowered his lashes as the man glanced at him. Juliana was tilting the bottle. Suddenly Yolande swooped at her and tipped the vessel so that the wine rushed out.

Gray rolled from beneath the swordpoint and jammed his feet into Osbert's chest. "Juliana, spit it out!"

Gray heard screams, but he couldn't take his eyes from the guard. Osbert flew backward and hit his head against the cave wall. He grunted like a stoat, but righted himself and charged Gray, his sword swinging over his head as he bellowed. Still weak from the blow to his head, Gray wasn't quick enough to avoid him. Osbert was almost upon him when Juliana rushed between them and thrust the end of a burning log in the man's face.

Osbert screamed, dropped his sword, and doubled over, his hands covering his face. Gray struggled to his knees and snatched the sword. He bashed the hilt against Osbert's head, and the screams stopped as the guard collapsed. Juliana stared at the prone man while Gray searched the shadows of the cave for Yolande. The girl was lying next to the fire moaning.

Juliana swooped down on him, her face red with wine stains, and began patting him all over in search of wounds. Gray wiped drops of wine off her cheeks.

"Did you drink any of it?" he asked. "Stop that, Juliana, and tell me if you drank the poison."

Juliana shook her head. "No, I spat it out. Phew, what an evil-tasting concoction. I should rinse my mouth."

A strange, animal cry echoed off the cave walls. They turned as Yolande rushed at them, a knife in her hand. Juliana was kneeling beside him, eyes round, body rigid with surprise and fear. Without thinking, Gray shoved her aside as Yolande bore down on her. At the same time, he grabbed Osbert's sword, which lay where he'd dropped it.

Yolande's strike missed Juliana, but she swerved and turned on him instead. Her mouth distorted in a snarl, she plunged at him, aiming for his throat. Gray shouted a warning, but she kept coming, and at the last moment, he raised the sword to ward her off. It shot up just as she reached him, and Yolande ran onto its point. Gray cried out and tried to withdraw as she lunged, but she was too quick. Her body sank onto the blade before he could avoid her.

Cursing and gasping, he released the sword. Yolande's head came up, and she looked at him. He pulled the sword from her. Her lips twisted into a grimace that resembled a smile. Blood rushed from her mouth. She choked several times as her body folded and dropped to the ground.

Gray threw the sword aside, stepped over Yolande. Juliana rose to her knees. He knelt before her and encircled her with his arms. They remained this way for long minutes without speaking.

"Oh, God, she almost got me," Juliana said, breaking their silence.

He could feel her body trembling.

"And you," she continued with her teeth chattering.

"I can't believe it was Yolande. She seemed so sweet."

"I know, I know. Don't you think I've been trying to make sense of it too? You didn't know her, and I suppose all along I just didn't understand how deformed her spirit was." She pressed her fingers to her lips, then took a deep breath and went on. "Since she came to us she was perplexing and full of crosswise qualities. Mother always said she'd been so indulged from a babe that she believed herself a person set apart from the rules that bind us all in Christian society. She played the simple maid with you, but she was far more."

Gray hugged Juliana closer. "And you thought Arthur the murderer."

"He could have been, but something Yolande said made me suspect her. She knew about the bloody sand in Edmund's throat. I didn't think about it at first, but later I realized that she and my sisters hadn't been allowed to see the body. And I was certain that neither my father, Richard, nor any other knight would describe the body to her. That would be unchivalrous."

"You suspected and you didn't tell me? Holy hell, Juliana, what a thing to forget. You remember my slightest transgression, but you forget a murderer. God give me patience."

Shoving away from his body, Juliana scowled at him. "Don't bellow at me, Gray de Valence. I've just been near poisoned and stabbed to death."

She was right. He'd almost lost her. He dragged her back to him, squeezing her as if to protect her from all harm with his body. She squeaked a protest, and he loosened his grip. With her head on his shoulder, she sighed.

He stroked her hair and mused. "God, she concealed her hatred well."

"We all thought she had changed," Juliana said. "When she first came to Wellesbrooke, she was selfish and cruel, but Mother corrected her evil habits."

Gray let his fingers trail through Juliana's hair for a while before speaking. "It seems she only concealed her real character behind a false one. Just God, if I had married her, in time she would have killed me for not complying with her most trivial wish."

"Yes." Juliana shivered. "We were all deceived into thinking she'd changed, but she never learned that wanting something isn't the same as getting it. I remember how she was before Mother taught her manners; if she wished for something, she thought that wish would be fulfilled without question or impediment. All this time I thought she'd mended most of her faults and had become my friend."

Juliana peered over his shoulder at Yolande's body, then closed her eyes and sank against him. He felt another shiver pass through her body and heard a sob.

"Come, my joyance. You can't stay here."

He led her out of the cave, then returned for her cloak. He set her the task of saddling his horse to keep her from trying to help him with the grisly work of moving Yolande's body and tying up Osbert. When he returned, she was waiting in the clearing with his hunter. He mounted and reached down, clasping her hand in his. She looked up at him with eyes bright with tears. He had to chase the fear away for her.

He bent down and asked, "Shall I toss you over my legs for old times' sake?"

At first she just stared at him. Then her jaw muscle twitched and she frowned at him.

"Arrogant Viking," she snapped. "There'll be no more tossing me over your saddle or your shoulder. Try it, and

I'll dose you with elder or bloodwort and you'll have to live in the garderobe for days."

He yanked her up into his arms and kissed her hard. Rubbing his nose against hers, he smiled softly. "There. I knew my fire-tempered wench hadn't vanished, she was only hiding."

Juliana glanced back at the cave, then rested her head on his shoulder. "Everyone thought I killed Edmund, after all my healing. They thought I was a murderer."

"You helped them think it out of perverseness, and you know it."

Instead of bursting into furious denial, she regarded him solemnly. "I wouldn't have wanted to live if she'd killed you."

His heart seemed to swell until it was too large for his chest. To mean so much to another, to know that his very existence was essential to her, this was a rare and wondrous gift.

"Oh, my joyance, my sweet, sweet love. I thank Christ and all the saints for sending me to your father's tournament, and to you."

Three weeks had passed since Yolande had died—three weeks during which Juliana had explained again and again about the girl's hidden character, her desire for Gray, and all the other unbelievable happenings that were nevertheless true. Her father had come near to war with the Earl of Uvedale over the girl's death until Gray intervened. And then had come the Stratfield messenger.

Gray's father was near death. His presence was required at home. Gray hadn't spoken of his family; his only comment was one whispered to himself that his presence hadn't been required for most of his life, and he damned well didn't see why it was required now. But he had gone anyway, swayed by Arthur's and Lucien's arguments of duty to his dependents if not to his family.

He left Imad with Juliana. "I know you, my joyance. Imad may be able to prevent you from sparking infernos with your temper while I'm away."

It was Imad who gave her a glimpse of why Gray seemed such a law unto himself. "When the master was accused of seducing his lord's wife, he asked his father for help. The baron sent back a reply at once; he said that for such a crime he would kill his son himself rather than live with the mark upon his honor. Once his family abandoned him, the master had no one to turn to, and the lord was able to do with him what he wished. The master says the Stratfields have always placed themselves on the winning side. They kill the weak of the family to make the strong stronger."

Thus Gray left to attend the deathbed of the father who had abandoned him to death. Juliana remained behind, and the longer he was away, the more doubts crept upon her. Once he returned to his family, would they and their dependents prevail upon him to make a better match? One of Gray's most admirable qualities was his care for those beneath him. Generous of spirit, angelic of soul, Gray might want her, but his family, the great and powerful Stratfields, wouldn't. He might not wish to put her aside, but he might be prevailed upon to do it for the sake of the barony.

As the days progressed, her old fears came trotting back like faithful hounds to the huntsman. They circled around in her heart, pawing at the soft places, and sat down to stay. What was she but a spiteful-tempered and malformed maid of too many years and too little beauty. She could never expect to keep Gray's heart and interest.

Such thoughts plagued her even as the castle prepared for her wedding. It didn't help that she'd made the same preparations only a little over a year ago. By the time word came that Gray would meet her at the village chapel on the morning set aside for their wedding, she was so disturbed she almost didn't believe he would keep his word. Mother and Bertrade made things worse with their incessant advice, which they dispensed whenever they encountered Juliana. She tried to avoid them, but they usually cornered her while she was being fitted for her wedding gown. Her mother found her in the solar the day before the ceremony standing on a stool while Alice tugged at the train of her overgown.

"This time I'm determined you shall conduct yourself as a right gentle lady," Havisia said as Alice took up the front hem. The overgown was of emerald silk shot with gold thread while the undertunic was of violet. "I've been remiss in your education, Juliana, but you're going to listen to me now, or you'll drive your betrothed away before the priest can complete the ceremony."

"I've done nothing to him!"

"You pushed him in a washtub. And don't bother to deny it. I heard the tale from nearly everyone in Wellesbrooke. Now, the first thing you must remember is to be courteous and meek, for doing so earns the favor of God and man. Be gracious to everyone, both the small and the great."

"I'm always gracious."

"Don't be absurd," her mother said. "And don't ever make yourself conspicuous. A difficult task for you, but you must try. You should walk becomingly, not stomp as is your custom. Look straight ahead with your gaze fixed on the ground ahead. Don't change your look from one place to the other, nor laugh nor chatter with everyone along the path. Don't talk too much or boast. And when you go to church, don't trot or run, but salute graciously all you meet."

Here Bertrade broke in. "But Mother, I think it more important that you warn her against scolding in public. And Juliana shouldn't travel without a proper retinue, or she'll get caught in compromising situations."

At this Juliana turned red and threw up her hands. "Thunder of heaven!"

Once Alice was done, Juliana donned her old wool gown and took refuge from this latest barrage of advice in the herb chamber, but Havisia followed her.

"I knew there was something I forgot."

Juliana sighed as she ground herbs with mortar and pestle. "That hardly seems possible."

"I thought you were going to try to be a courteous and gentle lady, Juliana."

"I can't," Juliana said. "It's against my nature, Mother. You know that. It's why you gave up trying to arrange my marriage. I can't abide fools, and there are just too many fools in this world."

"You must try, for your lord's sake, or you'll make him enemies."

Juliana stopped grinding and looked at her mother. "I hadn't thought of that. Hmmm. I'll try."

"Good, and there's one more thing."

"Only one? A miracle."

Havisia gave her a stern glance. "You must remember always to consider your lord's rank and fortune in your dress. By my troth, you're going to disgrace him if you continue to wear these old, patched gowns with stains on them."

"I wear them to work with herbs, Mother. Gray would rather I wore them than get my damasks and silks stained with the juice of flowers, berries, and roots."

"Oh, I wanted to talk to you about your manners at table."

Juliana dropped the pestle, which clattered into the

mortar. "Thunder of God, Mother! Leave off. I'm as I am, and Gray knows it. If he likes not what I am, he is more than man enough to say so, and he has my leave to withdraw from this betrothal."

Havisia drew herself up with a sniff and went to the door.

"After you're married you'll thank me, daughter. Your husband is a great lord, and he'll not appreciate being cursed with a scold and a drudge for a wife. Remember that, or you'll find yourself inviting a beating before your marriage is a week old."

Havisia slammed the door shut. Juliana sprang to her feet and shouted at the portal. "A scold and a drudge!"

She would have said more, but fear overtook her. Was she a scold? A drudge? She glanced down at her skirts. Stains decorated them from girdle to hem, mostly from the tincture of feverfew she'd made this morning. Sitting down again, she resumed her grinding, and with each pounding movement her worries and fears grew.

She went to bed worried, and woke on her wedding morn in a state of wordless trepidation. Gray hadn't arrived. While Alice, her sisters, and Havisia helped her dress, Hugo sent men down the road to Stratfield to search for the missing bridegroom. Juliana suffered, silently for once, while Alice fastened a girdle of gold links set with good-luck stones—sardonyx to prevent malaria, agate to guard against fever. At last her mother put a transparent, emerald-colored veil over the masses of her loose hair and secured it with a golden circlet. In too short a time, she was ready, and there was no word of Gray.

Mandrake

Mandrake root was used for the grievously pained. Whoever ate it was sensible of nothing for three to four hours. It was an ingredient in love medicines, a cure for devil sickness and heavy mischief in the home.

• *Chapter 23* •

HANDS COLD, KNEES WOBBLY, JULIANA FOUND herself mounted on a white mare and riding up to the front doors of the Wellesbrooke village chapel. Crowds lined the road, waving and shouting. She barely noticed the salutes of Piers and the other Vyne Hill villagers, or the cheers of Alice, or Eadmer and his companions. Her father rode beside her and helped her dismount. He held out his hand to her, and they walked up the steps as Friar Clement emerged from the dark interior.

He met her with tears in his eyes. "Dear Juliana."

Her heart banged against her chest, and she was barely able to get out a whisper. "What's wrong?"

The chapel door swung open again.

"Naught is wrong, my joyance, except that you look like you're going to a burial rather than our wedding."

Juliana's lashes fluttered, and she stared at the apparition before her. From surcoat to boots, Gray shone in the morning sunlight that reflected the gold in the chains at his throat, the heavy cloak pin in the shape of the dragon rampant, the chaplet that encircled his silver hair. Emeralds flashed in the circlet and on the signet ring on his finger. Yet despite the richness of his garb, he outshone the precious metal and costly fabric. Behind her, Juliana heard Laudine's whisper.

"Mmm, doesn't he make you shiver, Jule?"

Wearing his fine garments as easily as he wore chain mail, Gray seemed unaware of the murmur of appreciation that rose up from the crowd that had gathered to witness their joining. Juliana's gaze filled with wide shoulders draped in gold. She looked up at him, even more apprehensive now that she beheld this evidence of his rank, and met the teasing gaze of the man who had tossed her in the mud only a few weeks past. Fear melted away. Her knees stopped shaking, and she nearly strangled on a cry of irritation when he bent down and whispered to her.

"You thought I wouldn't come, didn't you? What a secret, whimpering little coward you are."

He kissed her hand, his tongue stealing out to taste her skin.

"Cursèd smirking savage," she hissed. "You hid inside apurpose to give me a fright, you tyrannical, arrogant Viking."

"I adore you as well, my love."

"Then let Friar Clement begin the ceremony, if you dare."

He did dare. To Juliana's astonishment, she found herself a new bride in moments. His green gaze flared as he consented to be her husband, and challenged her to say her own vows. How could she not accept his challenge? And so she married him. The shock pushed her into a fugue that lasted through the mass that followed and on into the wedding feast and the dancing and merriment thereafter.

What jarred her from her state of bedazzlement was the ribald jests that circulated from knight to lady to jongleur and baron. She was seated with Gray at the table of honor in the great pavilion set up before the castle while her sisters and their guests ate, drank, and danced. Raucous laughter recalled that of her first, aborted wedding and made her shiver.

The bedding of the bride. Its terrors were still to come.

At her feet were strewn roses and lilies. The air rang with joyous congratulations from damsels and knights, but all she could do was look for dark corners in which to hide.

Fingers trembling, she clutched the golden goblet she shared with Gray. Warm, strong hands wrapped around her cold one and held the cup to her lips. She drank sparingly and then glanced at her new husband. He was watching her with wicked amusement while she ached with fear. Her brows drew together.

"Thunder of God, how can you sit there and leer at me when soon—"

He rose suddenly, grabbed her hand, and shouted. "A dance, a dance for my new bride!"

Whistles and raucous laughter greeted them as he dragged her from the dais to the circle of dancers. Crowds of guests cheered them drunkenly. Juliana's gaze darted from one tipsy knight to another, knowing that soon they would huddle together and plan ways to embarrass her in her own bedchamber. She yanked her hand from Gray's.

"I don't want to dance."

He grabbed her hand again and, while she tried to free herself, signaled to the musicians. Flute, drum, trumpet, and lute struck a loud note. Gray nearly pulled her off her feet as he led the chain in a dash to make a circle. Around and around they went until Juliana thought she would never catch her breath again. She glimpsed Laudine's round cheeks and teasing eyes. She heard her father's loud laugh. Suddenly the music's pace doubled, and Gray increased the speed of their steps. Her vision blurred, and she almost stumbled.

Then there was a jolt. Gray broke from the circle and pulled her with him. She sailed after him into the crowd of revelers. It parted and seemed to swallow them as the guests cheered the lusty dancers and clapped in time to

the music. Lungs heaving, Juliana could only follow as
Gray threaded his way through the crowd to a shadowed
corner at the back of the pavilion. He tugged on her
hand and pushed her behind a trestle table piled high
with food. His arm came over her to push aside hangings.
She was shoved into darkness and then outside into the
fading daylight to bump into someone's back.

Arthur Strange turned around. "Well met, cousin."

He held out the reins of a horse to Gray. Lucien stood
nearby holding Juliana's mare and his own while several
other knights formed a concealing barrier with their own
mounts. Juliana turned to Gray, who was guiding her to
her horse.

"What are you doing?"

"Stealing my bride."

"But my father, the guests, the—the—the—"

A look from Gray made his cousin and his knights put
distance between them and their lord. He took Juliana by
her shoulders.

"My love, do you really want to stay here and endure
the bedding ceremony?"

"Help me mount."

"That's my fire-tempered wench."

He mounted his impatient hunter and they galloped
away from the pavilion, around Wellesbrooke castle and
over the east bridge. Juliana hardly slowed her pace until
they rode over the drawbridge of Vyne Hill. As they rode
across the deserted courtyard, dusk turned into night.
Gray dismounted and swung her to the ground.

Taking her hand, he said quietly, "I sent everyone
away."

The door opened, spraying warm candlelight over
them and framing a damask-clad Imad. The youth bowed
low.

"Welcome, O noble master and mistress. May the light of Allah bless you."

Holding her gaze, Gray drew her over the threshold without looking at Imad. He murmured her name in that rough, breathy voice that betrayed his intent. Liquid fire coursed through her veins, leaving behind an ache she knew would only grow.

"Does the master wish to dine? I have prepared roast peacock."

"No." Gray raised her hand to his lips and raked his teeth across her knuckles.

"Wine, master?"

"No." He placed her palm against his cheek.

"Sweetmeats?"

"Imad, you are dear to me, and I thank you for your service. Now go away."

Juliana was about to add her thanks when Gray swept her up in his arms.

"You may thank him tomorrow."

Her last glimpse of Imad was over Gray's shoulder as he raced up the stairs. Imad sank to his knees and touched his forehead to the floor, but Juliana wasn't fooled, for he was smiling as he called after them.

"Thy will is mine, O master."

Gray yanked open the door to her chamber, went in, and kicked it closed. He set Juliana on her feet. She turned around in a slow circle, unable to form words that expressed her consternation.

Her makeshift furniture was gone, and in its place were hangings of peacock-blue, -green, and -gold. Bronze lamps lit iridescent colors. A great bed sat against one wall, hung with blue silk bordered in green and gold. The old fireplace had been newly restored and a fire burned while her slippers sank into a carpet that Imad had extravagantly placed on the floor. She glanced at a flagon of wine and two goblets, then at the bed, then her gaze settled on the tips of her slippers.

She jumped when Gray came up to her silently, bent down, and touched the tip of his tongue to her cheek. He slipped his arms beneath hers and encircled her. His breath made the curls at her temples dance.

"Admit it," he said. "You were as frightened as a mouse cornered by a ferret at the thought of a public bedding."

"I—"

He nuzzled her hair back from her ear and began doing wicked things to her neck. "And you were afraid I wouldn't come back from Stratfield."

"No I wasn't."

"Liar." He lightly grazed her throat with his teeth.

Juliana swallowed, but found that she'd lost her voice when he placed soft little bites down the back of her neck. Without warning her gown loosened and his hand slipped inside the neck to rest just above her breast.

"No one knows where we are," he whispered.

"Your men."

"Value their lives and won't betray us."

"Then we're alone?" The idea was finally beginning to settle into her mind.

"Except for Imad, who is more discreet than an abbess."

She whirled around in his arms. "No priest is going to stand over us in our bed and mutter blessings?"

"Not even an acolyte."

She smiled then, in wonderment. "You knew how I dreaded the bedding. You knew. You're a devious knave, Gray de Valence, and I love you for it."

"I couldn't let you endure it, my joyance. I regret that I couldn't return sooner. I tried, but after my father died, there were so many obligations."

"Gray."

"Yes, my joyance."

"Shouldn't we speak of such things later, or perhaps you'd like me to mix you a potion to spur your desire."

He laughed, picked her up, and put one knee on the bed. "If you dose me with an aphrodisiac, you'll not get out of this bed for a week."

"Thunder of heaven, what a promise. My healing box, where's my healing box? There's mandrake in it."

Gray released her and she landed on the bed with a bounce. He sank down on top of her and took her mouth in a long kiss. She stirred when she felt his hand drawing her skirt up her thigh. His lips left hers and he looked down at her leg.

"No boots," he said.

"I have the heels of my slippers made specially—"

He placed his fingers over her lips, and she looked into the depths of emerald-green.

"No, my joyance. I meant that I prefer the boots."

"I do too."

"No, not under your gowns. Just the boots, and perhaps your stockings. By my troth, Juliana of the damascened eyes. I'll never forget the sight of you stripping off your gown and standing before me in your boots. I have dreamed of you that way."

Juliana trailed her fingers through thick, heavy locks of silver. "And I'll never forget that you noticed me and not my legs."

"Verily, my love, who could fail to notice such a fire-tempered wench?"

Their fingers intertwined, and Juliana's glance caught the gold signet ring he'd given her when they wed, a small version of his bearing the dragon rampant. His larger one vanished from her sight beneath the silk of her gown. She captured it as it slid over her breast.

"So," she said as she spread little kisses over his lips and cheeks, "I've captured the lord of the dragon."

"Alas, fair lady, captured, bound, and enslaved, willingly."

She released him and took his face in her hands. "Then show me the dragon, my lord. I want to see it, and feel it. Set the dragon free."

• About the Author •

SUZANNE ROBINSON has a doctoral degree in anthropology with a specialty in ancient Middle Eastern archaeology. After spending years doing fieldwork in both the U.S. and the Middle East, Suzanne has now turned her attention to the creation of the fascinating fictional characters in her unforgettable historical romances.

Suzanne lives in San Antonio with her husband and her two English springer spaniels. She divides her time between writing and teaching.

SUZANNE ROBINSON

loves to hear from readers. You can write to her at the following address:

P.O. Box 700321
San Antonio, TX 78270-0321

DON'T MISS THESE FABULOUS
BANTAM WOMEN'S FICTION TITLES